MAN-DAR
of Atlantis

Kenneth J. Sousa

outskirts
press

Outskirts Press, Inc.
http://www.outskirtspress.com

Paperback ISBN: 978-1-9772-4141-2
Hardback ISBN: 978-1-9772-4142-9

Dedicated
to
Laurie Meade

Book 1

Step Mother Earth Trilogy

ONE

Two pairs of lips chanted and two pairs of eyes watched a stream of blue smoke billow from the strings of the recently plucked miniature harp. The high-pitched resonance of the instrument vibrated through the still air of the prehistoric temple. The smoke from its strings circled and formed a large ring. Inside the ring of blue smoke a hazy image took shape, solidified and became the form of a sleeping man.

Suddenly the man's eyes opened and Patrick Hammel became conscious. Vaguely he recognized where the nightmare left off and reality began. Through lingering wisps of blue smoke, 3:00 AM came into focus on his digital clock, but he still heard a whispered voice call, "Pogul . . . Pogul." To Patrick the voice sounded distant, like someone calling him from a deep well. Although, in the seconds it took for his feet to reach the floor, the dream's content faded, leaving only a nauseous feeling of revulsion.

The nightmares had persisted for a month. The first and second a few days apart, but they soon increased to a nightly occurrence. The dream scenario never varied. A tall sinister looking man with piercing hate-filled eyes would enter his room. The man, dressed in a hooded black robe, would stand at the foot of his bed, and call him by the name "Pogul." Although an aura of evil shrouded this man, his manner was gently persuasive, compelling Patrick to respond with a submissive, "Yes, my lord?" Next, the man would walk to Patrick, slowly pull a revolver from his sleeve and hand it to him with instructions to *kill Mandar.* Instantly, Patrick would see himself standing in a doorway pumping bullet after bullet into a mustached stranger. Then he would wake soaked in sweat.

Since the onset of the nightmares, Patrick's nerves had frayed. His performance as assistant manager of a fast food outlet slipped, and he acquired a habit of thumbing his nose like a punch-drunk fighter.

Now, in a semi trance-like state, Patrick Hammel took a few swipes at his nose and began to dress. In slow deliberate motions he put on his pants, shirt and socks. Bending to tie his shoes, a blurred view of his clock informed him it was 3:10 AM. The blue smog, which clouded his thinking, totally excluded the question of why he was dressing at this odd hour. It did not let him wonder as to why he took his revolver from his nightstand drawer. It never let it cross his mind why he was methodically loading a bullet into each chamber.

A fuzzy-brained Patrick Hammel covered the gun and holster with his top coat, dropped a fedora on his head and walked out the door to his car. Without a thought he started the engine and drove several miles before realizing he had no idea of his destination. That disquieting thought slid instantly from his mind as he thumbed his nose and switched on the radio already tuned to a local country station. Through the blue smog clouding his mind he could not hear Tammy Wynette implore women to stand by their men, however, he clearly heard a voice gently ordering him to . . . *kill Mandar.*

San Francisco's Chinatown bustled with life but Shad Stone only saw death. It crept from racks hung with fly covered poultry and crawled from tiny alleys crammed with boxes, people and unfathomable odors. Shad ducked into a tiny side street jammed with pushcarts and produce. He needed to catch his breath. Hugging a wall, he breathed hard and watched an angry oriental women argue over the price of a few vegetables.

Shad had spotted the three dark suited heavies back near the Pyramid building. He couldn't be sure if they were Mafia, renegade FBI, or maybe fanatics from that crazy cult, the Center for the Elevation of Spirit and Mind. Any of them had reason to ice him and his partner, Muray W. Gordon, especially the Mafia. He knew his only chance of survival was to lose them and make his way to Sourdough Sam's and Muray. Peeking around the corner, Shad saw no sign of the three and moved into the milling crowd.

Two blocks later he exited Chinatown and breathed easier. Suddenly a suit blocked his way. A big suit. An ugly grin pulled across the man's face as he reached inside his jacket. Shad guessed what the suit carried and wanted no part of it. With a scream he kicked struck bit chewed killlllll........

"Aye carrumba, I hate it!" Manny Silva screamed as he punched delete on the worn keyboard of the old computer. Stroking his mustache nervously, he quickly undeleted the page and screamed louder. His tired voice ricocheting around the huge truck terminal building he guarded. Finally in complete self disgust, he slammed the computer's off button and jumped to his feet.

For six months, twenty-nine-year-old Manny Silva, a perfectionist who never believed he got anything perfect, had been attempting to write a novel. The book was based on a comet called Kohoutek, but so far all he had to show for his work was a rough outline and a dumpster full of scrap computer paper.

To earn a living, Manny worked night security at G&G Trucking Company of Boston. Located in the suburbs, the company consisted of a giant warehouse with offices surrounded by a large fenced-in yard for parking freight trailers. When first offered the position, Manny was thrilled. He felt security work was perfect for his writing career. He pictured plenty of quiet time in the empty warehouse and rows of computer keyboards to keep his fingers busy. Unfortunately, the job hadn't proved the boon to his career as he had first thought.

Aside from the exhaustion of all night watches, the security position held more complications than anticipated. Manny's responsibilities included locking doors and windows, answering phones, and logging in late arriving trucks. But far worse was making hourly rounds of the terminal grounds to check each trailer in the parking area.

Manny took a deep breath, glanced at the clock to calculate the time until his next pass through the terminal yard and sat down at the computer. He thought about how much he hated rounds. They dredged up unwanted memories of fear in similar situations while in the war. Back then, a sound or slight movement ignored could mean the difference between life and death.

Shaking off the unpleasant thought, the handsome, medium height, blue eyed, writer, ran his fingers through his dark wavy hair and switched the computer back on. He punched buttons to find his last page and began typing once more only to be interrupted by the insistent ringing of the phone. "What now!" he yelled at the instrument before he angrily tore the receiver from its cradle and growled into the mouthpiece, "Hello G&G Trucking, may I help you."

"Shit, Silva. Doesn't sound like you want to help anybody? Besides, is that anyway to greet an old lover?"

Caught off guard, Manny straightened in his seat and blurted a reply. "Carrumba, Iris, why are you calling at this hour?"

"Listen Silva, if you didn't have such a nice ass, you'd be useless. It's only midnight here in California and in your last E-mail you said to call anytime after eleven."

Chastised, Manny cringed slightly in a reaction reminiscent of two years earlier when they had lived together in San Francisco. That imperfection, that way of making him feel like a scolded child had driven him from her bed and back to Boston. Nevertheless, he had loved many things about her. He leaned back and pictured Iris; her beautiful tooth-filled smile, auburn hair, slender curvaceous body, and strong self-will. When they first met he had felt he had known her forever.

For quite a while after he left San Francisco, there was no contact between them. Eventually she sent greeting cards, a few E-mails, and now a call.

Laughing nervously, Manny fumbled for an excuse, "Carrumba, Iris, I completely forgot about that E-mail. I guess it's the weird hours I'm keeping. My mind's running on fumes half the time."

"Bitch, bitch, bitch. That's all you do, Silva."

Manny pulled a pencil from a box on the desk and beat

a nervous tattoo on the side of the computer. He anticipated another salvo.

"So tell me, Silva? Do you still have an opinion on everything? And do you still obsess on all your opinions?"

Familiar with Iris' baiting tactics, Manny refused to bite. Instead he chose to remain silent. It worked. Iris changed the subject. "So when are you coming out to see me?"

Manny caught a slight slur in Iris' voice and smiled. He realized she had a few drinks in her and the tap tap of pencil on plastic slowed. "I wrote in my last E-mail that I'll visit you before I go to Central America."

"So you did, nevertheless tell me again about this crazy trip to Central America."

The critical tone in Iris' question caused the taping to begin again. Manny wondered how he could still love this woman. Then he pictured her once again, her striking looks, her concern for others, even her caustic brashness added to her charm. And the love-making. He had loved the love-making. Sensuous memories of their hours in bed sauntered through his mind. He especially remembered the feeling of oneness with the universe their love-making created.

The tapping ended and he answered, his voice muted but even, as if speaking to a child. "I'm going to Central America to look for evidence of the *Lost Continent of Atlantis*. There's a diagram carved in the base of some pyramid proving it." Manny's mind instantly saw an array of books about Edgar Casey and Casey's belief that on the base of a pyramid in Central America stood proof that Atlantis had existed. That fact had instilled itself in Manny's belief system along with a deep need for him travel to Central America in a quest to learn of Atlantis for himself.

"Where the hell did you get a weird idea like that?"

Manny held the pencil still. "It's not weird. I learned about it while reading about Edgar Cayce, a psychic."

"You mean like the guy who used to bend spoons? What's his name Geller or something?"

The pencil moved again. "No, Cayce was a healer who gave what he called "readings," while in a sort of trance. During these readings he prescribed remedies for ailments, but more importantly, he told people of their past lives."

"Get out of town! You don't believe that reincarnation bullshit, do you?"

Tap tap…"I'm not sure. But a huge percentage of the population does."

"Well, say it's true. What's the Cayce, Atlantis connection?"

On more secure grounds Manny's tapping slowed. "In Cayce's readings he found many people had lived in Atlantis about twelve thousand years ago."

"Sounds a little thin to me, Manny."

"Carrumba Iris, it isn't! Cayce said Atlanteans were of the Amerindian race. He even described their political system. Two rival groups, the Sons of the Law of ONE, and the Sons of the Law of Billial."

"The idea still sounds weird. Besides, why go to Central America? I thought Atlantis existed on some sunken Greek Island?"

"No. According to Cayce, the continent of Atlantis lay in the middle of the Atlantic Ocean. Quit laughing. Even the Greek guy, Plato, wrote about a lost civilization which existed on a great island west of the Pillars of Hercules. The Pillars of Hercules being the rock of Gibraltar."

"I'm not stupid, asshole. I know where the Pillars of Hercules are. I've been there, remember? But that still doesn't explain how the diagrams ended up in Central America."

Manny hated it when she challenged him. "The Atlanteans traveled extensively. They founded colonies around the globe, Central America included."

"Listen, Silva. I know you. All you'll do is get to Mexico, find some hot tequila and screw some hotter chicks." Manny's trousers bulged when she added sensually, "You don't have to go all the way to Central America for that. Just get your ass out to San Francisco. It's waiting for you right here."

No taps, but laughing. "Don't get your panties in a wad, you probably won't have long to wait. My book isn't going so well and I've just about had it with this job. One more hassle and I'm out of here."

"Listen, asshole, why don't you forget about writing and this Cayce business. Come out here and settle down. I can get you a job with my 'repping' company and you could make some real bucks."

"We've been all through this before, Iris. I refuse to work the rest of my life for the sake of a pay check. I want to do something special with my life. Something no one else has done. Maybe I can prove Atlantis existed!"

Sarcasm crept back into the voice on the other end of the line. "You mean it's more like your obsession to save the world."

Tap! "Call it what you like! But I feel I have a special task in my life and nothing's going to stop me from fulfilling it!"

"Okay, okay, I get the point. I'm sorry; I know how sensitive you can be, especially about your obsessions." Coy teasing returned. "You just be sure you come see me before you head off on this crazy adventure."

"Don't call it crazy, and don't worry. I said I'd be there and I will. I always keep my promises. However, right now it's time for rounds."

"Shit Silva. Who the hell's going to come stealing at this time of night?"

"Iris, when do you think thieves strike, at high noon? Besides, it's part of my job."

"All right, all right, I know you're too much of a perfectionist to change now. Sometimes I don't know why the hell I fell for you."

"My nice ass, remember?"

"Okay, maybe it was that nice ass. But you better get it out here. Soon."

"I will. You're one of my obsessions, remember?"

"I hope so. I still love you.... Bye."

Gently Manny slipped the phone back on its cradle and the pencil back in its box. The thought of Iris waiting for him in San Francisco produced a wide grin which turned to a grimace when the clock on the wall reminded Manny of rounds again. In one quick motion he stood, snatched up his clipboard, hurried across the office, and bounded down the few stairs to the main terminal door.

Cold fall air smashed Manny in the face when he opened the door. Nevertheless, even the nipping cold could not prevent his pausing to glance up at the clear star-lit sky as he crossed the tarmac toward the parked trailers. Love for Iris saturated his heart, but was soon shoved aside by a totally un-expected feeling. A different chill engulfed him. Not the chill of fall, but the chill of fear. He felt watched. With a shudder he forced the new feeling from his consciousness, hunched his shoulders against the cold and hurried to the first trailer. Manny checked its number against his list, made a mark, and hastily moved on.

By the time he had looked up from his task, Manny had checked the second row of trailers. He tucked the clipboard under his arm and rubbed his hands together for warmth. Abruptly a loud scraping sound reached him from across the terminal. Immediately Manny froze in place. He held his breath and listened hard to recognize the source of the noise. Only the distant howl of a lonely dog and the rush of cars on the nearby highway found his ears.

After an intense moment he decided the sound meant nothing and went back to checking trailers. Manny reached the fourth row and heard the noise again. He challenged. "Who's there?" Whistling wind was the only reply. For anoth-er minute he listened intensely and again concluded the sound meant nothing. But, by reading faster and skipping a few trail-ers, Manny finished his rounds quickly and re-entered the ter-minal building locking the door securely behind him. Still, a slight hint of guilt slipped through his mind for not having done his rounds perfectly.

Back in the office, Manny gingerly brought up his last page on the computer when suddenly a resounding crash came from the cavernous warehouse. Instinctively his eyes strained to see into the gloomy light of the crate-filled building. With another crash Manny grabbed the three-foot long pipe kept behind the dispatch desk and leaped silently over the railing that separated the office and storage area.

Cautiously Manny made his way through the corridors of stacked crates into the maw of the huge metal warehouse. He climbed a forklift two-thirds across the structure for a better look and heard the crash only yards to his right, climbed down and moved in that direction. When closer to the sound he raised the pipe over his head as beads of sweat dampened his brow. Silently he moved down the last row of crates and paused behind a stack of boxes which separated him from the source of the noise. His arm rose higher, he squeezed the pipe tighter and rounded the boxes as another crash sounded. Startled, he jumped back. Slowly he peered around the boxes again, lowered the pipe and breathed a sigh of relief. The sound had emanated from an unlatched damper door. A back draft from the intensifying wind had forced the damper open, and closed it with a violent crash.

After he secured the damper, Manny wiped his brow and started walking cautiously back to the office. On passing the forklift again he remembered a night when his younger brother, Dave, visited the huge warehouse. With a mischievous grin Dave had suggested they each mount a forklift and race around. It had been a rousing time. It was Dave who was remodeling his old camper for his quest to find proof of Atlantis in the pyramids of Central America. And he also remembered it was Dave who had talked him into leaving Iris and San Francisco when he called him to tell him of finishing his first book. Manny had been living with Iris but their relationship wasn't going well. Iris believed he was wasting his time writing when he should be out making money. Manny had angrily shouted back that his unemployment paid for his share of the bills, and he had no intention of ever stopping his life's work, writing.

Manny is the oldest of ten siblings and realized he felt closest to Dave. He was aware their relationship had grown even closer since the death of their mother five years earlier.

When finally seated at the computer, Manny took a couple of deep breaths, shook the old memories from his head, and put his fingers on the keyboard:

"Chinatown was bustling with life, but Shad Stone only..."

Abruptly a loud banging came from the main terminal door. "Carrumba!" Manny screamed at the warehouse. "What the hell is it this time?" The pounding continued. Furious, he slammed SAVE on the computer and yelled towards the stairway, "Hold your horses!"

Manny stomped down the short flight of steps, unlatched the door and threw it open. With his body he blocked the doorway and glared at a short round man wearing an old wide-brimmed hat and a long overcoat. On his face the man held a lost but dangerous expression in his eyes which looked past Manny. To Manny he seemed like someone straight out of a mobster movie. "What the hell do you want at this time of night?" He demanded.

Slowly the man pulled back his coat, exposing a huge gun. "My name is Patrick Hammel. I have this 357 magnum, and I want to come in."

Manny didn't stir. He stared unblinking into the man's eyes. Rage, like back in the war, tore through his body. He wanted to hurt this man. He wanted to strangle him. It took every ounce of strength to keep from going for his throat.

Finally, in milliseconds which passed in slow motion, the rage spit through Manny's clenched teeth, "Get in your car and get the fuck out of here or I'm going to rip you to pieces!"

Manny's intense reaction shocked the man out of his stupor. He took a few swipes at his nose with his thumb, his eyes brightened, and his shoulders lifted.

"Listen fellah, I didn't mean no harm," he stammered. "I don't even know what I'm doing here. I'll go. I'm going."

Manny shook as his adrenalin rush subsided. Then he watched the man scramble into an old black Buick and drive off. Behind the car, tiny wisps of blue smoke turned to dust devils and disappeared into the cold New England night.

TWO

M anny Silva left Boston in his van on the twenty-first of November. Not long after Dave completed refurbishing his van at his auto garage and had sent him off with a mischievous grin. It also hadn't been long since his run in with Patrick Hammel. His plan was to take the southern route to San Francisco thinking it would be warmer. Manny's main intent was to spend Thanksgiving day with Iris before heading south to Central America. The first leg of the journey, south to Washington D.C. then southwest through Virginia into Tennessee, passed with ease. On the second stretch through Arkansas into Texas, a feeling of uneasiness began creeping into his consciousness.

Manny glanced at his odometer when he entered Arizona from New Mexico. He had driven 3,000 miles and by his calculations 700 more separated him from Iris. The trip so far was exhausting, although uneventful except for an eerie feeling of being watched. The uneasiness felt similar to what he had experienced shortly before Patrick Hammel had attempted to force his way into G&G Trucking. Worse still, advertising billboards attempted to sidetrack him with their seductive slogans of "Stop at Pablo's" or spend the rest of his life in some "retirement village."

Retirement isn't going to come early to me, Manny happily thought as he motored across Arizona. Even the soreness in his back from driving eighteen hours a day for four days while trying to sleep in his cold van at night couldn't prevent his good mood. *I set a goal to see Iris by Thanksgiving,* he thought, *and carrumba, I'm gonna make it.* As dotted white lines blurred to a single white and melded with the thumping of the concrete highway, Manny smiled. He felt free. Free to live adventures and free to write about them. With that thought he pictured the two facets of his plan.

The first wasn't far from fruition and he smiled at visions of Iris only a state away. He would spend time with her before traveling to Central America. The second facet, he wouldn't allow himself to think of; the possibility of staying with Iris. Although deep inside he knew love could make it happen.

To battle road boredom, Manny fantasized about the fame he'd garnish by locating proof of Atlantis, and thought about all he'd learned about Atlantis from the Cayce material. Facts regarding their development of flying machines and death rays. Cayce's claim that the Atlanteans controlled a cast of "lesser" beings. Manny wondered who those beings could have been. Maybe remnants of other races like the Neanderthal or Cro-Magnon he speculated. The matter of the "beasts" puzzled Manny even more. Cayce claimed the Atlanteans called a meeting of all races to combat a plague of beasts. What could these beasts be? Dinosaurs. Manny knew one thing for sure, if Cayce spoke the truth about the Atlanteans having a high technological society which destroyed itself, it could happen again, and he aimed to prevent that.

While his van glided down the highway, Manny's thoughts glided back to Iris. He remembered the good times they had, smiled, and drove the van harder toward San Francisco. In only hours he'd be holding her, Manny sighed to himself. In his heart he secretly knew if their old magic still existed, he might stay in the City by the Bay and never continue his quest.

As Manny Silva drove toward San Francisco, Jean Flack tugged on her earlobe, and then massaged her aching head. The pain was so bad she named it, *Migraine Gigantica*, which she told her boss after lunch. Jean was in too much pain to explain that *Gigantica* was the name scientists had given to nine foot tall ape bones found in caves in South Asia. Surprisingly human bones had also been found in the same caves and from the same time period.

Instead of the explanation, Jean could only think of the pain. It had crept up on her slowly, just as the others had over the past month. They always began when the word, Solram, scrambled threw her mind. She saw several doctors for the problem and all gave the same diagnosis, and the same remedy. They said she suffered from tension and prescribed pain killers. The pain killers worked temporarily but eventually Migraine Gigantica returned.

Frustrated with the doctors, Jean visited a counselor at the Center for the Elevation of Body and Mind, who told her she had bad karma left over from a previous life, and something in her present lifestyle triggered the headache response. For a fee, the counselor taught Jean a healing mantra and said the next time she got the pain to go straight home and repeat the mantra continually until her karma and headaches were cured.

Still the headaches persisted, along with the newly acquired habit of nervously tugging her ear. Today's headache felt the worst so far, and she pulled several times on her lobe while asking her boss for the afternoon off. Jean disliked leaving early. She was due for a promotion at Seager's, San Francisco's second largest importer of hand painted sushi bowls, and taking time off would certainly be held against her. If only the pounding pain would stop, she thought while backing out of the parking space and heading for her apartment in Daly City.

With tears of pain in her eyes Jean wheeled her big Chevy SUV like a Ferrari through heavy afternoon traffic. She couldn't wait to get home to a hot bath and her mantra. She tried the chant in the car but the traffic and the pressure in her head wouldn't allow her to concentrate. Suddenly a small Fiat cut her off. She jammed her foot on the brake and swung into the passing lane. As she sped past the little red demon, she threw the driver the meanest finger and angriest glare in her repertoire.

By the time Jean Flack saw her driveway, the combination of anger and the pounding pain in her head reached the crescendo of a symphony orchestra. However, at least I'm home, she thought. She need only drive through the tiny passageway between apartments to the garages in back and she'd be steps from relief.

Jean slowed, turned left into the driveway, and found the small blue Volkswagen belonging to the women in apartment 3A entering the passageway from the other end. Jean stopped and gave a gentle toot on the horn. It's too difficult for me to back into the traffic, she thought. All the woman in the VW need do is back into her garage space and let me pass. The woman in the VW stopped and tooted twice. Obviously she believed she had the right of way.

Again, the mere thought of turning her head to back into the traffic made Jean wince with pain. She attempted to calm herself with a deep breath then stuck her head out the window and called across the thirty feet separating the two cars, "Could you please back up? I must get to my apartment quickly." The other woman's head shot out her window and she yelled, "I have an important meeting to attend. Would you please get the hell out of my way?"

"I have a terrible headache, please let me through."

"Listen lady, I don't give a damn about your headache. I'm late for a meeting and if you don't move that piece of shit car, I'll come over there and shove it where it's too big to fit!"

At that remark Jean Flack snapped. The pain in her head felt like an elephant's stomp. She had almost been killed in traffic, and to top it off, some ball busting bitch wouldn't let her pass. Now the screech in Jean's throat matched the screech of her tires as she dropped the shift lever of the big Chevy into gear. Without thought she screamed the word, *Solram,* and smashed head on into the little blue Volkswagen bug.

Manny crossed the Arizona border into California exhausted but elated. Iris' state, he sighed to himself, and by dusk he saw the city of Los Angeles rise eerily on the horizon. The heavy yellow smog hanging over the city didn't surprise him, but the nauseous feeling in his stomach did. As he drove over a slight rise Manny suddenly gripped the van's wheel white-knuckle tight. Ahead of him the city shimmered and Manny saw it replaced by an immense fortress-like temple. From its walls rose huge geometrically shaped spires hung with mucous-like smog. A slime covered moat surrounded the structure and random movements suggested some massive denizen lurked below. Again, an overwhelming sense of being watched gripped him and a prickling sensation of fear rose on the back of his neck. The image lasted only seconds before a slight breeze turned the shimmering fortress back into a concrete and steel city.

In an attempt to rid himself of the dreadful apparition, Manny filled his mind with fantasies of his first night with Iris. But the image lingered until he reached the last set of mountains separating him from his love.

By the time Manny climbed half-way up the second mountain, his van had slowed to 15 mph, then five. Still he pushed on, crawling up steep inclines and coasting down the far side, until he reached flatter land on the outskirts of Fresno. Suddenly his engine gasped then clattered. The overheat light blinked fiercely and Manny swerved hard right, almost tipping as he just made it onto an exit ramp. Half-way down the ramp the engine died leaving Manny just enough momentum to reach a truck stop.

He didn't need to be a mechanical genius to figure out his engine had blown. Even before he lifted the lid to the smoking engine compartment, Manny had decided to leave the van and catch a bus. Nothing would stop him from sleeping with Iris that night.

The big Greyhound deposited Manny in San Francisco. Without hesitation he threw his bag into a taxi and yelled, "Take me to Daly City."

Upon arrival Manny dashed up the steps two at a time toward Iris' third floor apartment. As he climbed, he took little notice when passing a bandaged woman on the second floor landing who sat in a rocker tugging her earlobe. Only one thing occupied his mind and his heart soared with anticipation. When he reached Iris' door, he could barely control his excitement and called out while pressing her buzzer. "Iris, it's me, Manny."

It took three more presses and another call, before Manny heard an angry, "Wait a fucking minute."

When the door finally opened, Manny faced a vacant stare. Iris didn't rush into his arms, didn't even smile. She merely mumbled a barely audible, "Come in," and wandered into her bedroom.

Stunned, Manny stood in the doorway watching her flop onto her waterbed. Without even a look at him she asked for a glass of water while reaching for a vile of pills on the nightstand. Manny gladly filled the request; the activity gave him a chance to regroup his emotions. He hadn't driven himself and his van into the ground only to let a rough start ruin what could be a great relationship. It's late, he told himself, and she's probably just tired. It'll take a little time, but she'll soften up.

Wrong. When handed the glass, Iris gave a curt, "Thank you," and downed the water along with three pink pills. She added, "I have to get some rest. You can sleep on the bearskin rug in the living room. We'll talk in the morning."

Words caught in his chest, he couldn't speak. I pushed myself all this way and she won't even sleep with me, he thought. Crushed, Manny went into the living room, sat on the bearskin, and cried.

It had taken Manny four days to get from Boston to San Francisco and four days was all he could take of Iris. She wouldn't go out, not even for Thanksgiving dinner. She would only lie in bed and moan about how much she hated that bitch downstairs, who for no reason at all, smashed into her precious little VW bug.

The Monday following Thanksgiving, Manny took a bus to Fresno to tend his damaged van. After finding a garage, he called Iris.

"Hello, Iris Ivory." Her business voice.

"It's me, Manny."

Her tone softened. "Shit, asshole, where are you? When I got up you were gone."

"Weren't you listening yesterday when I said I had to get the van fixed?"

"Shit Silva, I forgot. I've had a lot on my mind."

"I know you have, and none of it pertains to me."

"What do you mean?"

"I mean, that I just spent four days with you. And in those four days, you barely acknowledged my presence."

"Since the accident I haven't been myself."

"You could say that."

"Shit, Silva, when you get back we'll talk about it."

"I'm not coming back."

"What do you mean?"

"Just what I said. I'm getting the van fixed, driving to Vegas and then to my cousin's in Dallas. Then I'm heading for Central America."

"I don't understand why you're doing this? Please come back."

Iris sounded like she was about to cry, but Manny couldn't remember her ever crying. His own voice, hardly audible, he croaked brokenheartedly into the phone, "Goodbye Iris."

Manny explained the hard-luck story about his first night in Las Vegas to Kersh, the man driving him to his van parked at Circus Circus. "I took my last quarter, broke it into nickels and dropped them into five different slot machines. I lost."

Low on gas and out of money, Manny had met Kersh while hitching back from an employment agency. Almost from the time he climbed in the pickup Manny had a strange feeling he somehow knew this person.

"Don't get too weirded out about it, man. Happens to half the dudes who come to this place."

"Ya, but I only paid for one night at the campground and I don't have a place to keep my van while I look for work."

"No problem, good buddy. You can park next to my mobile home. I live with my girlfriend and her two kids, but she won't mind."

With no money and no other choice, Manny accepted. Besides he thought, Kersh seems friendly enough. Except for his eyes.

Kersh had piercing eyes. Eyes that delved directly to a man's soul. Manny sensed vileness behind those orbs, even with the broad smile curling his lips. And, although Manny found the eyes unsettling, Kersh's friendly, let it all hang out, manner convinced him to accept the invitation.

It only took a few days for Manny to realize Kersh's friendly style masked a terrible evil. Manny decided to leave and told Kersh when he arrived home that night.

"Got great news Kersh. Found a job today. Problem is, it's on the other side of town and I'll have to move over that way."

"No problem at all, good buddy. But you'll have to stay at least one more night so we can have us a last supper."

With resignation, Manny accepted.

After dinner the evening progressed innocently over beer and a few puffs of what Kersh called, "lumbo." Pam, Kersh's girlfriend, stood at the sink doing dishes and her two small boys played with a pair of GI Joe dolls on the floor. Meanwhile, Kersh pulled open an end table drawer and showed Manny an item he had bought in Mexico. "It's an Akarri, an ancient ceremonial sword used by the Mayans." Something about the name instantly attracted Manny's attention.

The Akarri was short, more knife than sword. It looked about eighteen inches long with a spiked brass knuckle-like handle tapered to a point. The blade reminded Manny of a Bowie knife with the lower half serrated.

The inquisitive look on Manny's face encouraged Kersh to explain, "The guy I bought it from said the Mayans used the Akarri for human sacrifices. The serrated edge helps cut through the rib cage. With the ribs cut, they removed the heart and ate it."

With the explanation of the significance of the knife, Kersh's eyes changed. To Manny, they seemed to glow. As Kersh finished his narrative, his glowing stare moved from the Akarri to Manny.

Manny sat mesmerized by the eyes and a sinister grin

pulled Kersh's face into a grotesque mask. Abruptly Kersh rose. He stomped to one of the boys, pulled the GI Joe from his hand, and sliced off the doll's head. The boy yelled in protest at Kersh who hit him viciously across the back with the flat of the knife.

A scream of pain brought Pam rushing to the boy's defense. Without a word Kersh smashed her full in the face with the brass-knuckled handle of the Akarri. Manny heard a terrible thud as Pam's head hit the floor. She screamed and cursed at Kersh as blood poured from her cheek.

The brutality startled Manny out of his stupor. He sprung from his chair and jumped between Pam and Kersh. "Leave her alone!"

Kersh halted his assault on Pam, as a maniacal grin spread across his face. In a deep, reptilian-like voice he hissed at Manny. "Finally, the sheep come to their slaughter."

The glow in Kersh's evil eyes grew stronger. Manny couldn't tell if he was paralyzed by fear or some force created by the glowing hate-filled eyes.

Kersh' voiced hissed again. It sounded as if it rose from a deep well. "Your journey to past worlds ends here, warrior. I shall cut out your heart and destroy your soul."

The glow of power from the madman's eyes grew stronger as Manny's will grew weaker. He could barely move his feet in a backward retreat to the door. When he reached it, he lacked the strength to turn the knob. Finally Manny managed to tear his eyes from those of Kersh, but he could only focus on the hideous Akarri, poised to kill.

Manny forced his eyes from the Akarri and searched frantically for a weapon. His eye caught the glint of a can of furniture polish on a nearby table. Against the enormous power exerted by Kersh, Manny compelled his left hand to grasp the can. As Kersh raised his arm higher for the killing stroke, Manny lifted the can and sprayed Kersh's blazing eyes. With a scream, Kersh released the Akarri, his hands flying to his face.

Manny rushed to Pam who had already picked herself up. He grabbed a kid under each arm and scrambled for the door. Pam followed on his heels.

Outside, Manny yelled to her, "Quick, jump in the van. I'll get you to the hospital."

"No. I'm all right to drive. It's you he's after. Get going." Manny pleaded again as he noticed blood still pouring from under the hand Pam held to her cheek. "Let me drive you to the hospital!"

"I told you, I'll be fine. Get moving before he can see again!"

Still holding the side of her face, Pam herded the kids into Kersh's truck. As she peeled out of the gravel driveway, pebbles flew and Manny stumbled to his van. He pulled open the door and noticed his hands shaking. He still groped in his pocket for keys when Kersh bolted out the door towards him, Akarri raised, a terrifying scream on his lips.

With Kersh only seconds away, Manny finally managed to slip the key into the ignition. His hands still shaking, he turned the key only to hear the old van give a short grunt and die. Screaming hysterically, Kersh pulled Manny's door open, and waved the Akarri wildly. Panic stricken, Manny turned the key once more. This time the engine sputtered to life and Manny stomped on the gas. Kersh refused to let go of the door handle and fanatically held on while Manny dragged him across the yard. With panic still rising, Manny swung the wheel to the left and right. Kersh lost his grip and flew off the van. In the rear view mirror, Manny caught a glimpse of Kersh tumbling along the ground as he shifted to second and hit the tar road with wheels screeching. He didn't look back. He only prayed Pam and the kids had made it as he sped out of Vegas and away from Kersh.

Miles and hours later, Manny felt it safe to stop. He settled uneasily into the sleeping bag in the van's rear, but didn't notice a curl of blue smoke seep through a partially opened window and wrap itself around his head. Nor did he notice the memory of his encounter with Kersh mingle with the smoke, seep back out the window, and disperse into the cool night air. What he did notice was a feeling he had never experienced before. He felt it first in his bowels which almost moved. Then in his stomach which churned over, then through his chest which heaved as he gasped for air. Finally in his larynx causing a wail of pain that pierced the silent desert.

Manny Silva watched the dentist's nurse retrieve his file from a gray cabinet. Four months had elapsed since he vaguely remembered a stop in Las Vegas and five months had passed since Iris had broken his heart. Manny still hurt badly from his encounter with Iris, and he fought the pain of their last phone conversation by focusing his attention elsewhere. That attention fell mainly on the backside of the attractive nurse as he absentmindedly ran his tongue over the new cap on his front tooth.

Manny had broken the tooth in an accident on the construction site where he worked as a carpenter. Today's visit called for a final adjustment to a new gold-backed crown. As he followed the nurse towards the dentist's chair, he happily realized he'd soon leave the construction job to continue his quest.

He would head for Central America in two weeks, but since arriving in Dallas, Manny had made one change in his original plan. Experienced travelers cautioned that his van made a prime target for theft in Mexico and he had decided to leave the van with his cousin. In place of the van, he had bought a used suitcase, had attached straps for backpacking, and planned to hitch, take trains, busses, and if necessary, fly to wherever destiny led him.

Excited about the trip, Manny snapped back to reality when one of the nurse's ample bosoms brushed his shoulder as she clipped a napkin around his neck. After she placed a mask over his mouth and nose, the dentist entered.

"Hi, Manny. Guess this'll be your last visit. How about a little extra nitrous oxide to celebrate?"

Muffled through the mask came, "Beam me up, Scotty."

With gas hissing in his ears, Manny felt his head spin. When a breast touched his arm, sexual arousal electrified him as visions of a giant phallic symbol formed into an Atlas rocket which blasted into space. This led him to conclude that sex represented the evolution of humans. The destiny of the race would be to fecundate the universe. Humans could never die, they would expand, expand, expand. With every vision of expansion the spinning in Manny's head increased.

On the verge of passing out, the spinning stopped and

instead of the universe whirling around him, he passed through it. However, it wasn't a dentist chair he sat in, but the control seat of an airship. Through the cockpit he saw millions of stars.

An amber light flashing on the control panel caught his attention. Instinctively Manny flicked a switch. Promptly a man looking like an American Indian wearing a metallic jumpsuit and helmet fitted with feathers appeared on a screen. He spoke.

"This is STA-GEL from Poseidon base 763, Command Headquarters, calling Vector 513. Come in 513. Repeat. This is Poseidon 763, Command Headquarters. Come in Vector 513. Lieutenant Commander MAN-DAR, do you copy? Come in MAN-DAR."

Manny looked at the console. Stenciled in black letters he read, "Vector 513." It amazed him that he recognized the strange script. Furthermore, the man on the screen had not spoken English yet Manny had understood every word. A greater shock came when he flicked a switch and *he* responded in the strange tongue.

"This is Vector 513, Lieutenant Commander MAN-DAR speaking. I read you loud and clear. Over."

The man on the screen flashed a salute which Manny returned without hesitation. The man spoke again.

"Lieutenant Commander MAN-DAR, order number 387-0 has been rescinded. Intelligence reports indicate Gigantica Beast activity at the original rendezvous coordinates in Euroland. The liaison officer traveling with the Euro delegation has been informed. He will transport the ambassadors via Vector freighter to sector 27-6-304. Do you copy, 513?"

Great Baal! MAN-DAR cursed to himself. The alternate rendezvous is no safer than the original. It lays 800 kilometers further northwest and worse still, it lays in Angleland. The mere thought of traveling to a land ruled by accursed Zarharrab, High Priest of the Temple of Inanna, dampens my tunic. Besides, MAN-DAR thought, what of Gigantica Beasts in the vicinity? This new model Vector includes sensors to detect Beasts within a kilometer. Besides, a blaster will kill any Gigantica Beast. Baal, he cursed to himself again. He flicked a switch as his other fingers tapped irritably on his Akarri's scabbard.

"This is MAN-DAR. Does Poseidon Command realize where they sent the Euro delegation? Have they not heard of what happened to the last patrol that had the misfortune of landing in that sector? Over."

With brow knotted, the man on the screen spoke sternly, "I am acutely aware of your obsessivness when it comes to missions, Lieutenant Commander MAN-DAR. But may I remind you that this is merely a routine exercise. Besides, what Poseidon Command and the Atlantean Empire decide is of no concern to you. Your only concern is to complete the mission to the best of your limited abilities! Do you copy, Vector 513! Over!"

MAN-DAR's eyes burned into the image on the screen, his fingernails still tapping on his Akarri. STA-GEL stood as his fiercest rival since their school days at the Temple of Learning. Even now, as MAN-DAR looked at his rival's angry face, he could see the hatred. MAN-DAR piloted a new Vector Battler on a mission for the Empire while STA-GEL ran messages for Poseidon Command. Still, he knew STA-GEL could cause him trouble and possibly had something to do with the change of plans. Reluctantly, MAN-DAR flicked the switch while making a mental note to confront STA-GEL later.

"Lieutenant Commander MAN-DAR here. I acknowledge the change of orders. I will proceed to the new rendezvous point immediately. Over." Without waiting for further contact, MAN-DAR hit the switch and STA-GEL faded from the screen.

MAN-DAR wasted no time as he punched in the coordinates taking the ship automatically toward the new sight. When completed, he sat up and roared to the stars, "Great Baal, I know Zarharrab has something to do with this!" Then muttering to himself, "I have a hunch bringing the Euro delegation to the conference on the Gigantica Beasts concerns more than a routine exercise."

As MAN-DAR's angry words flew out at the universe, a large fair-haired figure seated in the rear of the cabin winced and raised his hands in protection from expected blows. When none came he slowly raised his eyes and went back to preparing the ceremonial helmet MAN-DAR would wear when he greeted the Euro delegation.

MAN-DAR never looked at the creature who sat to his rear. Instead he switched back to manual guidance, and reached for the controls.

"Mr. Silva! Mr. Silva! You're not allowed to touch the instruments. Mr. Silva, wake up." Manny Silva's eyes popped open when he finally heard the nurse's alarm. At first the room seemed tilted and out-of-focus. He blinked a few times and found himself in the padded chair, his hands grasping the dentist's drill.

THREE

M anny Silva heaved his suitcase into the back of an old Ford pickup and followed. He landed between a pair of teenage boys. Two hitched rides had gotten him 300 miles south of Dallas and the driver of the pickup had said he would give him a lift to Saltillo, Mexico. From Saltillo Manny could catch a train to Mexico City.

After hitching through southern Texas, during which Manny thought mostly about how far he was getting from Iris, the pickup finally stopped at the border. After he jumped from the truck to stretch his legs, Manny introduced himself. The Mexican American family named Arillo, included Arturo the father, Linda, his wife, and their two sons, Luis and Paco. Manny noticed bandages on Luis' wrists and inquired, "How'd you get hurt?" When no answer came he tried a lighter approach, "I bet the other guy looks pretty bad, huh?"

Luis stared at his feet still unresponsive. Linda took Manny by the arm and led him to the opposite side of the truck. "Don't think the boy lacks manners, Manny. His injuries cause him embarrassment."

"Sorry, I was only being friendly."

"I know. Your eyes show sensitivity for others. It's just that, well, Luis has tried to kill himself. Those bandages represent his third attempt."

Poking his long weatherworn face around the truck, Arturo waved, indicating they should go.

"Come, Manny," said the tiny but pretty mother, "ride with us in the cab. On the way we can talk."

During the 200-mile trip from the border to Saltillo, Manny and Linda with an occasional grunt of affirmation from Arturo, conversed about many things over the constant hum of the pickup and blaring Spanish music from the radio. But much of the conversation revolved around Luis.

Linda explained the attempts Luis made on his life and that a number of doctors and psychiatrists had examined him to no avail. "As a last resort, we're taking Luis to Saltillo in search of a faith healer who we hope can help."

The idea of a faith healer intrigued Manny; reminding him of Edgar Cayce. "What can you tell me about this healer?"

"Senora Marita Camilla. In Mexico they call her, 'Curendera de Saltillo,' Healer of Saltillo. Even before my parents moved to the States years ago, Senora Camilla had become a legend."

Fascinated, Manny pressed Linda further.

Linda glanced quickly at Arturo, whose eyes never left the road, and answered hesitantly. "Well, she claims to be the re-incarnation of a great mystic who visited Mexico thousands of years before the Mayans. She says a great Empire across the sea sent him to help heal the peoples of the region. You see, in that incarnation, she lived life as a man called Sol Ram. Even today, when she performs her healing rituals, she slips into a trance and her voice becomes masculine. Senora Camilla claims Sol Ram makes the diagnosis and prescribes the cures."

Manny became excited by the similarities between Edgar

Cayce and the Curendera in Linda's story. Maybe he had stumbled onto the first clue in his quest. Eagerly he asked to accompany them to the healing.

Again Linda's answered hesitantly after a glance at Arturo. "Well, I guess if it's all right with Luis. And of course, Senora Camilla."

Early the next morning Manny and the Arillo family searched Saltillo for the location of the healing ceremony. They had no problem getting directions since everyone in town knew of the Curendera, but although they quickly found the Senora's house, getting to see her proved another matter.

People seeking an audience filled her courtyard. The crowd grew so large, the overflow spilled into the plaza across the street where Manny and the Arillo family sought refuge from the blistering sun under a large tree.

After waiting hours, an aide to the Curendera led the Arillo family, followed by Manny, to Senora Marita Camilla, who sat on a small stool at the rear of her courtyard. The tiny old woman Manny saw had sunken eyes and gnarled hands. Her thinning gray hair slipped from a bun tied behind a wrinkled ear, and she wore a simple white peasant frock. In one hand she held a leafy branch.

Unspoken rules allowed no petition to directly reach Curendera's ear, so Linda explained her son's dilemma to an aide. She in turn bent, whispering the problem in Senora Camilla's ear. With a signal from the Curendera, an aide grasped Luis' shoulders and positioned him directly in front of the Senora.

Slowly rising, the Curendera closed her eyes and swayed slightly on her heels. Suddenly her eyes popped open. Shocked,

Manny saw the sunken orbs shine with vibrant life. Gingerly she lifted the branch and shook it rhythmically around the teenager. From her lips issued a deep masculine voice that chanted in a strange language. Soon, two more aides appeared. To one Senora Camilla handed the branch while she took from the other a glass of water and an egg. Still chanting, the healer rubbed the egg from the boy's forehead to his stomach. Abruptly ceasing the chant, she broke the egg over the glass of water. In disbelief, Manny watched a ball of hair fall into the liquid. The Curendera whispered to her aide who turned to Linda.

"The Senora wishes to convey to you that your son's body contains much agitation. She has removed some, but more sessions are necessary. Can you stay in Saltillo for a week?"

"I do not know. I must talk it over with my husband."

Senora Camilla whispered again to the aide.

"The Senora understands. You may return tomorrow with your decision."

The aide lifted her arm in dismissal, but before it raised more than a few inches, Senora Camilla sprang to her feet. Her spindly arm shot out and grasped the aid's wrist firmly and the old woman's head jerked sharply toward Manny. Her eyes met his and a deep male voice spoke in perfect English.

"In an age long ago, you were a great warrior. You accomplished much good for those around you and helped preserve the world from a great evil.

Continue your quest. But beware; the evil ones attempt to bar your way. Evil ones from the past who would change the course of history. Those with eyes that pierce and those with eyes of differing colors. They control the power to affect future events. You are not alone on your journey, but listen and remember. Accidents do not exist. Time and the physical universe are like rings of smoke. Each contains individual form, yet it takes but the slightest breath to blend or blow them apart."

Senora Marita Camilla's eyes closed her head drooping to her withered chest. Two aides helped the slumping old woman to her stool.

Later that evening, Arturo and Linda wished Manny, "God speed and good luck on your quest," as they dropped him off at the railroad station. His weak Spanish helped Manny buy a ticket, but the cryptic warning given by Senora Camilla still played havoc with his nerves. Even the rhythmic "chug chug" of the old slow moving wooden-seated train couldn't put Manny to sleep. Exhausted, he sat worrying about time, accidents, and evil eyes, until the early morning sun crept into the car.

After a morning of watching countless small adobe towns, desert cactus, and an occasional dead dog or donkey slide across his view, Manny craved liquid to ease his thirst. He also needed food to ease his hunger, and company to ease his loneliness. His lack of Spanish prevented his locating a dining car, but after watching a man walk by several times holding up a bottle while calling out, "cervesa," he realized the man meant beer and bought a bottle. Likewise, he curbed his hunger when the train stopped at a station and an old woman walked through calling, "tortillas."

The problem of company solved itself by late afternoon

when a red haired woman walked past him to the rest rooms at the far end of the rocking railroad car. Before she entered a door marked, "Damas," she turned and smiled sensually in Manny's direction. After her curvaceous rear passed through the door, Manny waited a few minutes, tucked his feelings for Iris in the back of his mind, and casually walked to the front of the car. As the woman exited the powder room, he allowed the rock of the car to bump his shoulder against hers. He apologized quickly.

"Excuse me, these trains get pretty crowded."

"You're not whistling on Staten Island, handsome. I've been stuck all day in a car stuffed with Mexican soldiers."

"You're an American?" Manny smiled widely. "Haven't heard a word of English all day and as much as I hate to admit it, my Spanish isn't perfect."

"Neither is mine," she answered, her sensuous smile brightening her face. "My name's Ginger Haskell, what's yours?"

"Manny Silva. Where are you from?"

"Brooklyn, as if you couldn't guess." She added without taking a breath, "Actually I was born in New Jersey but we moved when I was five."

As Ginger spoke, two soldiers pushed by, both scowling at Manny.

"I think we're blocking the isle. If you haven't anything better to do, how about joining me for a while? The seat next to mine's empty."

"Does the Pope live in Rome? I'd love to. Anything to get away from those soldiers. They haven't stopped babbling at me all day and I can hardly understand a word they're saying.

Although I can probably guess what's on their minds," she added with an extra dash of coyness in her smile.

Manny laughed at her joke as he led lovely redhead back to his seat. Standing aside to let her slide to the window, he couldn't help but notice her figure once more. No wonder those soldiers gave me such dirty looks, he thought, she's perfect.

Seated, Ginger wasted no time jumping into conversation. Among other things, Manny learned she was a nurse on vacation, how she disliked her parents, what her cat Fluffy ate, and that she was spacing around Central America to wherever adventure led her.

Manny sat captivated by the bubbly redhead with her gorgeous figure and intriguing eyes. Although oddly enough, each eye sported a different color, one brown one blue, but they didn't detract from her alluring appearance. Suddenly he remembered the warning from the Curendera about someone evil with differing colored eyes, but almost as quickly he dismissed it, rationalizing that in no way could this perfect creature cause him any problems.

After an hour of playing "getting to know you," Ginger's expression became serious. "Listen, Manny, seeing we're both traveling the same direction, why don't we join forces to save on expenses? Furthermore," she announced with a sultry smile, "why stay in cheap hotels as singles when we can combine our money and stay in much nicer places." Instantly Manny forgot about everything except the pretty redhead beside him and quickly agreed.

The couple found a beautiful old hotel in Mexico City. Decorated in marble and wood, the place had the ambiance of an older, more romantic age. Manny became especially excited when the desk clerk informed them Hemingway had once written there.

Manny and Ginger explored most of the usual tourist attractions in the first six days they spent together. Their tour included many restaurants, nightclubs, parks, and films, but on the seventh day they felt in need of heavier culture. Manny suggested the Archaeological museum downtown and Ginger concurred.

In the museum they meandered through halls and rooms jammed with artifacts. The couple each chose to linger over items which caught their eye. Ginger was particularly drawn to ancient medical instruments that Manny thought looked more like implements of torture than healing. But by early afternoon aching feet and empty stomachs convinced them to seek lunch. As they headed for the exit, a glass case filled with skulls seized Manny's attention.

"Ginger, look at this!" Ginger heaved a sigh of resignation as she followed him to the case. "Look at these skulls. They're shaped completely different than ours. Check out that one with the huge bones over his eye sockets. Amazing. And according to the plaque they're our ancestors. They used fire, stone tools, and lived in a social environment." Ginger gave Manny a blank stare unable to comprehend his excitement. "Don't you see?"

"No, Manny. I don't see anything but a bunch of bones and I'm starved. Let's get out of here and get something to eat."

Unmoved, Manny excitedly continued his obsessive discourse. "Did you ever read Tolkien, you know, with the hobbits and elves? You must have read the Lord of the Rings?"

Ginger's answer sounded unenthusiastic. "They got passed

around the hospital for a while. I picked up The Hobbit and read some of the Rings, but I really couldn't get into it. Can we go now?" Ginger started playing with Manny's shirt buttons in an attempt to seduce him from the museum. Manny wouldn't budge.

"Listen, Ginger, I'm not kidding. Can't you imagine these creatures? Scientists call them cave men, but can't you see them as the same creatures Tolkien wrote about? Picture the one with bones over his eyes being Gollum or an Orc. And that big one over there, with the large skull, Cro-Magnon. Can't you see him as one of Tolkien's elves?" Manny let his imagination soar while Ginger got angry. With her right hand still twirling a button, her left hand slipped into his rear jeans pocket. Gently tugging she attempted again to draw him from the exhibit, but to no avail.

"Tolkien wrote of elves as tall, intelligent beings. They lived in forests and knew magic. You know it was the Cro-Magnons who painted those famous cave pictures at Lascaux in France. And in his book, Silmarillion, Tolkien wrote that elves constantly migrated west to reach a great island where they could exit the earth plane body and soul. Atlantis!"

Pleadingly Ginger gazed into Manny's eyes while applying still more pressure inside his jeans pocket. "Come on honey, that's all speculation and I'm starved." Manny, no longer able to resist the beautiful nurse, took a last glance at the display as she steered him through the exit.

They strolled along arm in arm and in silence. Manny's mind was still filled with Tolkien and Cro-Magnons, but looking at Ginger he had no idea what filled hers. Her stare seemed millennia away.

Manny finally broke the silence with a cough. "So, now that we've done the museum bit, what do you want to eat?"

"I don't know, maybe a hamburger or something like that."

"A hamburger! The only places to get them are in the Hamburgesas and they're filthy."

"Come on Mannykins, what's the use of coming to a different country if you don't taste the culture."

"Culture. A hamburger? Listen, Ginger, so far we've managed to eat and drink safely. Let's not push our luck."

Ginger's hand slipped again into his jeans pocket. "I'm dying for a hamburger and it's about time we got down with the people."

Manny didn't answer, but found it impossible to resist the enticing redhead, especially when that certain gleam sparkled in her odd-colored eyes. They wandered along in silence a few more blocks when Ginger suddenly stopped.

"Look, there's the perfect place."

Manny followed Ginger's gaze. Between two dilapidated buildings on a small side street, Manny saw a faded sign, "Hamburgesa." Manny turned to Ginger. "Carrumba, that place looks condemned. There's naked kids' running in and out for Pete's sake."

Ginger scowled. "Manny. It's another culture. We have to sample what it has to offer."

Unfortunately for Manny, the sparkle in Ginger's eyes and her sensuous smile broke his resolve.

By the next morning he felt sick. After using the toilet for the fifth time, Manny eased himself onto the hotel bed as Ginger dialed a phone number.

"Hello. Is this the American Consulate? This is Ginger

Haskell from Brooklyn. I'd like to speak to someone in regards to the need of a visa for entering Guatemala. Yes, I'll hold." With her hand over the mouthpiece she said to Manny, "I'm trying to find out if you need a visa to get into Guatemala." Someone came on the line and Ginger asked again about the visa, listened, and then spoke once more. "Thank you very much, sir. I understand. Thank you, bye." Ginger hung up and turned to Manny.

"We're in luck. You definitely do not need a visa to get into Guatemala. We can leave tomorrow morning."

"That's great." Manny attempted to sound enthusiastic, but as he packed for the thirty-six hour bus ride to Guatemala City, he felt even sicker. Pain and the bowel movements increased steadily through the afternoon and into the evening. He considered getting something from a pharmacy to alleviate the symptoms but decided against it. "I only need to get my system used to the new environment." Manny called to Ginger from the bathroom. "Had the same problem in the war and got over it. This'll pass by morning."

The next day dawned bright, sunny and hot, but Manny did not feel better. Sweat dripped from his forehead stung his eyes by the time he and Ginger loaded their luggage into the overhead rack and found seats on the bus. After an hour's traveling, Manny's soaked clothes clung to his body and he greatly regretted not having stopped at a drug store.

In the twenty hours it took from Mexico City to the Guatemalan border, Manny endured the worst agony of his life. The temperature in the bus reached 120 degrees with humidity around the same. Manny's own temperature soared, and then chills began. After his ninth trip to the restroom, he told Ginger a permanent ring had formed around his rear.

Finally the bus lurched to a stop and the driver announced everyone must disembark for a passport and baggage check. Manny hauled their suitcases off the rack, and while handing Ginger hers, he stated, "I'll catch up with you later. I've got to find a toilet."

Relieved, Manny left the rest room but still sweated profusely. Unable to locate Ginger, he fell in line behind his fellow passengers. Up ahead a uniformed border guard sat behind a small table stamping passports with a heavy "thud thud." Upon reaching the mustached inspector, Manny pushed his passport across the table and waited for the expected "thud thud." Instead the man pushed his passport back without looking up and said in accented English, "Please stand aside, sir. You will not be allowed to enter Guatemala."

Manny's body shook from fever, as his fingernails beat an angry tattoo on the table. "The hell I can't! Nothing's wrong with my passport!"

"Si Senor, nothing is wrong with your passport," the guard answered still without looking up, "but you have no visa."

"The man at the U.S. consulate said I didn't need one!"

Slowly he raised his head and looked directly at Manny. "I do not care what the man at the consulate said. It is the policy of the Guatemala government to require a visa. You cannot enter the country. If you wish, you may go to Manzilla and get one."

"Where the hell's that?"

"About eight miles back."

"What about the bus?"

"You can return here for the next one. Please move along, others wait."

Manny protested once more, but another spasm of abdominal pain cut short his tirade. Resigned, he turned away from the inspector and searched for Ginger. Finally he spotted her in a line reboarding the bus. He shuffled weakly toward her.

"Ginger, they won't let me enter Guatemala without a visa."

"That's too bad, Manny. What are you going to do?"

"I have to go back to the last town to get one. The inspector said another bus stops here in a few hours. Will you wait for me?"

Ginger's odd eyes hardened and her sensuous smile turned sinister. "Gee, I'm sorry Manny, but I can't wait. I've met this nice English couple and I've decided to travel with them. Maybe we'll run into each other in Guatemala City. If not, enjoy the rest of your trip and I hope you find Atlantis or whatever it is you're looking for." She gave Manny a peck on his dripping cheek and boarded the bus.

He was too sick to argue, and, too sick to remember Ginger had made the call to the consulate. Dazed, Manny wandered aimlessly through the boarder station oblivious to hawking vendors and aggressive shoeshine boys. Slowly he became conscious of a voice echoing in his mind. He stopped. He ignored the barking dogs, the unmuffled engines, and the boy pulling his pant leg. He listened. Finally, when all fell silent save the echo in his head, he understood the words. The words of the Curendera *Continue your quest*. Somehow the vibrancy he remembered in the old woman's eyes and the intensity of her voice lifted him. His resolve hardened, he said to the boy putting black polish on his white sneaker, "I must push on with my journey."

Walking away from cries of "Fucking asshole gringo." Manny found a taxi driver, who for an outrageous fee drove him to Manzilla and back. Four hours later, another bus stopped at the station and took him to Guatemala City.

Still sick upon arrival, Manny sat, watching the other passengers disembark. After a harsh stare from the driver, he agonizingly pulled his suitcase from the rack and carted it to the station exit.

As Manny stood in the doorway, a burly cabby jostled through the crowd and asked if he needed a room. Manny nodded weakly and allowed the man to take his suitcase and lead him to a taxi. The driver threw his bag in the trunk and drove to a run-down wooden hotel. At the front desk, Manny managed enough Spanish to ask for a room, and then dragged himself and suitcase up to *numero tres* on the second floor. Once inside, Manny dropped his bag and rushed to the bathroom.

When finished, Manny painfully rose from the toilet and stripped off his remaining clothes while stumbling to the bed. He pulled back the yellowed sheets on the old iron four-poster and gently lowered himself onto the mattress. No sooner had he found a comfortable position when another spasm struck and he staggered back to the bathroom. This time the illness hit his stomach also and he didn't know whether to stand or sit. Finally through, he crawled back to the bed and used one iron post to pull himself erect. He then fell limply on the sheets.

Time lost its meaning as images circled in Manny's mind. His head spun and his stomach felt nauseous. Too weak to move, his thoughts ran from Iris to Atlantis then back to Iris with an occasional picture of Ginger's sinister grin as she dumped him at the border.

Ginger's grin reminded him of someone, but before he could grasp the image, another spasm of pain struck. Tears rolled down his face and he called out, "Please God, please make this stop." More pain and spinning ensued. He cried out once more for God to end his suffering and in his delirium he mumbled a name, "Lugaar." "Lugaar," he whispered, barely audible. Then, "Lugaar," loud enough to fill the room. Finally he roared out the name, his voice echoing throughout the hotel, "Lugaar!"

"Lugaar! Lugaar! Did you not hear me," MAN-DAR bellowed as he furiously tapped his fingernails on his Atarri's scabbard. "I said bring me the protocol tape on the Euro delegation!"

MAN-DAR cursed to himself as he turned his attention back to the controls of his Vector Battler, but the anger he felt at being forced to fly with a Lessor resurfaced along with the guilt. He remembered the smirk on STA-GEL's face when informing him of Poseidon Command's latest directive. "All first and second echelon flights, not formed for combat missions, will contain at least one Lessor in its crew." MAN-DAR knew his mission to pick up the Euro delegation definitely fell into the category of second echelon, forcing him to accept the lumbering Lessor, Lugaar.

MAN-DAR recalled the maneuvering by SOL-RAM at the last council meeting he had attended. SOL-RAM the physician-turned politician and leader of the Sons of the Law of ONE had altered a thousand years of tradition governing race relations. Although in the minority, the ONE's pushed through a law stating a percentage of Lessors must be employed by all agencies of the Empire. MAN-DAR although pressured by his conservative father, SAN-DAR, to vote against the measure, he secretly felt guilty over the treatment of the Lessors and had voted for it. SAN-DAR, beside himself with anger over MAN-DAR's siding with the ONE's, had banned MAN-DAR from his home.

Although the banishment hurt MAN-DAR deeply. He wished he had had the courage to stand up to his overbearing father years before. Thoughts of his father always pained MAN-DAR, especially when he remembered the happy days of his early childhood with his wonderfully loving mother and then happy-go-lucky father. The change came close to his seventh life celebration when his mother, KEL-MAR, had died while giving birth to a sister who had also died. The event caused SAN-DAR to turn inward and shut out MAN-DAR except to scold him for some minor infraction of his rigid rules or to demand a reason when MAN-DAR had not done better at the Temple of Learning or in some game. Although he excelled in everything, MAN-DAR could never please his father.

MAN-DAR, born into the Sons of the Law of Bilial class, had inherited a seat on the High Council of the Empire of Atlantis. The seat, originally granted to his great-great-grandfather, a hero in the First Galactica Beast War, fell to MAN-DAR when an accident forced SAN-DAR to temporarily cut back on his activities. Other than flirting with court ladies, MAN-DAR held little tolerance for the political intrigue, and rarely voted. He preferred racing high performance Vectors or practicing for the games. Although highly proficient in the use of the Attuchi assault rifle and the hand held Vappi ray, his greatest skill lay in the use of the ancient ceremonial blade, the Akarri.

MAN-DAR held the title of champion of the yearly games. The games and the use of the Akarri dated further back than record keeping. The rules of the game pitted one Atlantean against five heavily armed Lessors. With only an Akarri and shield for defense, the Atlantean must hunt and kill the five Lessors. The Atlantean performing the task in the shortest time was declared winner. MAN-DAR won an unprecedented five years running, and his Akarri became known as "Secura, Blade of Certain Death." But since the last games almost a harvest ago, MAN-DAR's views on Lessors had begun to change.

As the Vector hurtled through the sky toward Angleland, MAN-DAR could still see the sad eyes of the fifth and final Lessor he needed to kill in order to win six successive games. He had tracked the creature to a low outcrop of bush and rock in the huge games arena. MAN-DAR knew he was barely under a winning time and needed to dispatch this last one quickly. He expected the battle all creatures put up when cornered, but this one proved different. He was old and sat on a stone waiting for discovery. MAN-DAR raised his bloody sword to strike but caught the look in the Lessors eyes and hesitated. The old one's eyes showed strength, wisdom, nobility, and finally, resignation. He knew his hesitation had cost him the game, but if he failed to finish the creature his father would be doubly furious. Fear of his father overpowered his guilt and with a swipe of Secura the Lessor died.

Like all Billials, MAN-DAR had been raised to believe

Lessors lacked the intelligence to become anything more than slaves. Most Billials claimed the best use for Lessors were as conscripts in the Galactica Beast wars or in sacrificial rites. MAN-DAR found the creatures and their ways strange, but at the age of twenty-eight harvests, guilt and some sympathy for their plight had crept into his heart. Still, sharing his ship with one proved another story. The thought of Lessors reminded MAN-DAR of his mission, and he bellowed once more, "Lugaar!"

A crashing sound from the rear of the cabin spun MAN-DAR's head around. On the deck lay his ceremonial helmet and he glared fiercely at the green eyed, slope-shouldered, Lessor stooping to retrieve it.

"Lugaar, come up here."

Although a head taller, the light hair light skinned large-boned Lessor cringed under the glare of the bronze-toned muscular Atlantean who expected perfection. Another angry summons forced his appearance beside MAN-DAR. The slumped Lessor stood dressed in a drab brown loosely fitting tunic, which hung to his knees. Dark leggings led to ugly military boots issued to Lessors, and a huge crystal hung from a chain around his neck.

"I thought I told you to fetch the protocol tape on the Euro delegation?" MAN-DAR's question carried mostly accusation, yet he avoided the Lessors eyes.

"I did, Master."

"By Baal! Where is it?" MAN-DAR bellowed as he tapped his Akarri.

The Lessor cringed, again expecting a blow, and then feebly pointed to a blinking button on the console next to the view screen.

"Have you no tongue? At what does your shaking finger point?"

"Master," Lugaar answered a quiver of fear in his voice, "I sent you the protocol tape some time ago. This new model Vector can transmit material directly from the navigational station to the forward console. You need only press that button to access it."

MAN-DAR mumbled something about being unfamiliar with the new system, and then growled an order for Lugaar to return to his station. Before the Lessor took three steps, MAN-DAR growled again. "And get rid of the rock hanging around your neck. It violates uniform regulations."

His attention back on the instrument console, MAN-DAR set the Vector on autofly and pushed the blinking button. A bureaucrat from Intelligence appeared on the screen. He read from a prepared text. Besides protocol for meeting the barbarian delegation, the tape included a brief personal history of each member of the party.

"The Euro delegation contains only two member; Kirack, son-in-law to the chief of the tribe considered most important of the Euro barbarians, and his wife, Sulina, the only surviving child of the chief, Molack."

The tape continued, "Kirack, a cruel ruthless man, fought his way almost to the top of the tribal leadership. However, unable to displace Molack, he instead married the chief's daughter, Sulina. Sulina, a beautiful self-willed woman, considered a princess by the tribe, accepted the marriage out of filial duty to her father." MAN-DAR listened attentively.

"Although attaining only a rudimentary level of civilization, we consider the Euros important to the Empire as a buffer between the Galactica Beasts. They show an aptitude in combating the giant anthropoids, probably owing to their own primitiveness. We hope their successes will aid the Empire in eliminating the menace."

At the tape's end, MAN-DAR tried imagining a "beautiful barbarian princess," but realized he would soon meet her face-to-face, and quickly dismissed the thought. Then CHN-TIA, his latest love crossed his mind. She was extremely pleasing to the eye and extremely pleasant in his sleeping pallet, but she was also extremely selfish and he knew she would go the way of the others. Women did not last long with MAN-DAR he either discovered imperfections or they left for lack of attention. Sometimes he believed he was waiting for just the right one. One like the mother who had abandoned him by dying. Enough of that, he thought, all my attention should focus on the mission and guiding the Vector to the new rendezvous point.

While switching the controls from autofly to manual, MAN-DAR caught his first glimpse of the Angleland coast. Even from a distance, he saw a heavy mucous colored cloud shrouding the land. The cloud permitted little light to pierce the thick covering. Thirteen summers had passed since he last traveled this land and the memories made him view this visit with trepidation. MAN-DAR thought of the hatred Zarharrab held toward Atlanteans and hoped to land the Vector and complete his mission without making contact with the wicked priest. Deep in thought, he gazed into the thick clouds. Suddenly he sat dumbstruck as a huge image of Zarharrab's sneering face and piercing eyes appeared before him.

No sooner did the image become visible than a strong jolt

struck the ship's guidance lever. A quick glance at the instruments indicated a huge power loss to the ship. He knew at once the force beam from Energy Central had been interrupted. MAN-DAR automatically hit the auxiliary power switch. No response. Likewise for the visiphone and the emergency distress signal.

Without turning, the Atlantean yelled, "Lugaar, check the power supply relays!" But before the Lessor could answer, the ship crossed the cloud-covered coast of Angleland and all power ceased, plunging the Vector's cabin into semi-darkness.

As the Vector careened out of control, MAN-DAR yelled again, "Lugaar, lock into crash position!" His own safety straps engaged, MAN-DAR felt gravity pull the Vector toward a sudden end. Still unwilling to surrender, he yanked harder on the guidance lever nearly tearing the stick from its mounting. His action proved useless, the heavily armed Battler plunged faster toward the upcoming earth. Increased speed caused a whining sound as wind whipped past the fuselage.

With only seconds left, MAN-DAR prepared for collision. "If ye gods exist, show yourselves," he muttered. The whine of the descent increased when suddenly a new sound commenced. Its pitch like no other, hurt MAN-DAR's ears. He fought gravity's force and turned, searching for the sound's source. However in the instant before impact he saw only Lugaar's necklace and from its stone a blinding luminosity.

FOUR

In the milliseconds before crashing, a strange force lifted the nose of the airship. With nose lifted, the sturdily built Vector skidded on its belly for a kilometer, finally halting against the trunk of an ancient dead oak. The impact left MAN-DAR shaken but alive. With little time to consider what saved the ship, he pressed buttons to ascertain the damage to the craft. His actions proved futile. The Vector lay powerless. MAN-DAR shook his head in dismay and hoped they need not make a swift departure from Angleland.

Visually inspecting the operations compartment, MAN-DAR strained to see in the Angleland half-light. He found several gauges shattered and a row of navigation tapes scattered across the cabin floor. Finally, his eyes came to rest on the unconscious figure of Lugaar.

MAN-DAR unfastened his crash straps and moved quickly to the motionless Lessor. A swollen bruise on Lugaar's forehead indicated the heavy crystal worn by the Lessor had struck him during the crash. MAN-DAR considered the crystal no more than a good luck trinket and shoved it aside before he checked Lugaar's vital signs. Two fingers on the Lessor's aorta proved him alive. Roughly, MAN-DAR shook Lugaar and called his name.

Lugaar's eyelids fluttered open and his hand automatically massaged his swollen forehead. Finally he focused on

MAN-DAR and asked, "Is the ship still in working order, Master?"

"I know not. The damage scanners prove inoperative." Adding tersely, "I told you not to call me master. Master implies I have a responsibility toward you. Poseidon Command directive or not, as far as I am concerned, you do not belong on this mission." Then he growled, "Let me see that lump on your head."

Without looking directly into his eyes, MAN-DAR observed that the swelling and consequent bruising took the shape of the facets on Lugaar's crystal. Applying freeze spray from the ship's medical box, MAN-DAR asked brusquely, "Why do you wear that foolish stone? It might have killed you."

"I must. I have sworn to guard the sacred Crystal of Arrhamis with my life, as did my father and his father before him. I have special permission from Poseidon Command to wear it."

"I assume SOL-RAM had something to do with that."

"How did you know, Master?"

"A guess," MAN-DAR replied sarcastically. "And I told you not to call me, Master."

Lugaar ignored MAN-DAR's sarcasm. "SOL-RAM has done much to help my people."

"I should say he has," MAN-DAR replied again sarcastically, "But he is not much help now, is he?" With some concern in his voice, MAN-DAR added, "Are you able to stand? We must find the barbarian delegation and escape this accursed land."

"I am fine, Master." Quickly he added, "I mean Lieutenant Commander MAN-DAR." To prove his condition, Lugaar rose to his feet, ambled several paces while holding the crystal to his head, and turned to MAN-DAR. Already the swelling on his forehead had receded and the bruise almost gone.

Amazed, MAN-DAR inquired, "How did you heal so quickly?"

"The Crystal, Master, it holds the power to heal."

MAN-DAR looked at the large crystal in its symbol-laden gold setting and scowled. "I do not have time for absurd Lessor superstitions." MAN-DAR tossed a carrying sack to Lugaar and added, "Fill this with supplies. We must find the Vector freighter and the Euro barbarians before Zarharrab."

Lugaar promptly gathered necessary supplies while MAN-DAR prepared himself for the search. He discarded the ceremonial costume of kilt and tunic and pulled a lightweight combat jumpsuit of gray non-reflecting material and battle tunic over his muscular body. Worried about Zarharrab, he decided to travel heavily armed, but when flicking the readiness lever on his Attuchi assault rifle he got no response, likewise with his sidearm, the Vappi ray. All electronic mechanisms had malfunctioned. Undaunted, he reached for Secura, his Akarri and attached the scabbard to his uniform.

Manually opening the hatch, MAN-DAR and Lugaar jumped the two meters from Vector to ground. Behind the Vector, a long scar from the emergency landing had cut deeply into a devastated lifeless landscape. What MAN-DAR remembered as a green bountiful land now looked dark and foreboding. Not only was the tree the Vector leaned against dead, so were most others. The few trees still alive drooped, their leaves withered and mottled. Once lush grasses covered the soil; now they crackled under foot. What green which remained stood choked with vines sporting unattractive hand-sized red blossoms. Closer inspection revealed petals with jagged knife-like edges. Curious, Lugaar bent to pluck a blossom but straightened quickly when MAN-DAR seized his hand.

"Do not touch them. A strange aura permeates from these plants. Besides, we have no time to fret away with flowers."

Examining the horizon, both MAN-DAR and Lugaar noticed a curl of smoke rising lazily toward the murky yellow sky. Lugaar blurted out, "The Vector freighter, Master."

MAN-DAR, resigning himself to the Lessor's incorrigibility, ignored the word Master. "Possibly, but it might be a cooking fire from a village or perhaps a farmer clearing land. Do not make assumptions, Lessor. If I need your opinion, which I doubt, I shall ask. But, since no clear direction presents itself, we shall aim for the smoke. If only a villager or farmer, perhaps they have knowledge of the freighter and the party of Euros."

"Yes, Master."

"Let us move quickly, Lessor. Through this terrain, the smoke must be a good half-day's march and the hour grows late."

MAN-DAR glanced once more at the ugly vines, which he swore to himself had crept closer and gave an involuntary shudder. He then shouldered a heavy carrying sack, beckoned Lugaar with a nod and headed for the plume of dark smoke.

The pair traveled in silence, covering a good distance toward their destination without encountering another being. Much of the land lay barren except for the strange weed-like vines. Several times they came upon pathways but thickly woven clumps of vines or the path's state of disrepair rendered them impassable.

After they reached yet another of the overgrown trails at mid morning, MAN-DAR called a halt. "Let us rest and quench our thirst, Lessor. The smoke rises further in the distance than I believed. Pass me the water flask."

Lugaar lifted the flask's strap from across his large chest and inadvertently brushed the stone hanging around his neck. The crystal emitted a low hum.

MAN-DAR looked sharply at Lugaar's chest and then queried. "Did you by any chance hear a strange sound immediately before our crash?"

"Strange sound, Master?" Lugaar did not look directly at MAN-DAR. Instead he watched his large foot as it scraped at the ancient roadway.

"A high pitched whining sound?"

"No, Master. I heard only the sound of the wind."

"I heard the wind also. And something more."

Lugaar's boot dug deeper into the road. "I heard nothing, Master."

"Great Baal! Do not lie to me." MAN-DAR's voice rumbled with anger and his nails tapped loudly on Secura's scabbard. "I have the ears of a hunter. I did not imagine the sound."

Lugaar slunk low, trying to blend with the path, his voice barely audible, "But Master, you said never to speak of it."

"Speak of what? What do you sputter about, Lessor?"

"About the Crystal of Arrhamis, Master."

"That trinket around your neck? What has that rock to do with the sound?"

"I told you, Master. The Crystal has magical powers. I used them to lift the nose of the Vector just before impact."

MAN-DAR did not think it possible, but the Lessor

managed to slink even lower. "Why do you still insist on such drivel?"

"Because 'tis true, Master. The Crystal possesses the power to levitate objects."

MAN-DAR threw the water flask to Lugaar. "Enough of this nonsense. Take your drink and let us go." But as he reached the other side of the road, he wondered. He had heard the whine and seen the glow of the crystal. Perhaps something rang true about this magic, but he dismissed the idea with a shake of his head.

Further on, they found a deserted village, which contained a number of buildings surrounding a central marketplace. As they worked their way through the village, they discovered most of the houses plundered. Parts of broken doors and shattered furniture littered the village square making passage difficult.

"It appears a small army ravaged this village, Master," Lugaar commented as he scooped a broken homemade doll from the ground.

"Army or not, Lugaar, they had great strength. Most doors appear splintered or torn completely off their hinges."

Upon leaving the village, they spotted two children playing by a algae covered pond. One, a boy who looked not more than eight harvests, and a girl, five. Their clothes were hand-spun, ragged, and filthy. MAN-DAR hailed the children, but one glance at the travelers sent them fleeing in terror.

About to give chase, the firm grip of MAN-DAR held Lugaar in place. "Let the young ones go. We need only climb that small knoll to find the smoke's source." MAN-DAR nodded in the direction of the smoke and led Lugaar eagerly up the hill.

From the crest, the Atlantean and Lessor viewed a large, uncultivated field. "Lugaar, this field must be four kilometers long and at least two wide, a perfect site for landing a Vector freighter."

"Yes, Master, but what of that large mound in its center

The huge irregular shaped mound covered with weed-vines stood ninety meters long and three times the height of Lugaar. Behind the mound, from a stand of dead trees, rose the long dark curl of smoke. They moved to investigate.

By the time the two covered half the distance to the mound, they dragged along great tangles of the vines. "If I did not know better," MAN-DAR commented to Lugaar, "I would swear these vines attempt to detain us." When they reached the mound, they realized with astonishment the vines concealed the Vector freighter.

MAN-DAR pointed to the small stand of dead trees and the rising curl of smoke. "The ship must be abandoned. Most likely its occupants huddle around that signal fire in the woods. Let us make haste."

Hurriedly leaving the vine-enveloped freighter, they ran toward the stand of dead trees and the smoke. Weed-vines overgrown to massive thickness blocked their passage into the dead thicket. Without wasting time, MAN-DAR brandished Secura, and blazed a path until they reached an open glade. A lone man, apparently unconscious, lay surrounded by a ring of smoldering ashes. He wore the uniform of an Atlantean officer.

With hope of gaining answers to the deepening mystery which surrounded his mission, MAN-DAR slashed through the heaps of vines and leaped the smoldering ring easily.

Lugaar following stumbled upon landing and clumsily rolled against the disabled officer.

"Lugaar!" MAN-DAR roared. As he was about to admonish the clumsy Lessor, Lugaar looked directly at MAN-DAR who instantly recalled the clear eyes of the old Lessor he was forced to kill in the games and instead controlled his temper. His voice even, he ordered, "Hand me the water flask and rebuild the fire before the vines entangle us all."

MAN-DAR winced at the thought of what his father might say if he heard him speak to a Lessor with anything less than contempt. Pushing aside that ugly thought he turned his attention to the unconscious Atlantean and sprinkled water on the officer's face. When his eyes opened the man screamed in terror. MAN-DAR calmed him to silence. Finally gaining some of his senses, the officer identified himself as TAM-STX, but fell into unconsciousness again.

With the fire rebuilt, Lugaar returned to MAN-DAR whose hands probed TAM-STX for signs of injury. "Broken leg," MAN-DAR muttered to Lugaar who rummaged through the carrying sack locating the medical box. Lugaar kept his eyes to the ground as he held the box towards MAN-DAR.

"Get a splint and inflate it about his leg," MAN-DAR instructed the Lessor as he propped up the man on his carrying sack. "And do not allow your clumsy self to cause more damage than he has already suffered."

Next MAN-DAR took a spring-loaded ampule of medication from the medical box, put it to the officer's shoulder and pulled the trigger. As he did, Lugaar gently worked on the fractured limb and shortly the man regained consciousness. The medication had eased the Atlantean officer's anxiety and pain. With the discomfort gone, the officer unexpectedly gave MAN-DAR a mischievous grin and told MAN-DAR his story.

"I am an officer assigned to Angleland in order to watch for Beasts before they can invade Atlantis." TAM-STX coughed and asked for more water. After his drink that mischievous grin crossed his face again. He then continued. "Actually I wasn't assigned here, I was exiled here."

Somewhat astonished, MAN-DAR asked why.

Another mischievous grin appeared on the officer's face before he spoke. "I had been in charge of the Vector fleet in Poseidon. One day I got the bright idea to increase the speed of a Vector Battler by manipulating the magnetic field in its energy crystal. Something we were forbidden to tamper with." He coughed again, asked for more water and began with a grin again. "At any rate I was caught speeding over the Capital and arrested." He grinned once more and finished. "Long story short, here I am."

MAN-DAR spent some time digesting TAM-STX's words and finally decided that he himself had broken several rules of Poseidon Command but had gotten away with it. He didn't think that what this man had done warranted such an extreme punishment and told him so. Then he asked how he came to be in this particular spot.

"Yesterday, if one can discern day from night in this accursed land, I was not far off when I heard the Vector freighter land in yon field. In hopes I might be taken back to Atlantis I ran for the sound. Unfortunately I only got this far before being entangled by the vines." Without a grin he continued. "I soon realized the blossoms on the vines were gnawing through my cloths. As I struggle for freedom I fell and broke my leg."

TAM-STX coughed and MAN-DAR put the flask to his lips. He drank deeply, and in thanks, gave MAN-DAR another mischievous looking grin.

"But worse happened," TAM-STX continued, growing more excited. "The blossoms cut me with their petals. They sucked my blood! I thought my life over. Finally I remembered my fire-starter, played it on them and they retreated. I managed enough strength to build this circle of fire, and then passed out."

MAN-DAR thought carefully about the officer's words then questioned further. "You spoke of Beasts and some kind of forbidden causeway. What could Beasts have to do with any kind of causeway? I know of the Beasts, but I know nothing of a forbidden causeway.

TAM-STX closed his eyes as he tried to decide if he should tell MAN-DAR of the secret he had sworn to keep. Finally he realized that the Atlantean had saved his life and as an officer himself could be trusted with the truth. His eyes opened along with his mouth. "Few know of the causeway. It was built long ago. Even before the time of the Atlanteans. When given this assignment I was told it was possibly by the Lessors. They said the Forbidden Causeway was used to travel west from Angleland to a large island then even further west to the mountains of Northern Atlantis. From the mountains they would travel south to an area where both their bodies and spirits could leave the earth intact. I have no idea if that be true. But I do believe there is a Forbidden Causeway.

"What have the Beasts to do with the causeway?" MAN-DAR inquired.

"I have never encountered any Beasts," TAM-STX

answered. "But I was told they are extremely intelligent. It is believed by some that if Beasts were to reach Angleland they could use the Forbidden Causeway to invade Atlantis."

Directly, MAN-DAR asked, "How could a squad of men hold off a Beast invasion?"

"Obviously they could not. But many moons before even the fear of Beasts, Atlantis built booby traps at the entrance to the causeway to prevent Lessors from passing. As far as I know, they still exist to this day."

"Your answer gives me much to think about, TAM-STX. But what happened to the people on the freighter?"

"As far as I know, they are still in the freighter."

MAN-DAR turned to Lugaar. "Let us return to the freighter. I fear the weed-vines have the delegation and crew imprisoned in the air ship."

With his superior strength, Lugaar easily carried the injured officer as MAN-DAR led the way toward the vine enshrouded Vector freighter. When they had almost reached the point where they had entered the woods, MAN-DAR heard a large commotion in the distance. Instantly he dropped to the ground, signaled Lugaar to halt, and crept silently forward. At the edge of the field, he pulled aside a tangle of dead branches and froze. MAN-DAR blinked in disbelief as he watched the worst horde of demons he could have imagined tramp across the field toward the Vector freighter.

"What do you see, Master?" Lugaar called from behind. MAN-DAR turned, whispering sharply. "Set down TAM-STX and stay low." Looking back across the field he still felt shaken by the horde of brutes.

Unearthly monsters, half-animal, half-human stomped

toward the ship imprisoning the Euro delegation and its crew. Some looked like men with heads of bulls or bears and some had hooves for feet. One creature had a single eye centered in his forehead. All brandished weapons. Some carried clubs or axes, but a few held pikes and shields as well. In the lead strode a giant of a man. Clearly not one of the unearthlings, yet his face resembled that of a pig. He constantly swiped at his nose with his thumb as he led the march to the freighter.

When they reached the ship, the pig-faced leader bellowed, "They call me Pogul. In the name of the High Priest of Inanna, I demand you open the hatch and surrender."

MAN-DAR heard a muffled curse from behind the doorway, which several of the unearthlings had cleared of weed-vines. Sure the captain would have the hatch locked from inside, MAN-DAR felt the occupant's safe for now.

Unfortunately, MAN-DAR learned Pogul held no patience for waiting. When he heard the negative response, he ordered his henchmen to gather kindling and place it beneath the front of the ship. Once more Pogul called for surrender, and once more a curse flew through the locked hatch. Pogul signaled and flint met steel. Sparks caused a flicker of flame in the dead foliage, and more branches flew on as the flames grew. Finally, the weed-vines covering the freighter caught fire and a few moments later, MAN-DAR watched the hatch open.

With his crew outnumbered six to one, MAN-DAR hoped the captain possessed the sense to surrender. He had no chance against the unearthlings.

MAN-DAR's hopes proved groundless. For as the captain,

crew, and two delegates emerged coughing, surrender became impossible. The monsters attacked immediately.

Powerless to help against such odds, MAN-DAR knelt in horrified frustration observing the ensuing battle. He prayed the engagement would end with few casualties, but it soon became apparent the creatures wanted blood. Without warning a lion-headed unearthling pounced on a Lessor splitting him down the middle with an ax. Blood curdling screams sent chills through MAN-DAR as all the creatures intensified the onslaught. Instantly, one monster fell, spear in chest, hurled by the fur clad crimson-haired barbarian female. She is a fierce one, MAN-DAR thought with admiration, she must be the one they call Sulina.

The Cyclops, trying to ensnare her, died with the captain's Akarri piercing its single eye. Another creature fell tripping a comrade, whose head caved in when clubbed by a crewman's wrench. Pogul bellowed more orders and several unearthlings with shields attempted to force their way between the ship's crew and the Euro delegation. One lost his footing, then his head to the sword of a barbarian male who MAN-DAR assumed to be Kirack but immediately another unearthling creature took his place. Soon a dozen creatures traded blows with the crew and the two ambassadors. Another crewman went down with a single swing of the great club wielded by the leader, Pogul. A Lessor felled a ram-headed creature with a punch to his face. MAN-DAR found it hard to believe a Lessor possessed such bravery, but was soon forced to avert his eyes as a bear-headed half-man crushed the Lessor's skull between his tremendous jaws.

Dumbstruck, MAN-DAR saw the most despicable act he had ever witnessed. The male barbarian, Kirack, grasped the female, Sulina, thrust her toward Pogul while shrieking at the pig-faced giant to take her and spare him. The giant laughed horribly, thumbed his nose, and grunted, "I will have my way with you all anyway." And with a blow from his great club, he knocked the head completely off the crewman nearest the barbarian. At the sight of the blood pouring from the headless torso, the creatures went berserk. They roared while overwhelming the captain and the last of the crew, and hacked viciously at their remains.

MAN-DAR could control himself no longer. He commanded Lugaar to stay with the liaison officer, drew Secura, and charged screaming across the field at the monsters. Upon reaching the battle scene he threw himself between Pogul and the barbarians. The pig-faced giant laughed again, swinging his deadly weapon down on MAN-DAR who sidestepped, turned and caught the huge man in the lower back with his elbow. Not even a grunt issued from the giant. He merely laughed again while swinging his huge club in a wide arc. This time it caught MAN-DAR in the ribs. The blow slammed him to the ground, driving the wind from his lungs and left him in excruciating pain.

Unable to move, MAN-DAR watched in horror as the creatures devoured the crew. In their blood frenzy, several attempted to attack the two Euros but Pogul held them at bay. Enraged by the denial, one unearthling descended on MAN-DAR, a huge ax raised for the kill. "Do not touch him!" The leader's voice boomed across the field. "Leave that one to the blood-sucking weed-vines. 'Tis a fitting end for one from Atlantis." Snarling his disagreement, the unearthling slowly lowered his ax and rejoined the bloody feast.

Against the backdrop of the burning Vector freighter MAN-DAR watched Pogul signal his henchmen and march off with their two captives.

Even before the horde disappeared, the weed-vines covering the field, entwined MAN-DAR's legs. Panic filled him when he saw what looked like drool flowing from the hideous red blossoms as they inched their way to his throat. In vain he tried to wriggle from their grasp but unendurable pain prevented any movement. The largest of the blossoms reached his neck and sank its sharp petals into his throat. Suddenly MAN-DAR felt the bloom ripped away.

"I am sorry, Master," Lugaar exclaimed as he pulled the remaining vines from MAN-DAR. "I know you bid me to stay with the wounded officer, but I could restrain myself no longer." After a closer look at MAN-DAR he asked unsurely, "Do you live, Master?"

Through the pain MAN-DAR winced. "Barely. I think the big one hit me with a tree trunk. I cannot move."

"Move not, Master. Your ribs may be broken, or at least badly bruised. Breath easily, I am a trained healer, and will see to your wounds."

"Trained healer? I find that difficult to believe." Lugaar ignored the insult and opened MAN-DAR's jumpsuit. The Atlantean felt the icy coolness of the crystal on his side and protested, but silenced his tongue when he felt the stone vibrate and emit a shrill sound. Almost instantly the pain eased and in a few moments stiff movement became possible. Lugaar helped him stand, and with MAN-DAR leaning on the Lessor, they hobbled toward the other injured Atlantean in the dead thicket.

By the time they reached TAM-STX, MAN-DAR could

walk on his own, and Lugaar left him to help the liaison officer back to the protection of the fire. No sooner had the trio entered the circle of ashes, when the bloodthirsty vines encroached on their refuge. Lugaar once again rebuilt the fire, and returned to check on MAN-DAR's injuries.

After another treatment MAN-DAR asked curiously, "Lugaar, why did you not use the crystal to heal TAM-STX?"

"The bone had to be set before healing could take place, Master. Besides, you ordered me not to speak of Lessor magic."

About to chastise the Lessor, MAN-DAR cut himself short. He realized he had only himself to blame. Instead, he ordered Lugaar to check on the wounded officer's injuries. Presently, heavier matters burdened his mind. He needed to know where the unearthly creatures had come from and why they took the delegates captive instead of slaughtering them along with the Vector's crew. He felt Zarharrab somehow lay behind all this and vowed to make the priest pay for his treachery. More importantly he believed it imperative to retrieve the captured ambassadors, find a way to escape this evil land, and complete his mission.

The utter blackness of the Angleland night descended around the fire-encircled trio. MAN-DAR knew it impossible to locate the unearthlings in such darkness so he ordered Lugaar to set up a rudimentary camp and to keep watch on the defensive fire.

In the morning as the first faint rays of light pushed away some of the Angleland darkness, MAN-DAR found a tree branch the wounded officer could use as a crutch. He told Lugaar to take the officer back to their downed Vector Battler with orders to wait. MAN-DAR then set off alone, determined to find Pogul and free the barbarian captives.

FIVE

MAN-DAR paused as he discovered yet another of the huge upright stones. The megalith stood two heads over his own and carved into its surface were vaguely familiar symbols. As he ran his hand over the cool slab he felt the prickly sensation of an electric current.

Since leaving Lugaar and TAM-STX that morning, MAN-DAR had found three such stones, each covered with symbols and radiating a slight electromagnetic field. Testing further, he held Secura a few centimeters from the object and, as suspected, felt the blade magnetically drawn to the stone.

Still bewildered by the purpose of these monuments, MAN-DAR replaced Secura and continued his quest to find the unearthlings and their captives.

He followed their trail with ease until reaching a dry riverbed where the tracks ended. After he searched both banks for a good distance, MAN-DAR doubled back, but still failed to find evidence of his quarry. While probing the riverbanks, MAN-DAR felt awe at the desolation time had wrought in Angleland since his first visit many harvests ago. Neither this river, nor any he traversed, flowed with water eager to reach the sea. No trees, shrubs or blades of grass thrust shoots or seedlings skyward. No creatures scurried before him and no flushed birds took flight screeching. Even the air seemed dead as if the dirty yellow cloud cover absorbed its life. Certain

Zarharrab lay behind the ruin, MAN-DAR sadly remembered his other trip to Angleland when he was much younger, and his encounter with Zarharrab, the High Priest of Inanna.

MAN-DAR, as any young intern at the Temple of Learning, greeted the news of his first assignment with great enthusiasm. He knew a successful completion of the mission would almost assure his entrance into the Atlantean Temple of Flight. From the Temple, MAN-DAR would gain a commission in Poseidon Command as a Vector pilot, his life-long dream, and an accomplishment, which might even please his father.

His assignment included teaching basic energy production to the barbarians inhabiting Angleland. MAN-DAR, well versed in geometric construction, spent much time at the Temple building simple stone mock-ups. He learned concentric circles of stone slabs aligned with the Earth's magnetic fields could produce a useful current of electricity if captured and stored. This energy could run a simple thresher or grinder and MAN-DAR eagerly awaited the chance to test his skills in the real-life environment of Angleland.

Since his mother died, MAN-DAR's life had centered on his home in Poseidon, the capital of Atlantis. He knew little of Angleland other than a few facts gleaned from geography tapes. He learned the large island of Angleland stood East of Atlantis, and off the coast of Euroland. Except for a few Atlantean exiles, Angleland's population consisted of white skinned Euro barbarians, ruled by tribal leaders. As far as he could learn, the only access to Angleland was by sea or air.

Anxious to see the world, and escape the critical tongue of his father, MAN-DAR gladly boarded a small research vessel which deposited him and a crew of Lessors on a deserted beach in Angleland. As they traveled inland, the beauty of the countryside and its simple hospitable natives enthralled MAN-DAR. In time the natives became so hospitable they insisted on helping the Lessors carry the numerous supplies needed for the assignment. Sternly the young Atlantean lectured the barbarians on the proper conduct regarding Lessors.

"It is wrong for men to lighten the burden of the inhuman slaves. The Lessor's reason for existence is to suffer the weight of their master's tasks."

Upon arrival at the project site, MAN-DAR ordered the Lessors to set up camp while he explored the terrain. He introduced himself to the local leaders, explaining his project and inviting them to a demonstration of what Atlanteans could teach barbarians. He made no attempt to hide his belief in Atlantean superiority and treated the tribal chiefs with little more deference than he showed the Lessors.

Located on a high plain the project site held easy access to building materials quarried in nearby mountains. MAN-DAR did little physical labor but spent much time laying out the site. He also supervised the Lessors in lifting the heavy slabs of stone into upright positions then capping the huge rectangular columns with stone lintels. When completed, MAN-DAR and his crew had built a thirty-meter circle, standing four meters high and capped by a continuous circle of horizontal lintels. Inside the circle stood a smaller cluster of taller columns aligned in a half-circle. To complete the task, the only thing needed was to lower a huge bluestone into the center of the half-circle.

The demonstration day dawned on a plain filled with barbarians eager to learn what the burly young foreigner would do with his strange configuration of stones. The wait proved short for when the Lessors placed the lodestone into position, it began to emit a pulsating radiance. As the pulsating increased, so did the anxiety of the simple natives. When sparks flew from the object, the frightened crowd fell back in gradual retreat. A quick forming thunderstorm suddenly discharged an enormous bolt of lightning and the gradual retreat transformed into an uncontrollable stampede.

MAN-DAR, fearing for his life, darted behind a stone column and helplessly watched the unbridled mob trample three lumbering Lessors.

As the last of the frenzied crowd faded into the distance, MAN-DAR stood cursing in bewildered rage. He saw his dream of piloting a Vector disappear with the fleeing natives, and he could almost hear the stinging rebuke he would receive from his father. Never in his years at the Temple of Learning had he heard of anything approaching the disaster he witnessed that day. But he refused to let his dream slip away so easily, and vowed to solve the mystery. I must regain the confidence of the barbarian people he thought, and quickly made plans for another demonstration. He assured himself that next time the outcome would be different.

Unfortunately for the young intern, there would be no second demonstration. None of the tribes agreed to participate or even go near the plain. MAN-DAR, fearing his dream of flying for Poseidon Command might really be in jeopardy, sought answers from the village elder of a nearby clan. "Your people have nothing to fear from the stone configuration. I promise the next demonstration will go as planned."

"I am truly sorry, master Atlantean," the old man said lowering his eyes, "but a tribal shaman has convinced the people that an evil demon inhabits the stones. Even worse, he says anyone approaching the plain could lose their life-spirit to the demon."

"Tell me of this shaman who would make superstitious nonsense out of the natural laws of nature?"

"They call him Zarharrab."

"By what right does this Zarharrab's opinion weigh so heavily upon your people?"

"His father was a highly respected shaman and chief. When of age, Zarharrab replaced him. Zarharrab also possesses magical powers taught to him by his mother."

Undaunted, MAN-DAR learned the whereabouts of Zarharrab and wasted little time locating the shaman's thatched roof hovel. Barging through the door, he stopped abruptly, unable to see in the dimly lit room. When his eyes adjusted, he noticed a seated man surrounded by a group of young barbarians engrossed in animated conversation. With MAN-DAR's frame darkening the open entryway, the conversation ceased and all heads turned to the stranger.

"I am MAN-DAR of Atlantis. I demand to know who is the one called Zarharrab."

"I am Zarharrab," acknowledged the man in the chair. Although seated, he looked tall, lean, and about MAN-DAR's age. The mix of races had produced a handsome person with high Atlantean cheekbones but with a longer face, fine lips and delicate nose. The most prominent feature of the face was his eyes. Deeply set, the piercing pair of blue pools blazed with hatred.

"Why do you seek me out?" Zarharrab asked with a disarming smile that belied his burning orbs.

The smile put MAN-DAR at cautious ease. "Why does Zarharrab speak against the gift we Atlanteans wish to bestow on your people? The technology will only enrich Angleland."

Zarharrab's countenance changed abruptly. "By what right do the Atlanteans send young fools to blaspheme the laws of nature?"

"Blasphemy," MAN-DAR shot back. "This technology uses what the gods already provide. Nothing unnatural occurs while producing an electric current."

"If so, then why did a storm arise to mock your infernal machine? Why did lightning from the storm kill five in a nearby herd of sheep?"

MAN-DAR protested until suddenly a glow emitting from Zarharrab's eyes cut him off.

"The time of your teaching has ended, Atlantean. My people have no need of your demonic ways. Time has come for you to learn a lesson." With his words Zarharrab sprang from his stool and grasped MAN-DAR's throat. Several of his followers attempted to join the melee.

"Leave him to me, I shall handle this arrogant foreigner myself," Zarharrab ordered, as he began squeezing the life from the young Atlantean.

MAN-DAR struggled in vain, the glow from the mesmerizing orbs sapping his strength. It took only moments before the loss of oxygen made his head swim. He knew he must act quickly or perish. Gathering all his strength, he slammed his knee into the groin of his assailant. Instantly Zarharrab loosened his grip and fell, hands clutching his injured parts. Before the others could react, MAN-DAR drew his Vappi ray and fired a blast at the feet of the menacing gang. They stopped. Quickly MAN-DAR withdrew towards the door, but before his shadow crossed the threshold a shiver ran through his body as Zarharrab cursed him through clenched teeth, "You will pay for this humiliation one day, as will all Atlanteans!"

As the memory of Zarharrab's threat rang through his head, MAN-DAR redoubled his effort to locate the trail of the unearthlings. He had traveled half a day since leaving the riverbed without finding a sign of his quarry. Just as frustration drove him to conclude he needed assistance, he spotted a dwelling in the distance. A few pieces of wet laundry hung on a leafless bush led him to conclude it was inhabited.

Cautiously, MAN-DAR approached the hut. He had not yet encountered a native Anglelander except for the two children and he did not know what to expect when he did. He stopped a safe distance from the hut, and wished for a charged Vappi ray as he fingered his Akarri. Finally MAN-DAR hailed the occupants of the house. He received no reply and he called again, still no answer. After a third failed attempt, MAN-DAR gave up and turned to leave when a cackling laugh emanated from behind the closed door.

A slight creaking sound drew MAN-DAR's attention to a set of gnarled fingers, which wrapped themselves around the edge of the slowly opening door. Gradually a head appeared, then a torso. Finally the door swung full open allowing a bent old woman who leaned on a stick to take a few steps toward MAN-DAR.

Before MAN-DAR stood a wizened old hag with black teeth and tangled gray hair flying in all directions. A huge wart decorated her nose and her face carried the wrinkles of a hundred harvests. As she pushed down on her walking stick, her head slowly rose to gaze upon her visitor. The hag's eyes startled MAN-DAR. Clear and young looking, they were each a different color and somehow familiar.

Finally she spoke, "Why have you come to the abode of this poor old woman, handsome Atlantean? Perhaps you wish to learn the meaning of a toss of the bones, or perhaps of future adventures seen in the dregs of a goblet? Come now, tell the ancient Zerrina, for she grows weary easily when away from her seat by the hearth."

MAN-DAR stared at length before he spoke. He thought the old soothsayer harmless enough, yet something about her put a burden of suspicion on his mind. For although she seemed as ancient as the *Lost Land of Mu*, her voice bespoke of a woman not past middle age. At last MAN-DAR answered.

"No need to tire yourself with bones or goblets, ancient one. I wish only to know if you have knowledge of two Euros traveling in the company of a horde of unearthly creatures? If you have such knowledge, speak of it anon and I will keep you no longer from the hearth."

"'Tis always so," she cackled. "Atlanteans who come to this land leave hurriedly. Unfortunately, the memories of old ones do not move as fast as Atlantean feet. Come join me at the hearth for a sip of rube tea and perhaps as we sit the memory of those of whom you speak shall catch up."

With no recourse, MAN-DAR followed the old woman through her doorway. The hut consisted of only one room with a hay-strewn pallet in the corner for a bed. The table in the center was a rude affair with no chairs, and the hearth the hag had spoken of consisted of a small fireplace in which hung a kettle boiling over a lazy flame. MAN-DAR sat on one of the two stumps set in front of the fire while the women who called herself Zerrina prepared the tea and brought it to him.

MAN-DAR accepted a clay mug of steaming brew from one gnarled hand as Zerrina laid the other hand lightly on his neck. MAN-DAR shifted uncomfortably on the stump and began tapping Secura. Seductively, the old hag ran the hand along his broad muscular shoulders. MAN-DAR threw the woman a glance of displeasure causing gales of the hideous cackle he had heard earlier. Feeling ill at ease, MAN-DAR took a sip of the strong tea.

The cackle subsided as the old woman took her seat across from MAN-DAR. Both sat in silence for some time until Zerrina asked, "Has much time has passed since leaving your mother country, Atlantean?"

MAN-DAR, in no mood to exchange pleasantries, tapped quicker on Secura and abruptly asked, "What of the group I pursue?"

Silence again filled the tiny hut until Zerrina finally inquired, "The Euros of which you speak, could one be a beautiful crimson-haired woman?"

MAN-DAR pictured the fierce, red-haired wife of Kirack. "Yes, I have heard her called beautiful."

Catching MAN-DAR by surprise Zerrina asked, "As beautiful as myself?"

MAN-DAR could not hold back the laugh, which burst from his lips. Attempts to stifle it failed and he received a scowl from the woman, which produced still more half-stifled laughter. Soon, with eyes flashing hate, Zerrina hurled her mug at the laughing Atlantean, striking his forehead. With what MAN-DAR thought to be unbelievable agility, the hag threw herself at him, fiercely pummeling his chest and shoulders.

Still laughing, MAN-DAR stood to rid himself of the mad old woman, only to find himself leaping back in order to avoid a blow from the log aimed at his head. Off balance, he hit the table and fell, landing on the sleeping pallet in the corner. In a flash Zerrina leaped upon him. Not pummeling, not hitting, but with her mouth on his, kissing, sucking and biting.

Revulsion filled MAN-DAR as he felt her tongue fill his mouth. Angrily clutching her hair, he dragged her face from his, and without regard for age, heaved her from his body. With hand still entangling her hair he held her to the dirt floor demanding, "Where are those I seek?"

Hysterical hideous cackling commenced. MAN-DAR felt he was dealing with a crazy woman, and released her. To his surprise the woman regained her composure instantly and while rising, answered nonchalantly, "Yes, I know of those you seek. They camp not a far distance from this place," and added. "If the handsome Atlantean could set himself back on the pallet my dimming mind might remember the place."

Barely restraining himself, MAN-DAR's eyes blazed, causing the hideous cackling to begin anew.

"Where are they?" MAN-DAR shouted as he shook her like a child's doll. "I am on a mission for the Empire of Atlantis.

A mission that could affect the survival of humanity. I must find those monsters and release their captives!" With a deep breath, MAN-DAR fought to regain his composure and added almost calmly, "Please ancient one, if you know anything of them, you must tell me now."

Zerrina's coy smile turned sly and one of her odd colored eyes sparkled as she answered sarcastically.

"I had no idea how important your mission. I will lead you myself to the path which will take you to them." Without waiting for a response she found her walking stick and shuffled out the door.

MAN-DAR followed the old woman to the top of a small hill within sight of the hut. From the hill, Zerrina's gnarled finger pointed to a path leading into the distance toward a great forest. Without a goodbye, MAN-DAR started down the trail to the sound of the old woman's cackle. After a few steps he turned for a last look at the hag but she had vanished, leaving only the receding echo of her hideous laugh and a puff of blue smoke.

Once more MAN-DAR pulled a foot from the muck. Once more the putrid smelling mud of the swamp released him with a sucking sound, which reeked of disappointment, and he continued along the rapidly disappearing path. The light in the swamp, half again as dim as that on the outside, cast a pall of semi-darkness. Objects only meters away lost shape and blended into the vaporous gray bowels of the decaying swampland.

Where MAN-DAR had perceived a great forest, he found

instead a vast putrid swamp covered completely by the grotesque weed-vines. Repeatedly he used Secura to clear his way but so far the diminishing trail showed no signs of the party he sought. Still, feeling the path must lead somewhere and with no better alternative, he put his weight on what he hoped to be solid ground and moved forward.

Suddenly a slithering sound followed by a splash froze MAN-DAR in place. Fear jerked his head toward the noise, but he saw nothing, save an oozing ripple created by some unknown creature as it slithered through slime-covered water. The slithering-splash sound had begun soon after he had hacked through the weed-vines barring his entrance to the swamp. Along with the slithering-splash came a feeling of being watched.

As the path under his feet disintegrated further, MAN-DAR looked for identifying signs to keep from losing direction. He could tell the swamp had supplanted a once-vital forest, but now branches hung dead, their trunks standing dark and hollow, their life force sucked dry by weed-vines. Slime hung from decaying boughs and in some instances low enough to mingle with murky green pools. The stench almost overwhelmed MAN-DAR who breathed through his mouth.

Another slithering-splash brought MAN-DAR's head snapping left. Only ripples spread languidly across the slime covered water, but peripheral vision caught a slight movement among the dead trunks. On closer inspection he saw nothing but got a threatening feeling that he now stood as hunted rather than hunter.

The further MAN-DAR slogged into the swamp, the less perceptible became the path, until it disappeared altogether.

With no clear direction, he sloshed ankle deep in slime, occasionally slipping into the foul water up to his knees. After the third such slip he felt something graze his calf and immediately sought higher ground. When he stepped on a series of rotted logs, he was startled as a number of snake-like creatures darted from under foot. The last one turned and gnashed a deep gouge in his boot. MAN-DAR slashed at the ugly creature with Secura to no avail, then cursed himself for letting the old hag lead him into this swamp of doom. MAN-DAR, sensing the hopelessness of his situation, stared into the stench-ridden gloom and cursed out loud, "Great Baal, why have you done this to me!"

As the dull echo of his blaspheme was sucked into the deadness around him, MAN-DAR spotted a tree stump large enough to accommodate his bulk and decided to rest. Hunger filled his belly as he realized he had not eaten all day. He pulled himself out of the slime and opened his field pack. He removed only a small portion of the food ration, not knowing when he might escape the foul swamp.

While he ate, MAN-DAR cautiously eyed his surroundings. Movement constantly disturbed the green slime as if the denizens dwelling there hungrily anticipated his return. Now and again he heard the slither-splash sound and wondered if the same creatures that disturbed the slime below made it. And several more times he thought he caught a faint movement out of the corner of his eye, along with the sensation of being watched. Instinct told him the movement was not the slime dwellers but possibly a two-legged creature.

MAN-DAR repacked his rations, and was about to reenter the swamp when he felt something brush the back of his neck. Quickly he turned and stared down at the gently undulating slime but saw nothing. But again he felt something brush his neck. This time he looked around and up. Only centimeters from his face loomed a mass of drooling weed-vines. With lightning-like speed, MAN-DAR whipped out Secura, slashed at the vines, and jumped into the muck heedless of the rippling slime.

His feet barely embedded themselves into the muddy bottom when something wrapped around his leg. MAN-DAR wielded Secura once more and slashed at the unseen assailant, freeing himself just as the jumble of weed-vines reached him again. As swiftly as the murky waters allowed, he sloshed to the rotted hulk of an immense dead tree lying in the swamp. He managed to clamber onto its slick surface, and ran along it until clear of the vines and creatures seeking his demise. About to leap into the next body of swamp, he sensed trouble and stopped abruptly. As he did, a rough-hewn spear struck the log where his next step would have been.

MAN-DAR strained to see through the gloom in the direction the weapon had come from. He caught sight of a lone figure that ran full tilt away from him and into the dead swamp. With a last glance at the spear, MAN-DAR leaped into the putrid quagmire in pursuit of the would-be assassin.

It soon became apparent that his quarry knew the swamp better than MAN-DAR. The man moved swiftly through the quagmire and with a definite direction. To keep him in view, MAN-DAR willed all strength to his legs. He knew his survival depended on catching his assailant. Without whose help he might never find his way from the swamp. With great effort MAN-DAR slowly closed the distance to his quarry. At one point he saw the figure stumble and fall. As he rose again to flee, MAN-DAR noticed he splashed on with a definite limp. MAN-DAR gained on him rapidly now and knew if his strength held, he would soon catch the man.

Within fifty paces of his quarry, the land rose slightly and the man splashed onto a tiny island containing a thicket of decaying bushes. He disappeared into the brambles and MAN-DAR lost sight of him. Without hesitation MAN-DAR followed, bounding onto the soggy ground.

Once in the thicket, MAN-DAR paused and listened hard for the fleeing man. He heard nothing but continued to follow water-filled footprints in the sponge-like earth. He moved rapidly, confident the chase would soon end. Abruptly the tracks ended and MAN-DAR halted. Cautiously he proceeded another twenty paces and reached the end of the island where only empty swamp stretched before him. MAN-DAR turned to retrace his steps and heard a twig snap but had no time to react. A rough noose wrapped around his feet and lifted him into the air. The ground gave a deadened squish sound when his back and head hit the soggy earth.

At once MAN-DAR heard movement and squirmed around to see his quarry poised over him; in his upraised arms he brandished a massive tree limb. MAN-DAR winced, knowing his misery in the swamp would soon end. Involuntarily his eyes shut but they flew open when he heard a slithering-splash sounded in the nearby swamp. As the log crashed down toward his head, MAN-DAR twisted to the side. With a dull thud the weapon sank into the mud next to his ear. Then his eyes caught a more terrifying sight. From out of the slime shot a long thick mottled tentacle. It wavered only an instant above his assailant's head before it wrapped itself around his neck and dragged the man's thrashing body into the swamp.

Without a thought, instinct told MAN-DAR his survival depended on saving this man from the slime creature. A quick blow from Secura severed the noose binding his feet. Instantly on his feet he rushed into the water. As the man's head disappeared beneath the surface, MAN-DAR wielded Secura once more and severed the tentacle clasped around its victim's neck. With the last of his strength, MAN-DAR reached into the ooze, found the man, and dragged him onto the tiny island. As he bent to see if the victim lived, he felt a sharp pain explode in his head and the world went black.

SIX

MAN-DAR became conscious of pain first. He thought a woolly bison must have kicked his head until he remembered the chase in the swamp. Still, his eyes refused to open, and in an attempt to massage away the misery he discovered his hands were bound. Soon, the sound of movement around him aroused enough fear to overcome his agony.

He opened his eyes and tried to focus, but MAN-DAR could make out only a flicker of torchlight somewhere past an opening. When his eyes finally adjusted to the dim light, he found himself on the ground in a hovel surrounded by a group of ragged looking men dressed in mottled leather skins. They stared down at him with a mixture of fear and curiosity. Hoping to take his captors by surprise, he jerked violently on the thongs that held him. The bindings did not weaken, but his quick movement startled the men and they drew back in fear.

When it became apparent that their captive could not escape, the men ventured close again. One man, larger than the others, thrust his scraggly bearded face into MAN-DAR's. Immediately MAN-DAR recognized him as the man he had chased in the swamp, and demanded, "Why did you try to kill me?"

He did not answer. Instead he led the others to a corner of the hut. For some time they spoke among themselves with one or two occasionally gesturing wildly.

Finally they surrounded MAN-DAR again and the man who had flung the spear spoke. "We believed you were one of the creatures of the evil High Priest of Inanna. The one called Zarharrab. Up close we see you differently. "But tell us stranger," the spear thrower demanded, "Who are you and from where do you come?"

MAN-DAR thought before he spoke. Even in the dim light his captors looked pale and weak. But still, he thought, they are potential allies and could at least lead him from the swamp. He decided the best tact was to explain his predicament and ask their help. MAN-DAR ignored the pain searing in his head, and spoke slowly to insure they would understand.

"I am called, MAN-DAR. I come from the great Empire of Atlantis. I seek two Euros held captive by a horde of unearthly creatures of which you spoke."

The bearded spear thrower answered, "I am Reamann. I lead the swamp people. Why do you seek these Euros?"

"To escort them to Atlantis. A world meeting is planned to discuss combating the Gigantica Beasts."

"We know much of the creatures of Zarharrab, but little of Beasts, or Atlantis. Even Beasts fear Angleland. And in many harvests few Atlanteans have walked this land. How do we know you speak the truth? How do we know you do not spy for Zarharrab?"

"If I came to spy, would I have saved your life and risked my own?"

"That is why you still live, Atlantean. In this land, to risk a life to save another proves much honor. You saved my life and now I save yours." Reamann produced MAN-DAR's Akarri and severed his bonds. "Come share a meal, MAN-DAR of Atlantis, and tell us of the world beyond this wretched half-light."

"I shall, Reamann, and you shall tell me of what has destroyed this once beautiful land. But first I must hasten to find the Euro captives and free them."

"Leave not, Atlantean. Little time has passed since the blow to your head and you look weakened from the pain." A look of anguish appeared in MAN-DAR's eyes and Reamann added, "Do not brood, Atlantean, you have time to catch the unearthlings. The creatures of Zarharrab will surely bring the captives to the Temple of Inanna, and they travel slowly. It will take them at least four moons. Even if they do not stop to massacre a village or slaughter what few cattle still survive."

"Surely if Zarharrab ordered their capture they would return to the temple forthwith."

Reamann shook his head, "When these monsters leave the sight of Zarharrab his control of them grows slight, save for the vicious hand of his minion, Pogul. But not even Pogul can control the unearthlings when blood lust strikes."

Reamann's words eased MAN-DAR's anxiety, but in its place he felt the suggested weakness. With a shrug of resignation he followed the ragged band out of the hut to a roughly hewn log table where a few women, also dressed in mottled leather, kept busy arranging crude wooden bowls and a few pots.

In the dim daylight, MAN-DAR inspected the swamp men's impoverish encampment. It consisted of several tiny islands connected by rough log bridges. On the islands heavy logs embedded in the spongy earth kept feet from sinking. He guessed the camp could accommodate at least fifty people.

Above him, MAN-DAR noticed a series of burning torches mounted on poles. "Tell me Reamann, do these poles burn for extra light?"

"No, the torches keep the weed-vines at bay. Without them we would not survive their vicious blossoms."

With a wary eye on the vines above the flaming poles, MAN-DAR sat on one of the rough log benches surrounding the crude table. Reamann sat next to him and the rest of the scraggly crew fought for a place close to the strange foreigner. When the jostling for position subsided, MAN-DAR noticed the chunky stew the women dished into wooden bowls and turned to Reamann. "It appears you have much meat. I would think it scarce in so desolate a land."

The spear thrower answered with a grin. "The meat comes from the thordike. We hunt them for both food and skin, that is, when they do not hunt us. You met with this one yourself."

Gales of laughter rose from the men around him when the thought of eating the slime creature showed on MAN-DAR's face. Successful, after several attempts to swallow the grisly meat, he admitted to his hosts that thordike tasted better than it looked. However, before he could take another bite, the swamp men eagerly questioned him about Atlantis.

MAN-DAR felt anxious to learn of Zarharrab and how he came to hold such power over Angleland, but first he patiently answered the questions thrown at him from around the table.

"What size is Atlantis?"

"Scores of Angleland's could fit in Atlantis, but the whole Empire extends across the world. We have colonies in many lands."

"Does Atlantis have villages like ours?"

"Yes, Atlantis has small villages, but also many great cities. The capital is Poseidon. It is built of all white stone. Many of the buildings are adorned with huge white pillars as tall as a tree. Some of the stone buildings are as high as a small mountain. And surrounding the city are three huge moats leading to the sea. All the rules for running the Empire come from Poseidon."

"How can you travel about such a great area?"

"We have many means of travel, airships great and small, and ships that travel all the seas."

"But how can this be? What magic moves them?"

MAN-DAR attempted to explain Atlantean energy as simply as possible. "No magic. In Poseidon, the center of the empire lays a great crystal collector. This device gathers natural energy from the universe and changes it to a form that powers our machines. From Poseidon the energy travels through the air to smaller crystals. These smaller crystals release the energy that runs our devises. Devises like the Vector Battler which flew me here. That was before the magic of Zarharrab somehow disabled it.

The men around the rough table held bewildered looks on their faces, but their questions continued. "What of the colonies you spoke of? Do you enslave their inhabitants."

"No, never. Atlanteans believe in equality for mankind," in his mind MAN-DAR winced at the thought of the old Lessor's eyes. "We help the people of lands we settle. We build Temples of Healing to cure ancient diseases and eliminate afflictions passed down through generations. We also educate through Temples of Learning, and teach better ways to farm, including the way to read the stars to insure the proper time to plant and harvest."

Fascinated, the swamp men queried MAN-DAR further, "You spoke of the Beast menace. Tell us of these Beasts?"

"The Galactica Beast problem originated many generations ago. A warming of the earth caused vegetated areas where the Beasts dwell to enlarge. As the vegetation increased so did the Beasts. Their numbers have become so great, they battle us for food and territory."

"What are these Beasts? Are they demons?"

"No, not demons, but to do battle with them one might believe so."

"Then what ilk of creature be they?"

"Apes. Giant apes. Some stand many hands above a man, and they have the strength of ten."

"But you spoke of the strength of Atlantis. You own powerful weapons. Why can you not defeat a mere animal, no matter how large?"

"The Beasts are many and possess intelligence. They live by social order like clans and have leaders as we do. When on the attack, a pack will act as one, and with their strength and numbers they can easily defeat a well armed village or even small cities. We have had two wars against them already."

The swamp men quieted, fear showing on their faces. MAN-DAR saw the opening he hoped for and questioned Reamann further about Angleland and the unearthlings who captured the Euro delegation. Reamann hesitated, slowly pushed his half-eaten bowl of thordike stew away and answered. "The problems began many harvests ago, when POL-TAR first arrived."

MAN-DAR remembered the name from his internship so long ago. "POL-TAR? That name sounds Atlantean?"

"It is. She claimed misuse of sorcery caused her exile. We believe it true for when she arrived in Angleland, she bewitched the shaman and chief, Sealaac. When they married, she took the name Zerrina and had a son, Zarharrab."

"I have encountered Zarharrab in the past, and recently one who called herself Zerrina. But she seemed too old to be the mother of Zarharrab."

"It is said her magic powers allows her to change form."

"How did he gain such power over Angleland?"

"Let me continue Atlantean."

MAN-DAR tried to relax on the rough bench but his fingers slowly beat on Secura.

"About six or seven harvests after the marriage, Sealaac disappeared mysteriously. A council created by Zerrina collected tithe and conscripted men for an army. They governed Angleland until eight harvests ago when Zerrina's council named Zarharrab both shaman and chief. Together, mother and son built the Temple of Inanna, and through magic and treachery, their power has expanded. Now they possess all but a few sections of Angleland. Places like this swamp, where even the vicious weed-vines barely survive."

Emotion overcame Reamann and MAN-DAR averted his eyes to save the man from embarrassment. He noticed the lack of women in the camp and questioned why.

Reamann's face grew bleaker. "They are gone."

"Gone? Gone where?"

A tear ran down Reamann's gaunt face into his scruffy beard and his voice cracked. "At first but a few women disappeared, one or two from different villages. We believed they ran off with other men. Then Zarharrab sent strange men led by Pogul into each village. He demanded the villagers produce a maiden to work at the Temple. The maidens never came back. But, each time Pogul returned to a village for another female, fewer real men accompanied him and more of what you called unearthlings did. Finally when the villagers protested the loss their women, Pogul and his creatures broke into dwellings and took who they pleased. If they met any resistance, the unearthlings destroyed the hut and killed all within. Some even claimed the monsters ate their victims. At the time it seemed too horrible to believe, but we have learned different."

MAN-DAR needed to learn everything he could of his enemy and sympathetically pushed the grim-faced Anglelander further. "I know the story pains you Reamann, but you must tell me all."

Reamann struggled to hold back tears and continued. "My village lay a great distance from the Temple and Pogul visited only to collect the tithe demanded by Zerrina and Zarharrab. We paid and said nothing. But in time they took most of our harvests. When we could give no more and survive, they took our women instead.

"At this time the terrible weed-vines appeared. What Zarharrab did not take, the vines destroyed. Some even believe the vines spy for Zarharrab."

MAN-DAR shook his head, "I know these vines. It could be true."

Under forced control, Reamann continued. "Finally our village chief decided to act. When next visited by Pogul, he refused to hand over women or what little harvest remained. Pogul laughed a terrible laugh and with a swing of his club, crushed the chief's head. At the sight of the blood, the un-earthlings with Pogul went crazy and attacked all the villag-ers. Pogul attempted to stop them, but they listened not."

Tears again rolled down Reamann's cheeks. MAN-DAR, overwhelmed with compassion for the distraught man, sat in silence.

"We tried to defend ourselves but our struggle proved useless against the blood crazed monsters. Finally, I had no choice but to flee. As I sought to reach my family, I saw the creatures tear the limbs from their victims and toss them into the awful jaws of the weed-vines. The victims included my wife and small son. I could do nothing"

After revealing this final horror, Reamann broke down completely, and used his hands to cover his tears, grief and shame. Each face around the weeping leader bore witness to his story with their own pain.

MAN-DAR sat in silence, his heart filled with sorrow for the men. Yet his stoic rearing allowed no room for the expres-sion of empathy he felt for them.

Reamann regained control and spoke quietly, his voice ex-hausted by grief. "Those of us who survived escaped to this swamp. Others have since joined us and our numbers have risen to over four score."

"But I see only a handful in the camp."

"Most hunt the thordike and some stand guard against Pogul and the unearthling creatures of Zarharrab."

MAN-DAR seized the chance to draw the men from their grief and learn more of his old enemy. "What of this magic Zarharrab possesses?"

"The magic takes many forms and I know not the truth from

superstition. But many believe both Zerrina and Zarharrab read the thoughts of men. Some claim that mother and son change shape at will. Still others speak of seeing the pair fly on stones. They even speak of the pair being able to change the future."

MAN-DAR believed superstition lay behind much of Reamann's claims. Still, he thought, I have seen the unearthlings and they appear real. "Tell me more of the mother, Zerrina."

"No one sees her. But rumors claim she holds great beauty. Her face remains young and one smile from her can drive a man mad. They also say she has one eye colored different from the other."

MAN-DAR thought about the old woman at the little hut and remembered she did not act as old as she looked. "What more can you tell me of the unearthlings who captured the Euros?"

"The creatures appeared soon after Zerrina and Zarharrab built the temple. About the same time the women began to go missing. The villagers believed the pair to be evil demons and sacrificed sheep to the gods for help. No help came."

"You claim Zarharrab took the women as servants in the Temple. Did any return to speak of their ordeal?"

"No. Once they enter the Temple we never see them again."

MAN-DAR realized he could wait no longer to attempt a rescue of the two Euros, especially the female, Sulina. With a thought to his own plight he asked, "Why do you people not chance an escape across the forbidden land bridge to Atlantis? I have been told of this causeway. It could be no worse than your slow death here."

Reamann tugged on his rough leather sleeve and spoke for the swamp men again. "We know of the causeway. It has existed in our legends since the first Euro people came to Angleland. But, the legends also state the land between Angleland and Atlantis can be traversed by no man."

"Another ancient superstition?"

"Not superstition. We have sent scouts. Most never returned. Those who do, scream and rave and some have even burst into flame. Is it not better to live as a dog under Zarharrab than to chance death or life as a raving fool?"

MAN-DAR nodded his understanding, but knew if he could not get his Vector in the air, he and the Euro delegates would attempt passage of the *Forbidden Causeway*.

"The time has come for me to leave this Swamp of Doom, Reamann. My head no longer hurts and I have already accepted too much of your hospitality. I thank you and your people, but I must go now. Please show me the route from this place."

Quickly a pointy-chinned man volunteered for the mission. Reamann waved him off and turned smiling for the first time at MAN-DAR. "I will lead you from the swamp myself, Atlantean." Then his voice turned grave once more, "But you must travel carefully my friend. For the perils in this terrible land grow daily. The intrigues of Zarharrab drive the villagers who survive against one another. Many would befriend, then betray you, only to curry slight favor with the wicked Priest."

"Fear not Reamann, I plan to skirt villages to avoid detection." MAN-DAR stood to indicate his intention to leave and turned his gaze on the beaten people around the table. Then his eyes returned once more to their leader.

"I make a vow, Reamann. After I take the Euros to

Atlantis, I will return to make Zarharrab and his mother pay for the suffering they have levied upon your people and this once beautiful land."

Cautiously MAN-DAR moved toward the small village. From a distance he had heard screams of terror mingled with blood curdling war cries. By the time he covered half that distance he heard only an occasional war cry. Finally as he crept up a small hill separating him from the melee, he heard only the tiny squeal of an infant's life abruptly ending and the sound of crushing bones. His stomach almost emptied.

Perched on the rise above the village, MAN-DAR realized nothing he could have done would have helped. Most of the village and its inhabitants lay destroyed by the orgy of blood.

A huge fire burned in the village center and from his vantage point MAN-DAR observed some of the faces and forms of the ghastly creatures who had perpetrated the massacre. A few of the unearthlings lounged, picking their teeth with the bones of their victims or swilled a malted beverage fermenting in a huge vat. Nearby, some of the monsters swung great clubs at each other in sporadic drunken brawls, but it was obvious that like most of their compatriots, they would soon pass out from glut of mead and flesh.

Stealthily MAN-DAR crept from the ridge to the shadows of the remaining huts. Instinct told him he had encountered the horde that kidnapped the Euros and if they still lived, they would be close by.

Movement from the doorway of the hovel nearest the huge vat caught his eye. At once MAN-DAR dropped to one knee, and buried himself deeper in the shadows. Two creatures emerged from the hut. One had the face and torso of a large bearded man but from the waist down he had two legs and the tail of a goat. The unearthly creature accepted a bucket of grog from the other who stood taller but had the body of a man and a face which resembled a pig, although upon closer inspection MAN-DAR saw that the giant was actually human with an oversized head and a pug nose. As the goat-man swilled mead, the other swiped at the nose.

Then angry recognition tore through MAN-DAR as he remembered the battle at the Vector freighter. Pogul, he thought, the leader. That hut most likely holds the Euro delegates.

Pogul and the goat-man slid drunkenly down each side of the open doorway and continued to pass the bucket between them. Now MAN-DAR knew his plan. He would wait until the two passed out, sneak to the rear of the hut, find entrance and free the captives. A simple enough plan he mused in silence. He then glanced up at the starless sky and asked the gods for help.

In a short time great snores issued from the mouths of the two drunkards as they fell into deep sleep. MAN-DAR surmised the captives might be guarded by some other hideous monster so he approached the back of the dwelling soundlessly. Prying a slat from the wall, he peered inside with caution, and hoped for enough light to evaluate the situation.

Fortunately, light from the fire's dying embers allowed him to make out two bound forms on an earthen floor. Quietly he pried away several more slats and crawled through the opening to the first form. As MAN-DAR bent close he recognized the figure of a woman. He reached to cover her mouth with his hand to prevent a screaming alarm, but instead he had to stifle his own scream as the woman bit viciously into his hand. The pain reached to his elbow and yanked his wounded appendage from her jaws. Now he barely had time to duck when her bound feet struck at his head. Cautious to avoid more of her wrath, MAN-DAR moved as close to the woman as he deemed safe and whispered, "I am MAN-DAR of Atlantis. I came to rescue you and your husband."

When MAN-DAR sensed the woman relax, he untied her bonds. But, as he moved toward the other figure, she grasped his arm with an iron grip and whispered angrily, "His life is not worth the dirt he lies on. Leave him for the pig at the door." Her violent reaction startled MAN-DAR, but he quickly remembered that his mission called for delivering both delegates to Atlantis. Consequently, he ignored her plea and unbound the other figure that instantly woke. MAN-DAR motioned him to silence. He then led both captives through the rear opening into the blackness of night.

The trio traveled parallel to a path over the rough landscape. Reamann had given MAN-DAR directions for the quickest route to where the Atlantean believed his downed ship would be. They moved in silence with an occasional hand signal from MAN-DAR to indicate a change in direction or for a moments rest. Even in the half-light of the Angleland day they spoke in hushed tones only when absolutely necessary. Occasionally MAN-DAR glimpsed an angry stare pass between the Euros, and occasionally his own tentative glance fell on the beautiful redheaded barbarian princess. Sometimes she returned a look he somehow found familiar.

Within a day and a half MAN-DAR recognized features in the landscape and breathed a sigh of relief. His ship was within striking distance. Finally after another half day they came within hailing distance of the Vector, but a call to Lugaar received no answer. When almost to the ship MAN-DAR tried once more. Still, he heard no answer come forth. With a hand signal MAN-DAR stopped the Euros as he moved closer to inspect the Vector's interior. When he reached the ship's open hatch, MAN-DAR leaned to peer inside. Astonished, MAN-DAR saw the entire ship vanish before his eyes.

SEVEN

A day had passed since the Vector Battler disappeared. They had found no bodies of either the liaison officer or Lugaar. MAN-DAR surmised the carnivorous plants had completely consumed them. To his surprise he felt a large amount of grief not only for TAM-STX, but also for the lumbering Lessor, Lugaar.

The scowl on Kirack's face made MAN-DAR feel uneasy. Yet he understood the reason for the barbarian's anger. Since he rescued the couple, Sulina had barely spoken to her husband and had paid an inordinate amount of attention to MAN-DAR. Although he knew returning her attention risked his mission, MAN-DAR's resistance receded before the beauty of the Euro female. She had a natural curiosity about the world and could fathom deep concepts. They had discussed many topics including, the situation concerning the Beasts, what direct effect the conference would have on her tribe, and where the Euro's fit into the larger scheme of Atlantean politics.

The report on her had done scant justice to the being who was Sulina. MAN-DAR had never met such a perfect woman. Her flowing red hair, her fur-clothing cut to accent perfect curves, and her wild barbaric way. Besides beauty, MAN-DAR saw fierce self-will, strength of character, and an intellect beyond which he believed possible in any barbarian. Even though only a few days had passed since the rescue, MAN-DAR felt a special intimacy between them. An intimacy, which seemed to transcend time.

The trio camped for the night on a small hill capped with boulders not far from the downed Vector. Huddled together, MAN-DAR, Kirack and Sulina attempted to formulate a plan to reach Atlantis.

"As far as I can see, we have but two choices," MAN-DAR stated as he stirred the coals in a low fire. "Without the ability to contact Poseidon Command, we must either take the land route over the Forbidden Causeway, or find the Temple of Inanna and confront Zarharrab and Zerrina. I know their magic caused the Vector's disappearance and I will force its return." To MAN-DAR's chagrin, the couple paid scant attention to his words.

Kirack stood, paced a few steps and turned on Sulina. "You whore. I told you if your eyes did not lead the freighter captain to your body, we would have found a safer place to land."

"How can you say such things, you cowardly liar." Sulina screamed as she leaped to her feet. "You suggested we land here. And it is you who roams the land searching for anything to sleep with."

"For once you speak the truth. For I prefer any pallet to the cold one in which you lay with any animal available."

"Animals! By Kraal! Beasts! How many of them have *you* slept with?"

Like lightning MAN-DAR leaped up in time to stop a blow from Kirack aimed at Sulina's head. But as swiftly as he grabbed Kirack's hand, Sulina's foot caught Kirack in the ankle, tumbling him onto the fire. With his hand still on

Kirack's, MAN-DAR yanked the Euro from the fire unhurt. Then he stood between the couple as obscenities flew past his ears.

Finally he could take no more. "Desist! My mission is to take both of you to Atlantis, unharmed."

Sulina ignored MAN-DAR, and reaching across his shoulder she scratched Kirack's face, drawing blood.

"You whore!" Kirack screamed as he struggled with MAN-DAR to get at his wife.

"You Coward! Sulina screamed and once again her nails found their target. This time MAN-DAR turned and grappled with her thrashing body, but Kirack, taking advantage of MAN-DAR's hold on Sulina, reached across and pounded Sulina's face. MAN-DAR lost his temper, pushed Sulina aside and hammered Kirack to the ground. Kirack reached for a tree limb but Secura appeared in MAN-DAR's hand, its point pressed to Kirack's throat. The Euro dared not move, but both men's eyes blazed with hate.

"Kill him!" Sulina screamed.

The hysteria in the Sulina's voice snapped MAN-DAR out of his rage. Suddenly he realized by killing Kirack he would destroy half the reason for his mission. He sheathed Secura and helped Kirack to his feet once again.

MAN-DAR caught his breath and spoke to the couple with rare passion. "We must end this infighting. If we do not work together, we may never leave this land."

Sulina found her voice, "MAN-DAR speaks the truth, and we have more to worry about than the past." Then directly to Kirack, "Let us live a truce until we escape this dreadful land. For our fighting serves none but our enemies."

The simple logic of Sulina calmed the three and they sat once more to discuss their situation.

MAN-DAR stared into the dying coals of the fire and began, "As I said,.."

Kirack immediately interrupted. "I for one will not confront Zarharrab or his mother."

"You coward, Kirack. One scrape with the unearthlings and your nerve recedes like that tiny worm between your legs."

Quickly MAN-DAR held up his hand to intervene. "Be still Sulina. You asked for a truce. To Kirack he added, "Tell us your reason for an attempt across the Forbidden Causeway."

"I will not listen to the superstitions of ignorant farmers." He sounded nervous and his voice rose. "If they merely lost a sheep or goat near the overland route, they would embellish it to half a herd. I believe it safer to pick our way through the ancient trails than to confront the man who controls the hideous unearthlings."

MAN-DAR stood and paced before the two Euros. "If I believed only superstition motivate the farmers, Kirack, I would agree with you. But the farmer, Reamann, opened old memories in my mind. There are Atlantean myths about a Forbidden Causeway. As a young man, I studied this place called Angleland and read of its legends. The ancient Atlanteans blocked the causeway with both physical and magical shields to prevent hoards of Lessors from overrunning our land."

Sulina spoke up. "We must listen to the Atlantean, Kirack, he knows of this causeway and we do not. Besides, even if this Zarharrab knows magic, a spear through the heart will soon end his evil spells."

"I agree with your wife, Kirack," MAN-DAR broke in. "At first light we shall begin the trek to the Temple of Inanna."

There had been no more discussion on which plan to follow and on the second day the trio marched again in silence with occasional stares between MAN-DAR and Sulina. Any interaction between MAN-DAR and Kirack came in cross grunts and nods that facilitated their movement toward the Temple.

By the end of his turn at watch on the second night, MAN-DAR could not wait for daylight so he could once more gaze upon the face of Sulina. As they traveled the third day, they avoided a number of Zarharrab's patrols, only pausing occasionally to seek directions to the Temple from frightened farmers. Although MAN-DAR knew the risk, he and Sulina used every opportunity possible to gaze, brush or touch. Each occurrence brought him joy, but also anxiety for his mission. He feared Sulina might use her charms to provoke another fight between Kirack and him, which would prove fatal for the barbarian. Still, he could not resist her, for MAN-DAR found if they came within arm's length, he felt a magnetic attraction which not only raised the hair on his head, but also the lower front of his battle tunic.

On the third evening they set up camp a few strides from a defoliated forest. MAN-DAR believed it might prove useful if escape became necessary, and while Kirack gathered dead logs for a blind, he found himself alone with Sulina.

Together they busied themselves clearing dead brush from a once heavy thicket. As they paused to rest, their sweat covered bodies touched, sending shock waves of passion through both. Entranced, they stared into each other's eyes. Without hesitation Sulina took MAN-DAR's hands and pulled them around her, the silence between them broken only by a low moan from Sulina. Overwhelmed with emotion and lust, MAN-DAR wanted to take the barbarian princess where they stood, but instead he heard himself say, "We cannot do this. Kirack is your mate. Only he has the right to the sweetness of your body."

"This is true, I have sworn an oath of fidelity to my husband and I cannot break it. But I hate him. It is you I love, MAN-DAR. I feel I have waited my whole life for you."

"I love you also, Sulina. But I pledged my life to the Empire. My mission comes first, and I must get you and Kirack back to Atlantis. Already trouble brews between Kirack and I. And I fear without his cooperation, I may not accomplish what I began. I too am sorry, Sulina, and agree we cannot be together."

The hurt they both felt moved MAN-DAR. "If only I could find the words to speak of how I feel for you. We have known each other for but a few days yet it seems our time together has been endless. But alas, we cannot be together."

Sulina answered firmly, "Listen to me Atlantean. I do not understand your obsession with this mission. But no love exists between Kirack and me. He never visited my sleeping pallet, not even on the night of our wedding ceremony. He married me only to reach one step closer to tribal chief. Yet, he guards me from others and flies into rages if anyone dare look upon me. Sometimes I believe he tries to save me for another, but I can see no reason behind this."

"I have observed many men act thusly. He has a possession and means to protect it. Whether he wants you or not."

"But I hate him, and I hate myself for wishing him dead."

"But he is your husband."

Softening, "MAN-DAR, words come not easily to me either. But in our brief time together, I also sense something special between us. Something so special it feels as if I have known you for eternity."

"I know Sulina."

"You must believe what I say. I have visited no man's sleeping pallet, but if I could it would be yours, MAN-DAR."

"I know Sulina." MAN-DAR turned quickly and went to help Kirack as he entered the clearing with an armful of dead branches.

Sulina slept fitfully. She felt deeply saddened by her conversation with MAN-DAR, and had laid herself to rest without an utterance to either traveling companion. Sleepless hours later, Sulina thought she heard her name called. Although not yet morning, a dull illumination allowed her to make out forms around her and she clearly saw her husband's shape sitting against a tree. She knew he should be on watch but his breath rose and fell with the rhythm of sleep. As her eyes strained in the direction of MAN-DAR's sleeping place. It appeared empty. Again she heard the sound of a name through the darkness. It was unmistakably her name and had come from the direction of the nearby dead forest. Believing her bronze skinned rescuer wished to speak of his love for her one more time, her heart leaped with anticipation.

At the third call Sulina rose quietly and commenced stealthily in the direction of the sound. As she passed into the forest she saw movement ahead and stepped gingerly over the littered ground to reach it. One more time she heard her name and she leapt faster in its direction. By then she was heedless of anything save the beat of her heart and the heat of her loins.

Sulina found herself only few paces away when she finally recognized the figure of MAN-DAR. Without hesitation she threw her arms around him and gazed up into his smiling face. Immediately she sensed something wrong. It looked like MAN-DAR but the eyes lacked his kindness. The eyes she gazed into possessed an evil cruelty and an involuntary shiver convulsed through her body. But before she could will her arms to release their grip, she saw MAN-DAR's cheekbones wither, his nose thin, and the smile change to a sneer. Before Sulina could cry out, her nostrils picked up a strong scent as a rough cloth covered her face.

MAN-DAR awoke abruptly with a compelling sense of foreboding. In the dull light he saw Kirack at his post, asleep. Quickly he turned to where Sulina should lie and found her gone. He scrambled to his feet, stomped to Kirack, and shook him roughly.

"Wake-up you fool. Your wife sleeps not by the fire."

Kirack stared at MAN-DAR dumbly. "Ah, Atlantean, your concern betrays you. But have no fear, Sulina most likely relieves herself in the forest or perhaps searches for a trinket of adornment. Something to entice her lover. After all, she may feel her naked beauty not strong enough to attract the likes of an Atlantean officer."

MAN-DAR's blood boiled but he restrained his temper and growled, "At moments such as this I wish I wore not the uniform of an Atlantean officer. For surly the way in which you speak of your woman would put you in mortal danger."

Kirack jumped to his feet ready for a confrontation but MAN-DAR ignored him and searched the camp for signs of Sulina's whereabouts. He found fresh tracks leading towards the dead forest and hand signaled to Kirack to follow as he maneuvered into the trees.

Shortly they came upon a piece of ground disheveled by a scuffle. MAN-DAR felt sure Zarharrab or his minions had kidnapped Sulina again and growled to Kirack, "Hurry, we go to the Temple of Inanna."

Kirack complained again for the fifth time, "Why bother to follow the wench and her captors. We now have the opportunity to make for Atlantis, unimpeded." The look MAN-DAR gave Kirack stifled further enquiry and he doubled their pace through the desolate countryside.

They had marched nearly half the morning when the trail led them to the mouth of a long canyon. MAN-DAR reasoned the high steep walls surrounding the path made a perfect spot for an ambush and paused to survey the pass more closely. However, even as Kirack uttered the irritating words, "Why do we pause here?" MAN-DAR heard a band of unearthlings coming from behind. He looked once at the screaming horde and knew they had no choice but to enter the canyon. He took off at a run with a wide-eyed Kirack close at his heels. The ugly horde saw them flee, bellowed at their backs, and rumbled after.

MAN-DAR's sense of ambush proved correct. No sooner did he see the opposite end of the canyon when a cloud of dust informed him another contingent of unearthlings made egress in that direction impossible. MAN-DAR abruptly halted and Kirack almost ran him down. Promptly analyzing the situation, MAN-DAR looked at Kirack, pointed up the canyon wall and began to climb. Kirack protested, then saw the approach of the second horde and followed immediately.

The canyon walls proved steeper than at first glance, and they had barely climbed out of reach when the two hordes merged at their feet. Furious the unearthlings threw curses, screams, spears and clubs. One club nearly knocked Kirack from the cliff wall, but a quick grab by MAN-DAR saved him from the hands of the snarling creatures.

Halfway up the cliff, MAN-DAR and Kirack saw two bands of unearthlings charge out either end of the canyon. It was obvious they planned to catch their quarry as they clambered over the canyon rim. At that sight the Atlantean and Euro redoubled their efforts and reached the top moments before their pursuers.

From the advantage of the rim, MAN-DAR saw it was only necessary to dodge a few of the clumsy creatures to reach an open plain where they could easily outrun the unearthlings.

MAN-DAR hoisted Kirack up the last meter of canyon wall, but as he turned to flee, he found their way blocked by a huge creature with the head of a bull. As the unearthling made an attempt to seize him, MAN-DAR reached up, grabbed one of his horns and pulled it around hard until he heard the snap of the monster's neck. Subsequently another creature attempted to cleave Kirack with an ax, but before he could bring the blade down on his victim, MAN-DAR sliced through his leg with Secura. At once MAN-DAR and the Euro took off across the plain.

The two men matched strides and rapidly put distance between themselves and the howling horde of unearthlings who followed. Just as it appeared they would easily escape, MAN-DAR noticed a speck in the sky. The speck grew larger as it approached. At first, MAN-DAR believed it to be a large bird, but by the time they had crossed half the plain, MAN-DAR knew what followed was no bird.

From the object a high-pitched whine reached MAN-DAR's ears. The sound reminded him of the high-pitched whine he had heard prior to his Vector's crash. He looked up once more and saw to his amazement a huge flat slab of stone. Aboard the rude craft stood Pogul and one other creature with the head of a bear and the body of a man. The closer they approached the more their blood curdling war cries drowned out the sound of the whine.

When the huge stone reached to within twenty paces of MAN-DAR and Kirack, an assortment of weapons fell on the two fugitives. A club struck MAN-DAR in the small of his back and sent him tumbling along the plain. Kirack, without a pause, grabbed MAN-DAR's arm and dragged him until he could regain his feet. But, by then the creatures had positioned the flying stone nearly overhead and medium sized boulders rained down. One stone grazed Kirack and he fell. As he stopped to help, a well-placed rock struck MAN-DAR and knocked him flat.

Sprawled on the ground, MAN-DAR drifted half in and half out of consciousness. He became aware of the whine as it lowered in pitch and through blurry vision he saw the flying stone and its occupants slide to the ground not fifteen paces away. With the sound of the rude craft subsiding, MAN-DAR heard again the roar of the unearthlings who advanced across the plain. If Pogul and his crewman did not end his life, the rest of the unearthly horde certainly would.

As he drifted once more towards unconsciousness, the dying whine of the flying stone scratched a memory. He remembered the picture symbols on the huge upright stones he had encountered days ago. MAN-DAR's eyes suddenly opened with a start of recognition. He remembered the symbols represented sounds used in ancient Atlantis to levitate objects. The flying boulder and standing stones must be part of an ancient ley system, built for travel in a long-past attempt to colonize Angleland. MAN-DAR felt a ray of hope for escape as Pogul lumbered over to him laughing his hideous laugh and raising his gigantic club for the kill.

MAN-DAR feigned unconsciousness until the final instant and allowed Pogul to approach within striking distance. When he thought the giant had moved close enough. With all his might he kicked the huge mass of deformed man in the ankle. Pogul fell with a roar of anger. MAN-DAR leaped to his feet before his two adversaries could react. He put his Akarri through the bear creature and as Pogul rose, MAN-DAR slammed his stomach with an elbow. Pogul went down with a heavy thud. Yet MAN-DAR still had to smash a knee in his face as the giant rose for a third attack.

MAN-DAR heard a louder roar from the horde of unearthlings rumbling across the plain. In moments the creatures would set upon them and MAN-DAR had only time enough to hoist the unconscious Kirack to his shoulders and run to the grounded ley stone. When he reached the flat boulder he laid Kirack on its cold surface and jumped on himself. Meanwhile he prayed to the gods to help him remember the tone and pitch that would lift the boulder into the air.

As clubs and spears flew past his head, MAN-DAR cursed his lack of interest in history. Although he had easily passed his written exams, he had practically slept through classes demonstrating how the ancients used sound to defy gravity.

MAN-DAR hummed several tones and cursed again as the first of the unearthlings reached him. The creature attacked with sword in hand but MAN-DAR slammed a foot into his stomach and sent him sprawling into those who followed. Quickly, MAN-DAR coughed to clear his throat and once more hummed. The stone vibrated slightly. As a blow from a club whooshed by his ear, he hummed a tone one octave higher. This time the huge flat boulder raised half a man's height from the ground and emitted a sound that matched the one issuing from MAN-DAR.

The unearthlings surrounded the crude airship, but MAN-DAR increased the pitch one more octave and the large stone floated up over their heads. MAN-DAR raised and lowered the pitch of the tone and the boulder matched his rhythm and moved away from the angry horde of unearthlings who cursed and threw weapons in a useless attempt to retrieve their lost prey.

Now the ley stone took on a life of its own and the pitch and speed of the flying vehicle increased with no help from MAN-DAR. Soon wind rushed through his hair and forced him to lay flat. With the loss of control, MAN-DAR could do nothing but grab the unconscious Kirack and hang on. The stone, its eerie whine increasing, flew faster and faster and where it would stop, MAN-DAR knew not.

EIGHT

Sulina searched her mind for pleasant experiences to alleviate her extreme discomfort. She remembered her homeland, and the happy days of her youth. She thought of the period before her father became chief of their clan.

She remembered herds of woolly bison growing fat and plentiful on the plain. Sulina smiled as she thought of how she would shun the quiet games of the other girls in order to run with the boys. How she had learned the skills of a tracker and sat around the campfire enthralled by the ancient tales of great hunts and of the heroics of combat in the constant tribal wars. While her peers dreamed of the day they would meet their first love, she had dreamt of the day she would kill her first bison.

One spring in particular rushed colorfully through her head as she fought the pain emanating from her wrists. That year her breasts swelled like new melons on the vine and she first noticed blood staining the soft leather undergarment she wore beneath fur-covered hides. She especially remembered the awe she felt standing next to her father as they watched a herd of bison stretched across the horizon. Even though night forced them into camp for safety, the next morning found the huge herd still passing before her eyes. That year she would make her first kill and set events in motion, which elevated her father to chief of the whole Uxmal tribe.

The great herd had grazed on the plain for half the moon's cycle. The numbers killed filled larders to the brim before the hunt ended. A period of feasting and performing of tribal rites began. Everyone celebrated save for Sulina who sulked in her family's bison skin hut. Impatiently she sat beside her mother, Mojecca, as Mojecca chewed a hide, the method used to soften skins for clothing.

"Why can I not kill a bison, mother? All the boys my age got their first kill."

Mojecca ceased her work, brushed a wisp of stray hair out of her eyes and spoke seriously to the younger of her two daughters, "You know the rite of passage belongs only to boys entering manhood. You are but a girl, Sulina."

Sulina's scowl drew deeper. "But mother."

"You are a girl," the elder explained somewhat exasperated by Sulina's unwillingness to accept her fate. "You must stay behind with the other women." Mojecca turned to Josecca, Sulina's older sister and instructed her further in the curing of hides.

Sulina interrupted once more with her complaint. "I do not understand. Why can I not partake in the hunt? After all, I can run faster and throw a spear truer than any boy my age."

Sulina's sister, Josecca, pulled a section of wet rabbit-skin from her mouth and teased, "You should spend more time learning to catch a man rather than catching a bison."

Sulina screeched at her sister, "I am not interested in catching a man! Someday I will be a great hunter."

Josecca continued to tease, "Maybe you think no one will want you because of that ugly blemish on your thigh."

The insensitive remark about her birthmark proved too

much for the already angry girl. Sulina grabbed Josecca's hair, dragged her face to the earthen floor, and commanded, "Lick dirt."

Pinned to the ground, Josecca screamed while Mojecca attempted to pull Sulina from her eldest daughter.

Just then, Molack, Sulina's father, rushed into the crude summer dwelling, and roughly separated his two angry daughters. "What madness comes over you two! Must you fight like chickens and geese with each turn of my back?"

Josecca continued to cry but Sulina took a chance and pleaded her case once more. "It is not fair. I cannot participate in the hunt simply because I am female. I am as good as any of the boys and stronger than some."

"Sulina, my child. You are a girl and the hunt for the woolly bison holds much danger."

"But father," Sulina pleaded, "I am of the same age as Uljeck and he killed a cow this very day."

Molack tried to explain once more of the danger incurred on a hunt, but the sorrowful look on his beautiful daughter's face melted his heart. "All right, I will take you on a hunt in the morning. Perhaps you can kill a calf or maybe one of the ancient bulls. I am sure the elders could see no harm in that."

The next morning, before the first light, Sulina awoke filled with excitement. She dressed quickly, went to Molack and shook him gently. "Awaken father. The gods throw light into the eastern sky."

Slowly Molack rose from his sleeping pallet, careful not to wake Mojecca. Still groggy from the previous night's revelry he attempted to snatch two spears leaning by the entrance but one fell loose. Before it hit the ground he saw a flicker of movement and the weapon held in Sulina's hand. A smile of love and admiration curved his lips.

Once outside he pulled two hairy bison robes from a pole and led his youngest child toward the plain and great herd of woolly bison.

By the time they traversed the small pass between the two hills separating the clan's camp from the herd, they had donned the hides Molack had brought to disguise their outline and scent from the grazing animals. When they entered the plain, a sudden thrill shuddered through Sulina's young body as the first rays of sun spread across the great pack of bison.

Father and daughter crept close to the animals. Molack used hand signals to direct Sulina to a small patch of bushes while he slipped into the herd to separate a small calf from its grazing mother. Silently, Molack drove the calf toward Sulina.

As the young bison wandered in Sulina's direction, a commotion arose among a portion of the herd, which grazed near a small stand of trees. Slowly Molack stood in an attempt to find the cause of anxiety among the usually peaceful animals. While searching the horizon, he failed to see a huge bull which had lay hidden by the body of the cow. The enraged animal instinctively moved to protect its mate and calf and charged directly at Molack.

Molack, absorbed in his search for the source of the ruckus, still did not see the huge animal bearing down on him, but Sulina did. Her reaction proved as instinctive as that of the bull. She screamed, half in fear for her father and half with the cry of a warrior, as she threw her spear with all her strength. It entered the gaping maw of the bellowing bison, crashed through the back of its throat and came to rest in its brain.

The great animal heaved itself in the direction of the two-legged intruder in a final attempt to protect its offspring, but collapsed at the feet of the astonished Molack.

Sulina, following the flight of her spear, flung her arms around Molack. "Oh father, I thought he would kill you!" Molack did not respond. Instead he pulled her arms from around him and stared intently across the herd of bison. Tears stained Sulina's face.

"Something is out there," Molack muttered without looking at his daughter.

Sulina's reddened eyes followed her father's gaze as the entire herd began to stir. Suddenly Sulina realized the cause of their uneasiness and pointed. Above the backs of the huge bison, so distant that only specks of shoulders and heads stood visible, they saw Beasts.

"They drive the herd toward our encampment!" Molack yelled. "Run to the sentry and see why the alarm has not sounded."

Sulina had to scream above the noise of the frightened bison. "Where is he?" Molack pointed to a lone tree atop a small hill west of the two hills, which formed the gorge leading to the camp.

"If they stampede into the camp, our clan will be destroyed! I shall try to move the herd in another direction." Molack picked up two leafless sticks and beat them together. His action caught the attention of the nearest animals but pressure from their rear forced the herd closer to Molack and the entrance to the clan encampment.

Sulina still stood frozen with fear at her father's side. Molack noticed and yelled above the din of beating sticks and bellowing bison, "Get to the sentry, the camp must be warned!"

Shaken from her inertia, Sulina raced toward the lookout post. Breathlessly she reached the top of the hill and saw one of the older boys, Kirack. He lay asleep beneath the tree, an empty mead bowl by his head. Without hesitation Sulina fiercely kicked him awake screaming, "Beasts are stampeding the herd!"

Stupidly Kirack looked up, rubbed his eyes, and chastised her. "How dare you awaken me, girl. Do you not see that I rest? I guarded this important post all night."

Sulina shook her head in exasperated disbelief and pointed toward the place where her father stood futilely attempting to turn back the herd. "We must warn the camp, Beasts are stampeding the herd!"

Kirack screamed in terror as he followed Sulina who ran for the pass which led to the camp. Halfway down the hill he fell and struck his head on an outcrop of rock. Sulina heard the thud and a cry of pain from Kirack. She turned to see him sprawled on the ground and screeched scornfully as she raced back to the sentry. Roughly she dragged Kirack to his feet and pulled him toward the encampment. When they reached the entrance to the pass, they turned in time to see Molack, followed by the stampeding herd, heading directly toward them. While on the run, Molack signaled them to head for the camp.

At the far end of the pass, fear for her father's life forced Sulina to stop and turn once more while Kirack ran for his life. She watched in awe as Molack ran up one of the boulder-strewn hills enclosing the pass. When he reached the crest,

Molack used a huge log to pry loose a boulder, which crashed upon others carrying them down the hill in an avalanche that filled the entranceway. Blocked, the stampeding bison turned in a wide arch and ran straight back at the Beasts.

That night all in the camp sang songs of praise to Molack, the man who saved the clan. And to Kirack, the young man who said he received a severe head wound while single-handedly fighting off two Beasts. Everyone ate much meat and drank much mead, but no one listened to the story told by the budding young woman. She was merely a girl.

Thoughts of Kirack brought back the awareness of the pain in Sulina's shackled wrists. She craned her neck upward and followed the chains to where they connected to bolt driven into the cold stonewall at her back. She pulled on the chains until trickles of blood ran down her wrists before she gave up. Resigned to captivity, her thoughts fell again to Kirack and the clan.

Sulina recalled with pride her father's election to the tribal council the spring after he had saved her clan from the bison stampede. The spring after that Molack became the new leader of the Uxmal tribe. Kirack also rose to a position of power. For with each telling of the story of his battle with the Beasts, the tale became further embellished. Soon Kirack's reputation as the Beast slayer had spread throughout the plains tribes.

By the fourth spring after the incident, Sulina's sister Josecca became betrothed to the son of the one who speaks to the spirits. It was a powerful position in the clan. As the three women sat in their hut working on Josecca's trousseau, Mojecca lectured her youngest daughter.

"Is it not time you stopped hunting with the boys, Sulina. You are at an age to pick a marriage partner for yourself."

"But I love the hunt, mother. Besides, no one in the tribe attracts me."

Mojecca added pointedly, "Many fine suitors live among the clan. Most would gladly marry a tribal chief's daughter, but I see only one truly worthy, Kirack."

"I shall never marry that coward!" Calmer she added, "If I choose anyone, it would be Uljeck. I consider him a good hunter and a kind soul."

Josecca threw up her hands and laughed. "Everyone knows Uljeck prefers to hunt flowers rather than woolly bison."

"You speak lies, Josecca."

"Besides," Josecca added sarcastically, "his family can provide little dowry."

"I will never marry Kirack!" Sulina screamed as she ran from the hut.

Later that day, after gathering roots for the evening meal, Sulina met Uljeck as she entered the camp. Boldly she took his hand, "Will you walk with me to my father's dwelling, Uljeck? "

Red-faced he stammered, "But Sulina, you know what that gesture means to the clan."

"Yes, I do Uljeck. It means we shall marry." Uljeck hesitated, blushed, but finally grasped her hand and walked smiling with Sulina through the center of the Uxmal camp.

In her mind's eye, Sulina could still see the look of rage on Kirack's face as she and Uljeck marched hand and hand past him while his friends pulled the woolly hide from a fresh kill.

The thought of Uljeck and the soft touch of his hand brought a stab of pain to Sulina's heart. Only one moon had passed after their betrothment, when a foraging party found his body at the bottom of a cliff, his neck broken. Some clan members believed Uljeck had wandered off in the night to relieve himself and never saw the edge. Some believed Beasts caught him. But Sulina believed the killer to be a man, Kirack.

Within the passing of three moons from the death of Uljeck, Sulina's mother and sister left the camp for a walk along the river. Josecca's marriage approached and she had questions about her wedding night. They never returned. A search party gathered early that evening but the women remained missing until the next morning. They were found dead in a thicket near the river. It appeared a Beast had killed them.

Beyond despair, Molack ordered every man in the clan out in search of the Beast. He wanted its head brought to him and as a reward he offered his prize possession. His only surviving daughter's hand in marriage.

The sun set and rose seven times before the men of the tribe returned, without the head of the Beast, and without Kirack. Still another sun went by without a sign of the Beastslayer and the tribe resigned itself to the possibility that he too had been killed. Sulina prayed to the god Muckdah that it be true, but after two more sunsets, Kirack arrived in camp. He walked directly to the dwelling of Molack and ceremoniously laid the severed head of a Beast and a bit of hide, dyed the color of Mojecca's headband at the grieving chief's feet. Of all the members of the Uxmal tribe, only Sulina wondered why a Beast would keep anything belonging to its victim. But it mattered little, for she and Kirack married on the next full moon.

Suddenly a shrill feminine scream, half pain, half pleasure, wrenched Sulina from her revelry once more. Her ears strained to discern its direction, and for the first time since her captivity, she examined her cell.

The room was twice the size of her father's hut with high stonewalls and a barred window which only allowed dull Angleland daylight to pass. On the walls hung rugs, but, woven into the fabric, Sulina noticed scenes of men and women performing grotesque forms of the marriage act. In some scenes animals performed the acts and Sulina tore her eyes from the rugs and focused on what looked like a sleeping pallet. But unlike the fur-strewn mats used by her people, this one stood off the floor on wooden pegs and had post at each corner. She wondered about use of leather thongs hanging from each post.

The sleeping platform stood very near and Sulina reached out with her foot and touched it. Astonished, she found the coverlet of the sleeping pallet smooth, almost like the slickness of bear grease but not wet. The color looked like fresh blood and had a shine like the sun on new ice. As her toes felt the coverlet, she realized for the first time her feet lacked her hide sandals. As she followed the line of her leg from the toe up past her birthmark she found herself dressed in a garment of the same hew and material as the pallet cover.

With hands painfully shackled above her she examined the tightly fitted garment. Two wide swathes of material held it on her shoulders, but a partial split in the front exposed half of each breast. The material continued down her midsection, joined, and passed tightly between her bare legs. Suddenly she realized each bodily movement caused her tiny waves of pleasure similar to when she looked upon MAN-DAR.

She thought of the Atlantean. Never had she an attraction to a man as she had for MAN-DAR. The instant she saw his muscular form in daylight, she could think of nothing but him in her arms and on her pallet. Never before had she thought of a man that way. Compared to the emotion MAN-DAR brought forth, her love for Uljeck felt like that between two cubs at play. As for her husband Kirack, only loathing and disgust filled her heart. Despite her discomfort, a tiny smile crept across her face as she recalled kicking Kirack in the groin on their wedding night.

Shuffling her feet to relieve the weight on her shackled wrists, Sulina felt a new twinge of pleasure whelm up in her stomach, but another muffled shriek of pain or pleasure, drew her attention to the chamber door. Her eye caught movement as the door slowly swung open and a small woman slightly younger than herself entered. The woman wore a look of permanent sadness on her dirty face as she hesitated at the doorway and stared at Sulina. Her clothes, filthy as her face, were of rough hand-woven cloth and hung on a frail body. The woman carried a mug and bowl of food. Without a word, she set the bowl on a stand in the corner and approached Sulina. Meekly she raised the mug to Sulina's lips.

Without warning, Sulina raised a leg, put her foot against the woman's stomach, and pushed savagely. The woman flew across the room and slammed against the opposite wall. Sulina heard a whoosh of air leave the woman's lungs as her knees buckled and she slid down the wall to the floor. Tears streamed from her eyes but no sobs left her lips. She merely sat and stared dumbly at Sulina while she tugged on her earlobe.

Sulina glared down at her and demanded, "Who are you and where am I?"

With her tear swollen eyes now fixed on the stone floor she answered slowly, "I am called Marrina, a scullery maid. They call this place the Temple of Inanna." Another flood of tears streamed down her face as she fiercely tugged her ear.

Sulina's heart melted at the sight of the pathetic woman, but before she could utter a sympathetic word the door opened once more. This time a man entered, a hunchback with an ugly pock scarred face. After a glance at the broken mug, he cursed Marrina and reaching down, slapped her viciously across the face. Marrina raised her hands and pleaded for mercy but he only replied with another slap.

Marrina ducked a third blow and attempted to retrieve the broken crockery. The hunchback roughly hauled her to her feet, and threw her onto the silk covered bed. With a drooling grin he sneered, "Me think you need a little something to make you less clumsy, scullery wench." He then tore open her filthy tunic and exposed her tiny breasts. Too frightened to move, a pall of resignation covered her face as the hunchback unbuckled his belt and released his pants.

Before the pock-faced man touched Marrina, Sulina acted. She lifted herself off the floor by her shackled hands, swung her legs out and wrapped them firmly around the hunchback's neck. With all her strength she squeezed the deformed man until he lost consciousness.

As the hunchback slumped to his knees, the door to the cell suddenly flew open. Sulina's head turned with a start. In the doorway stood a tall hooded man with a charming smile and deep sinister eyes.

Sulina writhed in her shackles and cursed the man she guessed to be, Zarharrab, the High Priest of Inanna. The movement increased the pain to her wrists, and the undeniable pleasure of sexual warmth from the garment stretched between her legs.

About to leave, Zarharrab turned languidly at the doorway, a sneer pursing his nearly white lips. "Struggle all you like sweet barbarian princess, it only serves our future goals."

The evil smile on his face made Sulina struggle harder. "If I could get my hands on you, I would claw out your wicked eyes." Finally she accepted the futility of struggle, calmed herself and questioned Zarharrab.

"Why have you brought me here? What is to be done with me?"

Zarharrab paused, he seemed to ponder Sulina's question. "You are here for a very special purpose. If you cooperate, you will receive an opportunity given only a few in all man's existence. That is if we receive your cooperation."

Sulina spit at Zarharrab and struggled once again against her shackles. Zarharrab merely laughed and as he led the gasping hunchback through the door he added, "Keep fighting sweet princess, the harder the better."

NINE

Shrieks from ghastly torture combined with screams of erotic passion rose from the bowels of the Temple of Inanna. Shriek followed screams as waves of sound filled the lower rooms of the fortress temple. Ever expanding, the horrendous cacophony careened off thick stone and climbed winding stairways to scores of grotesque spires studding the godless temple walls. The sound entered cells where women of all forms hung in excruciatingly tortuous positions while experiencing costume causing masturbation. Huge tapestries decorated with ungodly acts absorbed some sound. Some entered rooms where creatures, half man, half beast, took their pleasure with unwanted experiments who were the missing women of Angleland. The sound traveled up a long staircase and reached a huge portal. A doorway, carved with symbols depicting the keys to a world no man dare enter. Finally the shrieks burst through the entrance to an enormous vaulted chamber where Zerrina and Zarharrab stood, exalting in the crash of sexual ecstasy coupled with convulsive waves of agony.

POL-TAR remembered why she summoned her son, Zarharrab. She screamed above the din reverberating from the dungeon, "I told you, those two must never meet!"

Zarharrab did not answer. His ears lost the sound of pain and his eyes wandered the huge ceremonial chamber as he plied each crack in the cold masonry for an avenue of escape from POL-TAR's caustic tongue. He longed to scream back, to tell her the fault belonged to others. To tell her he never intended to allow an encounter between the scullery maid and barbarian Princess. However, his fear of the woman he called, "mother or Zerrina," overrode his rage.

"Their destinies entwine. Together in this lifetime they could combine to destroy our chances of completing the *Trinity of Waves!*"

"I told you, Mother. If you foresaw the scullery maid as a problem, you should have gotten rid of her. The underworld creatures would happily make a meal of the wench."

"No! I want her. She satisfies my needs. Without her I would go mad in this place."

Zarharrab's eyes wandered to spaces in the chamber's floor as he dwelled on his mother's needs. Her need to inflict pain. Her need to satisfy her insatiable sexual appetite. Her need for revenge on Atlantis. She needs this wench, like she needed me, he thought. Oh, but how sweet that need felt at first. Short visits in the dark of night after Sealaac snored. Short visits where she would stroke my head, my young chest, and my maleness. The need felt good. Yes, the need felt sweet then; before what she did to Sealaac.

"Look at me when I speak. Do not lower your head like a cur. Like Sealaac, the dog whose seed fertilized your worthless life."

Zarharrab's eyes wandered from the floor to the ornate stone alter in the center of the chamber; then to the chair of torture with its leather straps and spiked iron head retainer; across the long chamber to stands holding her magic runes and books of gramarye he would one day possess. In the center of her scrolls, on a pedestal by itself, his eyes settled on the *Harp of Agron*. The harp with its power to see forever, with its power to change shapes, with its power to summon the *Abominable Blue Demon*. Finally to the skull encrusted throne where POL-TAR sat in her long black gown sporting upswept shoulders in the style of an Atlantean priestess. Finally he met his mother's cold stare.

Still beautiful, he thought. Shorter than Euro women, but with the regal bearing of the Atlantean Billial class. Her coal black hair still shines as it did on those nights long ago when she used those tresses to stroke my face to wakefulness.

Her mouth, although still sensuous, forms a permanent frown from her bitterness towards Atlantis. Her nose and high cheekbones, unmistakably Atlantean, shape her face and accent her eyes. Eyes of two different colors which I try to avoid. I remember how those eyes looked on the special nights when her fine black hair woke me. I can smell her scent, feel the pricks of her sharp nails. Even the pain gave me comfort, *then*.

Never the less, he hated what she had said about his father, and he spoke up, "Why must you always bring Sealaac into these arguments? I remember him as a strong man."

"Huh! He did not perform like a man. He could not make me feel like a woman. I longed for the strength and hardness of real men, Atlantean men."

Zarharrab could not understand this contradiction. Many times he heard her state that she hated the Atlanteans. Hatred she had passed on to him.

Cold orbs locked, he could not pull away. Her eyes held more power. Power like his but stronger. A power she had told him he would someday possess. A power to control, to rule, to become emperor of the world. It was her desire and to please her, it became his.

Zarharrab remembered words, chanted ritualistically in an unfamiliar tongue. Following the chant, POL-TAR would hum a tune; a tune which grew in intensity until his hair prickled and fingers, tingled. Even then he feared her magic and always tried to hide from her eyes, but always failed. For in those eyes images formed. Images of people, his father, his mother, him, all committing unnatural acts. And although he had only seen his sixth harvest, his man part would swell. It swelled to an enormous size, a size that scared him. She would see his fear and laugh. She would stroke the grotesquely swollen member, prick it with her nails, and laugh again at his wince of pain. She never apologized. His pain only made her hips move wildly and soon she would pull back her robe and mount his young boy's body.

Once more Zarharrab became conscious of the shrieks convulsing through the door. "Kill her now, Mother. The scullery wench is not the One. Why leave her around? Certainly by now she has fulfilled every need you can imagine. Especially after that bastard, SOL-RAM, working through that organization *The Center for the Elevation of Body and Mind*, used her spirit as Jean Flack to disrupt our plan to keep MAN-DAR imprisoned in the future."

"Quiet!" POL-TAR rebutted brutally. "I have put a spell on the wench and wish to savor the sound of her pain."

Zarharrab felt no compassion for Marrina, but wished to learn more of his mother's magic. "Which spell, Mother?"

"Merely a light memory spell. It forms a loop in her brain. Right now she constantly relives the memory of the instant she collided with that tiny blue vehicle in the future."

"Very amusing mother, but why that particular memory?"

"Idiot. As you said, her soul has fallen under the influence of my old enemy, SOL-RAM. Many lifetimes will pass before she forgets that pain."

"Did you use the harp?"

"Do not be a fool, Zarharrab, and do not treat me as one. When the time falls right, you shall know all I know of magic, and of the Harp of Agron. Unlike the cur, Sealaac, your training began early. You have almost mastered the discipline necessary to control the nether forces. Be patient, my son."

The shrieks of pain and mention of Sealaac reminded Zarharrab of his father's murder. He attempted to resist the memory but each sound wave of terror brought that night more clearly into focus; that night he first saw the Abominable Blue Demon summoned by the use of the harp.

Suddenly Zarharrab realized POL-TAR's lips moved but he heard no sound. Fear shook him as he realized a memory spell came from those lips. A spell aimed at him. He fought fiercely to avert his eyes from POL-TAR's, but he lost. Her eyes became pools and in those pools he saw the reflection of a boy of eight harvests. The young boy was him and in his mind, he became that young boy. A young boy who awakens from sleep by screams of terror from the next room.

Zarharrab's fear kept his young body frozen in his sleeping pallet. He knew the shrieks of terror issued from his father's lips but still he could not move. Gradually, mixed with the horrible cries, he recognized another sound, the beautiful sound of a stringed instrument accompanied by the chanting voice of his mother. The music swelled in intensity as the cries of pain subsided. Finally Zarharrab's curiosity overcame his fear and he slowly slipped from his pallet and crept to a crack in the slats which separated the two rooms of his parent's rough hut.

At first he saw only the dancing shadow of his mother, POL-TAR, thrown on a wall by the flickering flame of a tallow lamp. The cries of pain had turned to whimpers by the time he shifted his position for a better view. Still fearful, he swallowed a gasp as he spied his father. Sealaac lay staked to the earthen floor with long wooden splinters protruding from all parts of his body. Between legs spread eagle, stood POL-TAR, her naked body painted scarlet and blue, her hair woven into braids which moved like snakes. With one hand she clasped a tiny harp to her breast, with the other she plucked its strings. From her lips issued the strange chant and with each stroke of the harp, the splinters embedded in Sealaac quivered causing a scream.

As the chanting, strumming and the movement of splinters subsided, Zarharrab could hear the pleas of his father.

"Why POL-TAR? Why do you do this terrible thing? Have I not given you all I had? Have I not loved you with all my heart?"

POL-TAR laughed hysterically, suddenly stopped and snarled at her husband. "You skulking dog. What have you given me? A filthy hut in a land even Zeetron would not spit upon. Given me love? You mean that shriveled pole bean you squirt inside me when it pleases you? Do you not know that I am a priestess, royalty, and daughter of the Billials of Atlantis? You gave me nothing. Nothing but that whelp who sleeps away the same worthless life as yours."

POL-TAR again strummed the golden harp and chanted in a strange tongue as Sealaac pleaded for mercy. Zarharrab turned his head from the crack and bit his lip to keep from crying out to his father. He wanted to rush to his side, to tear the harp from his mother's hand, to pluck the splinters from his body, but fear held him still. Fear of his hideous mother.

The intensity of strings and chant grew once more, as did the shrieks of Sealaac. The pandemonium drew Zarharrab's eyes once more to the crack in the wall.

As Zarharrab stood riveted to the horrifying scene of his father's torture, blue smoke began to rise from the vibrating strings of the harp. Slowly the curl of smoke formed a ring. The ring, as tall as his mother, contained a blue smoky haze. In the haze a blue shape formed. Slowly the form solidified and Zarharrab saw a creature so terrifying he could not stop his water from spilling down his leg.

Except for the scales on its face and a huge mouth filled with dragon-like teeth, the blue demon took the shape of a human from waist up. But below his waist slithered a thick blue snake whose tail melded into the haze of the smoke ring. The awful creature spoke, its voice, a low rumbling hiss, echoed in the tiny hut.

"Whoo hasst ssummoned the Demon of Agron."

Zarharrab heard his mother answer. "It is I, POL-TAR your servant. Daughter of BOL-TIN, priestess of the Temple of Souls."

"Why dosst thou call mee now."

"The stars command it. They claim the time has come."

"Of what time do you sspeak?"

"Time for the second level of the *Trinity of Waves*," POL-TAR boldly answered.

The demon laughed in a low rumble, which vibrated the wall Zarharrab felt glued to.

"Good. Thou hasst done mee a great sservice. The world will one day be mine."

"It shall be, Master of the harp. It shall be after we perform the ritual of the Second Wave of the Trinity. I have prepared myself, and the sacrifice."

"Who iss thiss ssacrifice? What qualifications doth he carry?"

"My husband, sire, Sealaac. Although low, he acts as chief and shaman for his tribe of earthbound. He possesses an aura stronger than any found among them. His spirit can fulfill the Second Trinity."

"Good. Let us proceed with the ritual."

"Wait sire. Before I sacrifice this earthbound, I must hear you state what I shall receive in return."

An angry rumbling hiss roared through the hut. Zarharrab again felt his own wetness, but his mother stood unmoved by the terrible tantrum.

"You. Earthbound creature, dare quesstion Agron! You dare bargain with him!"

"Yes. I dare bargain. For I have learned you cannot complete the Trinity of Waves without the help of an earthbound. You need me, as I need you."

Another hissing roar issued from Agron. "Thou iss more clever than Agron hass antissipated. What iss thy wissh?"

"Upon completion of the third ceremony of the Trinity; when we have unleashed the army of unearthlings from the underworld; when we have conquered Atlantis, I wish to hold the fate of each Atlantean in my power."

"Sso it sshall be, daughter of BOL-TIN, priestess of the Temple of Soulsss. Now, begin the ceremony, free your sspirit of Ssealaac sso we can be as one."

Zarharrab continued to watch as his mother's chant began anew. Soon the chant reached a fever pitch, which hurt his ears, but still he could not take his eyes from the ritual unfolding before him.

As the pitch reached a crescendo, Zarharrab saw his father's male part swell. At the same time the demon, which thus far had remained in the circle of blue smoke, began protruding from the mist into the room, although his snake-like tail still blended with the blue mist. As the creature moved toward his parents, his split serpentine tongue flicked to the flow of the harp's rhythm.

Sealaac screamed as his wife jabbed more splinters into his spell swollen member. She too flicked her tongue and as she leaned forward to lick Sealaac's face. She then moved back, making room for the hideous blue creature. The demon extended from the blue circle and reached POL-TAR. Upon the demon's touch her body slowly began changing shape and turning blue. In an unhuman-like fashion her body twisted and her tongue flicked Argon's tongue. As the tongues met, sparks flew, and POL-TAR's hair again became alive with movement. The rhythm of the harp reached a peak and POL-TAR body changed further into the same form as the blue demon. Suddenly hissing sounds emanated from both Agron and POL-TAR. POL-TAR's snake-like body gyrated wildly from the touch of the monsters' split tongue. As POL-TAR's writhing mounted, the demon's tongue left POL-TAR. He then extended himself further and dropped his lower jaw. With his mouth extended completely he reached down and engulfed the head of Sealaac. He continued to swallow Sealaac until he reached his stomach. Agron then reared back and pulled Sealaac's remaining torso into the ring of blue smoke.

Zarharrab watched in horror as the new form of Agron consumed the rest of Sealaac. The rhythm of the harp slowed, the pitch changed, and the blue smoke ring dissipated. From his position, Zarharrab could only see a blue fog floating close to the floor. Slowly the fog gathered and a rough form of POL-TAR appeared. The harp's rhythm changed again and POL-TAR transformed back into herself. Zarharrab, soaked, terrified, and still unable to draw his eye from the crack, watched as his mother stood naked, her voice taking up the rhythm of the harp in her hand. Gradually the Harp of Agron ceased to emit sound, leaving POL-TAR chanting alone in the center of the hut. Abruptly the new chant on his mother's lips reached a fever pitch and the new pitch turned to horrifying shrieks.

Shrieks from the dungeon dragged Zarharrab back to the present. For some moments he continued to stare into his mother's eyes, while impressions of that terrible night flitted through his brain. POL-TAR had not been the same since. Any semblance of good had vanished with her demonic encounter. Her visits to Zarharrab's bed became a nightmare of pain he was forced to accept. From that night of Sealaac's death her excuse for the horrible sexual aberrations she subjected him to included the pretext of teaching him the ways of Inanna; the way to unlock the underworld, the way to raise a soulless army, and the way to inflict revenge on Atlantis.

Gradually, as Zarharrab pulled himself from POL-TAR's spell, he thought, my mother's power still holds sway over me, but when we perform the third Trinity of Waves, I shall make my move. The strength I gain when I know all her secrets will give me power over the world.

"Mother, you have sharpened my memory of the night you performed the *Second Level of the Trinity*. Why?"

"Because I see the time grows near to the third and final level. The planets line the sky with the pattern necessary for us to jump physically to the dimension of the underworld. And, we have Sulina, whose extraordinary sexual aura will allow us both to travel with her spirit into that dimension."

"I know the plan, mother, but you never explained how you came to possess the harp or why the Atlanteans exiled you."

"No reason exists for you to know."

"But, Mother, if I am to participate in the ceremony to reach the third level, should I not know about the first?"

Both Zarharrab and his mother fell silent. Zarharrab could see his mother arguing with herself about how much information she should release. For what seemed an eternity to Zarharrab, the only sound he heard was the cacophony of sounds from the dungeon.

POL-TAR thought long and hard before she decided to tell her son of the *First Trinity of Waves*. She knew of her son's ambition. She had built it into him. However, she also noticed the closer it came to the time of the ceremony, the more inquisitive he became. She suspected his true interest lay in acquiring power for himself. Never the less, she thought, he should know from whence the power came.

"Very well, I shall tell you the story."

"Do not trouble yourself, mother. I will not press for answers from the past."

"Hush! I have decided. It may become necessary for you to know more of the harp, and the demon it controls. For you see, the harp controls the demon, and he who controls the harp retains the power. The demon must do the bidding of he who plucks its strings."

"Then I will listen, and learn."

POL-TAR paused, searched for the correct words and seated herself on the throne. "I come from a cursed family."

"What kind of curse?"

"A curse put on my father, BOL-TIN, shortly before he reached full manhood. A curse from a Lessor."

"How could a lowly Lessor put a curse on your father? I believed you high-born."

"It is so, but still, it happened."

"Tell me of the circumstances."

"BOL-TIN was highly spirited and traveled with a group of the same ilk. One afternoon they crossed paths with an ancient Lessor who begged by the roadside. The young men made sport of the Lessor and his bumbling ways. Soon the boyish teasing grew rough and from rough to vicious. So vicious in fact that the young men used their Akarri's to carve small cuts in the helpless old slave." The thought of the pain gave POL-TAR a shudder of pleasure, but she continued. "Finally they decided to castrate the old one and they tore off his clothes. From the filthy rags fell a large crystal mounted in gold. BOL-TIN quickly snatched up the bauble and joined with the others as they hacked at the ancient Lessor's genitals. As he bled to death the old Lessor cursed BOL-TIN and his family, stating that his first-born would bring a terrible shame on him and all his family. BOL-TIN paid no heed to the useless creature, but, as the ancient Lessor died, the crystal in BOL-TIN's pocket became warm. Soon the warm became hot and with the death of the ancient one, the crystal burned like fire. BOL-TIN threw the crystal into some brush. To his surprise, a young Lessor who had witnessed the torture grabbed the crystal and ran off. BOL-TIN and his friends laughed at the young slave and the crystal trinket and went on their way." POL-TAR paused, shifted her weight on the rough throne and continued.

"When BOL-TIN grew to manhood, he married MON-SUN a high-born Billial priestess in the Temple of Souls. Soon MON-SUN conceived a child. MON-SUN had a difficult time carrying the baby and died at its birth. Grief stricken, BOL-TIN climbed a Temple spire and leaped to his death. Suicide being a horrible offense in Atlantis, BOL-TIN and MON-SUN's families would have nothing to do with me, the surviving child, as they blamed me for the death of my parents. Unwanted, they placed me in the custody of the Temple."

POL-TAR coughed lightly, but felt no remorse for the unjustness. She merely stared unmoving as Zarharrab fetched her a goblet of wine, which she accepted without acknowledgement, took a sip, and continued her narrative.

"I grew into a beautiful young girl but did not adjust well to life in the Temple. They claimed I had a sadistic streak and that I never failed to hurt someone's feelings if possible. Of course they were correct, but to avoid punishment, I switched to inflicting as much physical pain as possible onto Lessor slaves, an act never punished. Unfortunately, I had only female Lessors to persecute, as males never entered the Temple, and all females who did, never left. Most became sacrifices to the gods. But a few, considered holy for some reason I never understood, had their womb removed in a cleansing ritual and became guardians of sacred objects.

From early age, I aspired to join the surgeons who performed the sexual rituals or at least one who cleansed the slaves. However, the elder priestesses, jealous of my beauty, would allow me to perform only the least important tasks. I soon grew to hate life in the temple. Everything tired me except the torture of temple mice, but even that grew old, and soon I became more defiant of all Temple rules. In the dead of night I began exploring areas of the huge Temple not open to novices. I became obsessed with what secrets those areas held. I let nothing stop me. I even befriended wretched Lessors to ply from them some minor bit of information which could lead to the magic powers I knew the elders possessed. Eventually I learned of an area called the *Keep of Souls*, and I felt sure it held the secrets I longed to know."

POL-TAR sipped more of the wine and waited as Zarharrab poured himself a goblet and returned to his place.

"One night I stole into the Keep where I found an gnarled old Lessor kneeling over a miniature harp, apparently asleep. I stood silently in the doorway and wondered what secrets could be attached to the tiny instrument. Suddenly a powerful yearning to pluck its strings gripped my fingers and I crept to within arm's length of the harp. But as I reached to touch it, the sinewy arm of the slave grasped my hand. I reacted with fury.

I screamed at the Lessor. "How dare you touch the body of a sacred priestess of the Temple of Souls? I shall have the rest of your life for that, ancient slave."

Barely audible the Lessor answered, "No one must hear the sound of the harp of time, the *Harp of Agron.* Its powers reach beyond earth."

"You old fool, if its sound was not meant for ears of man it would not exist. I order you to hand it to me."

"No. The harp belongs to those not of this world. Its sound will summon a terrible demon ruled by Inanna. I guard this instrument with my life. Your hands may not touch it. Go!"

"I will not. Give me the harp." I flung the old Lessor aside, and seized the instrument. Immediately a warmth ran through my body and I knew I must stroke the harp. But before I could, the old Lessor, much less feeble than she looked, grasped my arm. Without a thought, I drew my ceremonial Akarri and slashed the old one's throat. I dragged her body behind a pillar and ran from the chamber clutching the Harp of Agron to my breast.

"Back in my chambers, harp in hand, I felt its power surge through me. The harp vibrated and I heard bits of a melody. Cautiously I put my fingers on the strings, looking for the chords, which matched those I heard. Once, twice, a third try before I found the proper sounds. As I did the golden harp began to glow. Soon a small curl of blue smoke lifted from the harp. Before my eyes the smoke circled and in the circle the shape of a huge serpent appeared. It had a split tongue of deep scarlet and a blue hew. Its eyes glowed as red as its tongue, and I stood mesmerized before the serpent, a fever growing in my body.

"Suddenly the demon's tongue streaked out, licking my forehead, nose, and lips. Uninhibited, I returned the kiss of the reptile and slowly its upper body protruded from the blue smoke and wrapped around me. I did not call out, nor did I attempt to escape. My body responded to the undulations of the demon engulfing me. Excited beyond compare, I believed I would scream when the reptile's actions ceased. Still coiled about me, it's great head reared back as if to strike. For the first time I became frightened and my throat contracted to scream.

"Hussh my ssweet prettee," the serpent consoled in a rumbling hiss. "I mean to cause you no harmm. We musst not conssumate thiss relationsship too ssoon. We sstand only on the *Firsst Level of the Waves*. When the sskys fill with four planets in the Easst, we will fill our bodies with each other and complete the *Second Trinity of Waves*.

The Unholy Sscion chose you to free the ssons of Beelzebub. Much power will come to you as consort of he who reignss the underworld. Lissten clossely to my words and you sshall rule the world."

Still mesmerized I stood motionless, following every raspy hiss spoken by the terrible demon that held me in his deadly embrace.

"You sshall take the harp from thiss place. You will be caught. But in the catching you will esscape. You will claim the Sonss of the Law of ONE sstole you and the harp from the temple. The sstory will seem true, for you will be with a ONE.

"Hiss name iss COM-GEN, one of the Unholy but not of high caste. You will sseduce him to obtain hiss loyalty, and then kill him. Claim he sstole the harp, but you ssaw not where he hid it. Go now and fearr not, for the touch of my tongue hass imbued you with powerss to make otherss believe."

Slowly the serpent uncoiled itself and dissipated into a stream of blue smoke, which reformed in the shape of the tiny harp.

"I stood motionless for an instant, picked up the harp and made straight for the Temple exit. At each guard mount I wished the guard to look elsewhere and they did. Once outside I went to the barracks where I found COM-GEN and seduced him easily. As my last kiss still lingered on his lips, I could not slit his throat as I had the ancient Lessor. I then ran screaming to the street. I told the authorities of my kidnapping and of the theft of the sacred Harp of Agron which I had attempted to protect.

They believed, and the Billials almost went to war against the Sons of the Law of ONE until SOL-RAM proved that COM-GEN had nothing to do with the theft. They exiled me to this dung heap under a sentence of death if I return. They never located the harp, but you Zarharrab saw it on the night of the coming together of the three planets, the night of Sealaac's death. The night of the Second Level of the Trinity of Waves.

"Come to me Zarharrab, "POL-TAR cooed. "The shrieks of the scullery wench excites me, handsome son. Come to your mother."

Zarharrab retreated from the throne. He knew his mother and he knew well the scullery maid's agony wet her desires. But the time of the converging of the planets swiftly approached, the time when he, Zarharrab would rule the underworld and its army. The time had arrived to prepare the Euro barbarian for the ceremony to reach the *Third Level of the Trinity of Waves*.

TEN

Zarharrab winced as he dragged the sharp blade across his arm. He let the blood flow into a golden goblet and noticed the quickening heaves of his mother's breast. She gets aroused, he thought, I suspect the bloodletting element of the ceremony is necessary only for her gratification. With the goblet half filled, he handed it to his mother who lustily downed the warm drink. Then together they walked to the pedestal holding the tiny Harp of Agron.

Zarharrab studied the harp closely for yet another time, for his mother's use of it never failed to fascinate him. POL-TAR would pluck its strings and with her voice, match its wondrous frequency, which would somehow materialize visions of past, present, and future in the blue smoke ring emitted by the harp. Curious, he again queried about the instrument's magic.

"Mother, may I question you about the harp?"

Zarharrab saw annoyance in his mother's countenance but felt it necessary to learn all he could of the instrument's power. Someday he would depend on the Harp of Agron and the time might come when he might need to use it against POL-TAR, herself.

"If you must, but the knowledge will come in time anyway."

"I have witnessed your magic for years. I have seen you use the harp to create and control the weed-vines so we may spy on the primitives. I understand how you use it to see past and present events for they do physically exist. But to see into the future astounds me most. The future contains so many probabilities. Even the slightest accident can change a future event. But yet the harp can sift through eternity and find one event directly connected to our plans. Tell me, how did it locate MAN-DAR's future at the exact time we needed to delay his trip to the place called Central America?"

"Be wary of the questions you ask my son. For some subjects weigh heavily on my mind. The question you should ask is why you failed to kill MAN-DAR when I sent your soul into the entity called Kersh. That failure caused us much grief. For if MAN-DAR had not reached the place called Guatemala he would not exist in this lifetime."

Zarharrab grew angry at the place of blame, "My failure. I seem to remember a wench named Ginger Haskell who also failed to rid us of the Manny Silva entity!"

"Remember to whom you speak, my son. For it is still I who control the power of Agron. Besides, the harp did not show me that SOL-RAM would intervene. His warning elevated the inner strength of Manny Silva enough to overcome my poison."

Zarharrab shook his head in exasperation, "Let us not place blame, mother. The deed is done and I have sent Pogul and the unearthlings to capture MAN-DAR as you ordered. Use the harp now to show us their progress."

"Very well, Zarharrab, I know you are eager to practice the exact resonance needed to activate the harp. However, remember the strength of the instrument grows weak with use. At least until after we have performed the Third Trinity."

"I understand, mother, but we must know the whereabouts of MAN-DAR if we intend to thwart his attempt to overturn our plans."

Zarharrab felt a slight shiver when his mother took his hands to form a circle around the Harp of Agron. "Listen to my pitch, Zarharrab. If the resonance finds the proper level, energy displacement is minimal when viewing the present. Much more of the harp's power is displaced when we manipulate the future. Now picture in your mind the image of MAN-DAR and chant with me."

As POL-TAR chanted, Zarharrab lifted his voice imitating the sounds of his mother. After a short while the Atlantean priestess released Zarharrab's hands and plucked the harp's strings. POL-TAR's fingers easily found chords to match their chant. Slowly blue smoke rose from the harp and curled into a large circle. In the blue mist of circle, images took form. The forms grew more solid and a scene of MAN-DAR gaining control of the flying stone took place in the ring. It soon became apparent that the Atlantean had eluded the unearthlings and had escaped on the ley stone.

Suddenly the scene exploded in a puff of blue smoke as Zarharrab screamed, "Great Kroll! That cursed Atlantean escapes us again! I will have the head of that oaf Pogul when I get my hands on him!"

"Calm yourself, Zarharrab. The barbarian wench interests us most, and she stands chained in our dungeon. Do not worry, my beautiful weed-vines will keep watch on the mischievous Atlantean, and you will have your revenge on him soon enough. We both will have revenge on all Atlanteans soon enough."

Frustrated Zarharrab stomped across the ceremonial chamber and turned to his mother. "I do not trust those creatures from the underworld. They possess much brawn but no brain. They consume most of the stores, and have already devoured half the subjects we gathered for the Trinity conversion experiments. Even the giant brute, Pogul, has no control over them, and he looks like one of their kind. Why, please tell me, do you believe we will have any control when we acquire a whole army of the creatures?"

"Because, my wretched non-believing son, it is written in the great book of Kroll that if a mortal reaches the underworld with soul intact, he shall rule over all the underworld possesses. And it possesses all the lost souls since time began. We shall control a vast army of unearthlings whose only existence will be to serve us. Their vast number alone will overwhelm Atlantis. We shall rule the world, and the Atlanteans will rue the day they drove me from my home."

Zarharrab turned from his mother's wild-eyed countenance and gazed through one of the few slitted windows of the ceremonial chamber. He could see past the great courtyard, past the wall embedded with huge manned spires, past the treacherous moat and out into the gray gloom of Angleland. He also hated this land. Its backward natives with their backward superstitions. He longed for what he imagined to be the splendor of Atlantis, and he imagined himself Emperor. For whatever his mother believed, it would be he who ruled the world. He knew that after their descent to the underworld, he and his mother would share equal powers. He vowed to himself that her reign of terror over him would end.

He recognized his mother's sorcery made it possible for

him to rule Angleland. He even shared her sadistic thrill for watching Angleland and its people disintegrate before their eyes. He cared not that his mother used the women of the villages in satanic rites copied from rituals she had seen used on the Lessors. He cared not that the primitives starved or died of illness caused by the spells his mother wrought, and he cared not at all that the land had become almost barren except for the weed-vines spies. Through POL-TAR's magic they had usurped the life of Angleland to increase their own power. Angleland sat as a stepping-stone. A stepping-stone to the world. And not only for his mother's reasons, but for his own power.

Zarharrab longed for the power above all else. The power of life and death, the power to make men and gods worship his every word. His mother merely wanted revenge. She wanted to destroy Atlantis. He wanted to rule it and wallow in its vast splendor. Save for MAN-DAR, his mind held not the dream of revenge against all Atlanteans, but it held a greater thirst for power. A thirst, which overshadowed the plans of POL-TAR. A thirst so strong, not a life, not a thousand lives meant anything if it would offer him one more step toward his goal. Only one life meant something to Zarharrab. His own. He smiled to himself as he thought of the day when his mother would see who held the real power in the Temple of Inanna.

Calmed, Zarharrab turned back to his mother who stood busily chanting. The huge blue smoke ring appeared again and Zarharrab saw shapes take form in its blue mist.

"The harp sees all time my son. Come see the precious soul mates as they meet in the place of the future called San Francisco. Watch and learn, see how their souls entwine. It is this power of soul love that we will use to destroy them both, and gain an empire."

Still amazed at the harp's power to see the future, Zarharrab stood spellbound by the scene unfolding inside the blue smoke-ring.

Rocket, a large barrel-chested man with a handlebar mustache, continued spinning yarn after yarn until Manny Silva suggested they head for another bar on Union Street. "Perhaps I'll meet my first San Francisco lady."

"You might be right, little brother, nothing's doin' in this place, that's for sure."

Rocket paid the tab and led Manny out the door and into the next bar, a place called Slater Hawkins. They sat at the long horseshoe shaped bar, ordered drinks, and watched as the first two female prospects of the afternoon walked in.

One woman looked as tall as Manny, she had a large-boned face, strawberry blonde hair and although attractive, Manny didn't think her especially beautiful. The other one had auburn colored hair, flashing eyes, and a smile to match. They sat at the opposite side of the bar, ordered drinks and talked quietly to each other.

Rocket looked at Manny who nodded in agreement and Rocket called across the bar in an accent befitting Long John Silver. "Well, me fine beauties, I see by the trinkets you wear that you like fine jewelry."

The two women looked at each other and the dark haired one who sported a beautiful silver and turquoise necklace spoke back casually, "Of course you dumb shit, all women like jewelry." Her brilliant smile while making the comment took the sting out of it.

"Well in that case ladies, why don't ye join us for a wee bit of a cocktail and I'll show you some of my own handy-work. This fine young friend of mine will escort you to a table while I pop out to me truck and fetch me wares."

The women laughed at Rocket's phony accent as he bounded out the door while Manny walked around the bar to escort the women. The tall woman spoke for both and introduced herself as Gail and said her girlfriend's name was Iris. Manny retuned with his own name and led them to a table.

Manny played the role of a Mafia don out to paint the city red and ordered drinks for everyone. Soon Rocket returned and started his act. First he took out a cigarette and with a flick of his finger, popped it between his lips. Next he balanced a table and chair on his chin. Finally he asked the bartender for a butcher knife. When the man said he couldn't accommodate him, Rocket snapped open his briefcase and tried to sell the bartender jewelry. The man wasn't interested in anything except a large crystal in a symbol laden gold setting.

"Sorry, me bucko, the crystal's not for sale. It's far too precious to let go. Unless I someday have a son, and to him will I pass on this crystal. And all its magical powers."

Manny laughed at Rocket's tale and ordered another round of drinks. He soon found himself caught up in a discussion with the woman who called herself Gail. As he and Gail chatted, he could hear an occasional, "Ah, me proud beauty," as Rocket proffered his wares to Iris. Astrology became the topic of conversation between Manny and Gail.

"I'm an Aries, Gail offered, as she spoke swiped at the

reddish gold hair hanging half over her eye. "But I don't have any of the baby-like traits usually seen in the sign because of my rising, its Sagittarius."

Manny thought a second and remembered someone had once done his chart, "I'm a double Pisces," Manny told her proudly. "Actually I'm just like the Pisces Linda Goodman described in her book, Sun Signs." The talk of astrology soon led to Edgar Cayce.

Swiping hair out of her eyes again, she asked, "What do you think of Cayce's predictions about a forthcoming cataclysm, Manny?"

"Carrumba! You've got to be kidding? A publishing house brought me out here to finish a book I'm writing about a family forced to move from Boston to Southern Illinois after the cataclysm occurs. Basically, they have to fight their way through all the destruction."

"That sounds great. You'll have to come with me to see Betty Bathard at the Center for the Elevation of the Body and Mind. She speaks a lot about Cayce and does life readings just like him. She says that lots of Atlanteans are reincarnating into this particular time period."

Manny found he and Gail shared many interests. The conversation had turned to electromagnetic energy and the oneness of the universe, when it happened.

Suddenly Manny lost his voice. He felt a strange force grab him. The force seized his head and compelled him to look at Iris. Their eyes met, but they didn't speak. After a long stare, Manny's blue eyes returned to Gail, "I'm sorry. I know you and I seem perfect for each other, but something incredibly strong attracts me to your friend."

Gail hesitated a second, brushed the gold hair from her face and smiled wanly. "I understand, Manny, go ahead and do your thing. However, I must warn you. Be careful of Iris. She has a strong will, and can be tough on men."

Manny barely heard Gail's words as he turned to Iris. Rocket ignored the intrusion and merely moved his seat closer to Gail and opened his jewelry case, exclaiming that such a pretty lass surly deserved one of his pieces.

Almost immediately Manny found himself in deep conversation with Iris. He wanted to know everything about this beautiful auburn-haired woman who said she was thirty-three, seven years older than Manny.

Manny shifted his position for a closer look. "Carrumba. There's no way you're more than twenty-five."

"You shithead," Iris said with a twinkle in her green eyes. Why the hell would I tell you I'm thirty-three when I could have said twenty-five?"

Manny squirmed slightly at her somewhat caustic answer and changed the subject. "So what brought you to San Francisco, you don't sound like you're from here."

"Neither do you, Beantown. But if you must know, I grew up on my father's ranch in North Dakota. I split at seventeen."

Manny wanted to know more, and as he waved to the bartender for another round of drinks he asked, "So, how come you left the ranch?"

"Are all you proper Bostonians such nosy shits? Naturally, I left the ranch to see the world. I lived in most of the major cities and worked as a stewardess for World Airlines ferrying troops to the war and back."

"Carrumba, I was in the war."

"No shit. I felt pretty bad for the boys I met going over there, but a lot worse for the ones coming home.

"Ya, I know what you mean."

"As a matter of fact, that's where I met Gail, she worked for World, too."

"How'd you like the warring country?"

"I thought it was okay, except for the war. After I left World Airlines, I decided I had seen enough of war. "

"Ya, that's about how I felt. But what's kept you busy since then?"

"Hell, I did a lot of things. I hitchhiked through the Mid-East and then got a job in business as a medical equipment salesperson. Things went great too until they promoted some man with less seniority and experience over me. As it turned out, I sued under the equal rights laws and won the case."

"You still with them?"

"Shit, no. The chauvinist bastards still found a way to get rid of me. So now I 'rep for another company and do law school at night."

Manny looked directly into her strong-willed eyes, "You know Iris, even though it's only been a few hours, I feel like I've known you for eternity."

As the figures from the future dissipated to blue mist, Zarharrab turned from the harp, and watched POL-TAR prepare the ceremonial chamber for the Trinity of Waves, which she claimed stood not many moons away. She had sent servants to scour the Temple for candles, and su-pervised their positioning. At the same time she scolded others until they placed nine goblets on short pedestals in the perfect place around the sacrificial alter. She had already driven them unmercifully while they practiced chants needed to evoke a breach in the dimensional barrier to the underworld.

He, his mother, and Sulina would make the journey. The book of Kroll contained no design for three to make the passage, but through experimentation POL-TAR had discovered that a woman with a high sexual aura could increase transport capabilities. The three would pass through seven vibration levels before gaining the underworld. On each level the host spirit, Sulina, would lose a portion of her soul-life and when reaching the underworld it would die. The host spirit, and remainder of its physical body would end its eternal existence impaled on an iron stake.

The mere thought of Sulina, the beautiful barbarian princess impaled on a stake aroused Zarharrab. Quickly he turned from his mother to hide his passion. He knew they must conserve their sexual energy to carry out the ceremony. A ceremony, which would lead to his rule as Emperor of the World.

The fantasy of his empire helped his obvious arousal subside and he returned his attention to POL-TAR. "How do you know the barbarian princess possesses the sexual aura necessary to make the leap, mother? We have tried so many times with little success other than to transport a few score of unearthlings."

"Do not fret my son. I have scoured the earth and heavens for the one we need. I divined the where and when of her birth and have kept track of her since. You think it by chance the Atlantean freighter landed in Angleland? Do you not believe me cunning enough to employ spies? Those who would think they gained by the loss of the barbarian, Sulina. You underestimate your mother. That, my son, could prove dangerous."

"But if she is not the one, the danger falls on us."

"She is the one. During the Second Trinity, Agron informed me of one who would be born with a birthmark shaped like a rose on her thigh. The birth would occur in the land to the east in the year of the skull. I found her and have had an agent keep watch ever since."

"But how did you know she would come here now?

"The Kroll states she must come of her own free will. As she must enter the ceremony of her own free will. Their relentless wars with the Beasts gave me the idea to use the Atlanteans themselves in their own destruction. They ferried her to us. I now see we will even have help from the cursed Atlantean, MAN-DAR."

"MAN-DAR? How could he help us? He wishes to free the wench. We tried our best to prevent his return to present time."

"Kroll works in strange ways. In different lights circumstances change. I now see we will use him to complete the very task he tries to prevent. He will help us reach the underworld."

"How can that be?"

"Fate works in our favor. MAN-DAR has once again met his soul mate, Iris. In this time she is the anointed one, Sulina. We shall use that love against them. Eventually Sulina will gladly assist us."

Zarharrab immediately understood his mother's words, and they both laughed a sinister laugh. A dreadful laugh which filled the ceremonial chamber. A hideous laugh which reached the lowest dungeons where it drowned out even the terrible shrieks and screams emanating from the bowels of the Temple of Inanna.

ELEVEN

Sulina believed she would go mad if Marrina continued to scream. Suddenly the terrible shrieks stopped and the little scullery maid bolted upright on the crimson covered sleeping pallet. She sobbed pitifully as she tugged her earlobe.

The screams had begun immediately after the hooded priest, Zarharrab, and the groggy jailer had left the cell. To Sulina it seemed that Marrina's cries had lasted forever. She had tried everything to coax the young woman from her hysterics but nothing helped.

For a long time Sulina managed to steel herself from the young woman's pain but its intensity broke Sulina's resolve. Finally the scullery maid quieted for a short while, but soon the shrieks resumed and Sulina realized Marrina continually relived some horrible nightmare. Again, without regard for her own pain, Sulina pulled herself up by her shackled wrists and lifted a foot to the sleeping pallet. She reached Marrina's leg and gave her a sharp kick. Almost immediately Marrina came out of her hysterical revelry.

"There there little one, all is well. All is well," Sulina whispered soothingly while she stroked the troubled young woman's leg with her foot. With a final scream, awareness came into Marrina's eyes and the look of terror left her face. Soon recognition of Sulina brought her to full consciousness and mere sobs burst from her lips as tears fell from her eyes and she tugged on her earlobe.

"It is all right Marrina. It is over. The hooded one has left and the hunchback with him."

Slowly Marrina's sobs abated.

"What caused you so much pain Marrina? The pock faced jailer barely touched you."

Marrina spoke through her sobs. "He did nothing compared to the usual. The witch, Zerrina caused my pain. She has done this before. She weaves spells, which force me to view terrible scenes of violence. She enjoys my pain, and sometimes she touches me in bad places while I live it."

"How does Zerrina's spell cause you such pain?"

"In my mind I see this horrible scene. I know not where it comes from. But I find myself in an iron machine traveling as fast as the wind. Suddenly I see a smaller blue machine in my way. Without thinking I give a terrible scream and crash painfully into the other iron machine."

"How long have they treated you like this, little one?"

The concern in Sulina's voice brought an end to Marrina's sobs and her speech steadied. "Almost since I came here."

Sulina shook her head in sympathy. "What brought you to this terrible place?"

"As Zarharrab and his mother grew in power, the crops in the field grew less. Soon my family starved and were forced to sell me as a slave to the Temple."

"Why you? Why not a male?"

"Zarharrab only wanted females. He claimed he had all the men he needed for his army, but he needed women for maids and kitchen help. I grew frightened. I knew Zarharrab took other girls to the Temple and none returned. Some believed them well-taken care of. Maybe ever kept as virgins for

Zarharrab to wed. I believe the villages looked for excuses out of fear of Zarharrab and his henchmen. Especially the giant with a face like a pig, Pogul."

"What happened when they brought you to the Temple?"

"They treated me well at first. Zarharrab even brought me to meet his mother. She smiled at me. She told me if I obeyed her wishes, life in the temple would go easy. Her attention pleased me, but gradually she turned mean. She would do little things to hurt me and take pleasure in it. With each encounter the pain grew sharper, but she always said she was sorry. One night she had me strapped to a stone alter and did terrible things to me until I could not help but reach a burst of orgasm. Zerrina grew horribly angry and beat me mercilessly. She kept screaming I was not the One."

Marrina sobbed again, but regained control. "Then she allowed those horrible unearthlings to hurt me. I thought they would devour me, but she stopped them. She still likes to watch the horrible things they do and laughs her frightful laugh the whole time." Marrina broke down again.

Sulina soothed the young woman as much as possible with her extended leg. "You spoke of the unearthlings. I have witnessed their inhuman attacks, but from where do they come?"

Marrina stifled her sobs in order to answer. "Through magic. Zarharrab and Zerrina conjure them from the underworld. I have seen them appear suddenly in the Temple, and always after one of us females disappear."

"Why do you accept this treatment? Why do you not escape?"

"It is not possible. Guards stand at every entrance and many watch from the towers. Besides, who would have me on the outside? I am ruined. No man would have me and I know not how to care for myself."

"What of your father, your family?"

"They exist no more." Marrina wept and tugged her ear once more. "Zarharrab sent for my sisters, but my father refused to give them up. Zerrina laughed at my grief when she told me the unearthlings killed my whole family."

Marrina sobbed uncontrollably while Sulina attempted to calm her. "If they held you prisoner all this time, how do you know she spoke the truth?"

"I heard Zarharrab scream at Pogul. He said they needed all the women they could get and could not afford to kill them needlessly. Pogul said the fault was not his. The unearthlings got out of control. Then to lessen the blame, he told Zarharrab he brought other women in their place.

"Zarharrab told Pogul he had finally put his deformed head to use, and offered me to him as a reward. That night Pogul forced me to drink great mugs of mead while Zerrina stood by and watched as he did beastly things to me." Marrina sobbed harder, "I pleaded for her to make him stop, but she only laughed louder. Finally I got dizzy and blacked out."

"Marrina, you can stay here no longer. You must try to escape no matter how terrible the conditions outside this dreadful place."

"What can I do? I am but a lowly scullery maid. How could I ever hope to overpower the guards?"

"I will help you." Marrina's sobs subsided. "Free me of these shackles and we shall escape together."

"But, I.. I.. I cannot." Marrina stammered, while tugging her earlobe. I am afraid. What if we get caught? You don't know the awful things they can do to you. They would feed us to the unearthlings, or worse still, the horrible weed-vines. Zerrina and Zarharrab know everything, we cannot escape."

Sulina looked straight into Marrina's reddened eyes, "I now know they have something evil planned for me. I must escape and you must help."

"But I.."

"Did I not save you from the hunchback. At least you could help me from these shackles. I will attempt to escape, with or without you."

The look on Marrina's face told Sulina a terrible battle raged in the young woman's mind. She pushed harder. "Please Marrina, you know what they can do to me. I need your help."

Finally she gave in. "You have treated me kindly. Since I entered this place, no other human has. And you are right. How much worse could it be outside this Temple of misery? I will help you." Resolutely she added, "We will escape."

"Good Marrina. Now, help me out of these shackles."

Marrina frowned hopelessly; she had no idea what to do.

Finally after a search of the room Sulina's eyes fell on the belt the hunchback had dropped during his attack on Marrina.

"Look Marrina, on the floor in the corner, a belt with metal buckle. Fetch it." Marrina scooped up the belt and held it in her hand with a questioning look. "Do you not see, put the buckle between a crack in the wall and bend it until it breaks." Marrina complied immediately and broke the buckle as ordered. Again she stood motionless, waiting for her next order. Sulina saw that Marrina still did not understand, and explained. "Fit the broken end in the keyhole of the shackles and twist until the lock has broken."

After a quick look through the bars on the door, Marrina carried out Sulina's directions.

It took longer that Sulina had imagined, but finally she heard a click and the shackles fell from her wrists. She rubbed the soreness from her hands. At the same time she felt the sexual tension between her legs slackened. A rumble from her stomach reminded Sulina she had not eaten. Quickly she searched the floor for the food she had knocked from Marrina's hand, found it, and wolfed it down. Finally she went to Marrina who sat helplessly on the sleeping pallet tugging her earlobe.

Sulina threw her arms around the ragged young woman. "Thank you my friend."

Marrina appeared startled by the statement. "I have not heard that word for many harvests. I almost forgot its meaning. A friend is what I shall be Sulina. I will stay by you always."

"Always may not be long if we do not find our way from this place. Now think hard Marrina, you must have heard rumors of other passages from the Temple? I cannot believe the evil ones would not have built a hidden escape route."

Marrina tugged on her earlobe as she thought. Finally her face brightened and she looked up at Sulina who tried to have patience with the pathetic woman. "I do remember talk of passages under the Temple. Supposedly they lead to the moat. But, it is said those who wander into the passages never come out. Besides, even if we get to the moat, there are still the *gall worms*."

"Gall worms?"

"I do not know exactly what they are, but they live in the moat and protect the Temple. Some say they wrap themselves around a captive and bore a hole in his stomach to suck out his innards."

"That sounds like superstition, or a rumor started by Zarharrab to keep people from the moat. But even if true, we will find our way around the gall worms when we reach them. Do you know the way to this passage?"

"I am not sure, but one time in the kitchen, as a pig was prepared for a feast, it wiggled free and I was sent to fetch it. The animal ran fast and I had almost caught it when the pig scooted through a hole in the floor of a pantry near the kitchen. I could have followed, but did not."

"Why? You must have known they would punish you for losing the pig."

Marrina tugged her earlobe, lowered her eyes and answered, "I would have, until I heard a terrible squealing come from the hole. I thought the pig merely injured until I heard bones snap. Back in the kitchen they beat me terribly for the lost pig, but I knew if I said the pig went down that hole, they would make me follow." Marrina sat still, her eyes glued to the floor.

"The hole you speak of sounds like our only chance of escape. Could you find it again?"

Eagerly, Marrina looked at Sulina. "Oh yes. After they beat me, I crept back to the pantry and pushed a large cupboard over the hole. I did not want to lose another pig."

"Good, we have a way out."

"But Sulina, what about the passageway? What about the thing that got the pig?"

"We cannot worry about that now. Just get us to that hole and we will deal with whatever man or monster we find."

Marrina found it easier to sneak Sulina through the Temple than she had imagined. When they came upon a guard, Marrina, who knew them all intimately, merely distracted their attention while Sulina slipped past. When they finally reached the door to the kitchen she peeked around the corner and found it crowded with busy workers. She knew passage to the pantry would prove much more difficult. The kitchen help would most likely harass them as they squeezed between the cooks, helpers, counters, tables, and huge ovens.

Marrina's thought more quickly as the hope of freedom filled her mind. It seemed forever since she heard the word friend, and meeting Sulina gave her a surge of energy along with the hope. If necessary Marrina felt she would help this wild and endearing woman, even at the cost of her own life.

She turned to Sulina and whispered, "Quick, follow me, I have a plan." Marrina led Sulina down a hall and past several rooms until they reached a small closet filled with cleaning implements. Marrina reached into an old sack and pulled out an armful of rags. "Put some of these around you. We must cover that scarlet costume and disguise you as a new scullery maid."

Marrina found a rag large enough for a skirt and tied it around Sulina's waist. Then she tied two filthy clothes together for a blouse and finally wrapped one around Sulina's head. When Marrina saw that Sulina looked as ragged as she, she handed Sulina a wooden bucket and bade her new friend to follow.

As they passed through the kitchen, the chief cook took

no notice of the two shabby scullery maids, but as they passed his assistant, an ugly man with a severe limp, he reached out and grabbed one of Marrina's breasts, holding her firmly in place.

"Well, what have you brought us wench? Another chicken to pluck? I hope she be a little fresher than you." He laughed lewdly.

"This is Ulna," Marrina replied, she removed his hand with a new confidence. "You are not to lay a finger on her."

Quickly his hand slammed across her face. "Who do you think you talk to!" About to strike once more, the man found his hand stayed by the meaty fist of the cook.

"Leave them alone, we have much to do. The high priest has ordered a special supper for this night. And you two," he gestured with his head to Marrina and Sulina. "Get out of my kitchen before I feed you to the unearthlings."

Without another word, Marrina grasped Sulina's hand led her to the other side of the kitchen, down a hallway and into a small chamber which contained a few stacked stools and a large cupboard.

"This is it, Sulina," she whispered. "Help me move the cupboard. I know we will find the hole."

With Sulina's help the large cupboard slid slowly across the floor and Marrina wondered how she had ever found the strength to have moved it by herself. As foretold, a large opening, crossed with cobwebs, led diagonally downward. Abruptly they heard the sound of footsteps approaching from the kitchen. Marrina heard her name called, but before she could answer she felt Sulina's arms grasp her waist and shove her down into the black hole. Sulina followed.

The two slid down a long greasy chute, and landed on a hard stone floor. Rats squealed and scurried from the landing site, and the room was midnight black. Frightened, her voice shook as she whispered to Sulina, "What do we do now?"

"There must be a door someplace. Take my hand. We shall walk to a wall and follow it until we find one. Unlocked I hope."

With one hand in Sulina's and one on her earlobe, Marrina followed her friend. They had taken only several steps when Sulina gasped and fell forward dragging Marrina with her. Marrina loosened her hold on her earlobe and reached forward to break her fall but landed hard on a round object she frightfully recognized as a skull. Bones flew everywhere and rats squealed and scattered. Sulina stood quickly, pulling Marrina with her. Marrina felt the barbarian Euro's hand again as she led her through the darkness. Finally Sulina whispered the fact that she touched a wall.

Cautiously they followed the stone until they reached a large wooden door. Sulina found a handle and both she and Marrina pulled with all their strength. At first it would not budge, but pulling harder the door groaned on its hinges and moved a bit. The door's slight movement gave them hope and with an extra effort they pulled until a crack grew large enough to allow dull light to filter into the room. Unfortunately for the already frightened scullery maid, the crack also brought in distant screams, groans and cries. Marrina began to doubt her choice of action until Sulina widened the opening, grasped her hand, and led her into a long low passageway.

At the far end of the tunnel-like corridor, Marrina saw flickering light from a bend in the corridor. Also from around that turn came the horrible sounds of pain.

Marrina let Sulina lead as they passed other passageways along the tunnel, but all were black as night. They continued toward the flickering light at the turn. As they reached it, Marrina felt Sulina's lips close to her ear, "Peek slowly around the corner for guards. If they recognize you, they may not sound an alarm."

Marrina's hands shook as she grasped the cold stone corner and slowly poked her head far enough out to see and empty passageway. The tunnel looked long, but torches burned at intervals. Terrible cries issued from doorways, but she waved Sulina forward. They hugged the wall and cautiously worked their way along the passage.

When they reached the first doorway, Sulina again motioned for Marrina to check for safety. She complied but after a quick look, she gasped and flung herself against Sulina. Marrina barely held the contents of her stomach in place but eventually she whispered, "The room overflows with horribly misshapen women. I have heard Zerrina speak of failed experiments. She said they dispose of the bodies by feeding them to the unearthlings. These must be some of the experiments." Once again Marrina held her mouth to keep from retching. "What is worse, some have been chewed by the unearthlings, but others still live! We must help them."

"No. We can do nothing for them, Marrina. Save to escape and find MAN-DAR. He will help avenge these poor women and put an end to the evil priest and his mother. You must be strong, Marrina. We must escape. Did you see any unearthlings?"

"No, but they must be close. Some of the women still bleed." The memory of what she viewed filled Marrina with terror. "Need we go further, Sulina? Other unearthlings might lurk ahead."

Marrina felt her arm grasped hard, "We have to take the chance. Do you want to end up as those you saw in the room? We will go on."

Sulina's strength helped Marrina regain her confidence and she spoke again. "I have a better idea. Let us take a torch and return to one of the darkened passageways. I have seen how flame seeks the air near a chimney. If the torch flame draws into a tunnel, it might lead to the outside."

"Now you use your head. Let us move quickly before the unearthlings return."

They took a torch and traveled back towards the room with the hole and checked each opening for a way out. The flame flickered toward none of the tunnels and Marrina began to panic. With only one more passageway to check, she grasped Sulina's hand for strength. When they reached the black opening Sulina held the torch up to its entrance. A gasp of joy left Marrina's lips when the torch flame flickered wildly into the tunnel. They followed.

To Marrina the tunnel seemed endless. She knew they had walked at least half the distance of the width of the Temple when they found their way blocked by a crisscrossed series of thick twine.

"What could this be?" Marrina whispered to Sulina nervously.

"It is nothing. Simply some old twine probably blown here by wind through the tunnel. Help me and we shall quickly clear a path."

Gingerly, both Marrina and Sulina grasped the strings.

"It sticks, Sulina. I cannot remove the twine from my hands."

"I too have trouble. I cannot loosen my leg from its grasp." Sulina gasped. "Marrina touch no more of the twine. Try to free your hands from it. I believe we have fallen into a trap!"

Marrina managed to loosen her hands. She held the torch high and became distraught when she found Sulina firmly bound in the mass of sticky twine. "What will we do, Sulina."

"Use the torch to burn away the strings."

Marrina had burnt through several of the many strings binding Sulina when a commotion at the other end of the passageway caught her attention. Almost at once she recognized the voice of Pogul. "They followed us. We will surely be caught!"

"No, Marrina, I am caught. You can still gain your freedom. Look at the bottom of the trap. Some of the twine has pulled loose from the stone. You need only burn away a small portion in order to slip under."

"I shall not leave you to them. I will die before I let them have you!"

"Do not worry. They will not harm me, at least not right now. Zarharrab has something special in mind for me. You must save yourself. You must find the Atlantean called MAN-DAR. He is strong and brave. Tell him what has happened. Tell him of Zarharrab's plans to overthrow Atlantis. He will help you. He will save me. Hurry, Marrina. Pogul and the unearthlings approach. Go!"

Reluctantly Marrina burned a few more threads and slid under the web-like twine. She tossed the torch aside, and fled into the black tunnel just as Pogul reached Sulina. With one last look at her trapped friend Marrina felt her way along the tunnel until she saw light ahead. Cautiously she moved forward and had almost reached it when she realized unearthlings pounded down the passageway behind her.

Marrina ran the rest of the way to the tunnel's end, only to find it barred with a heavy iron grille. Frantic, she squeezed her tiny body between the bars just as the unearthlings reached her. With their huge mass they were unable to fit through the grate. They could only snarl and claw at their lost quarry.

Marrina felt their sharp nails scrape her back as she dived into the slimy moat. She gasped as she struck the cold water but swam with all her strength for the opposite shore. Half way across something touched her leg. She turned in time to see an unearthling's hand outstretched in an attempt to drag her under. She caught a glimpse of others who stood on the shore and realized they must have forced the grate.

Frantically Marrina pulled herself faster through the water, but the huge creature gained on her and she knew she had but a few more strokes to live. Panic stricken, Marrina barely managed to dodge the next grab by the unearthling. Suddenly a large wave washed over her head. By the time she found the surface she saw the unearthling high above the water. A huge worm, thicker around than the unearthling, had coiled itself about his body and lifted him from the moat. Again Marrina swam with all her might but turned once more at the sound of a horrible scream. The head of the gall worm had plunged into the unearthling's stomach.

Marrina had almost reached the shore when again she felt something touch her leg. Its slimy feel told her it was not another unearthling and she felt sure she was doomed to the gall worms. Soon another slimy stroke caressed her leg just as her hand touched the steep bank of the moat. She could not take the touch of the worms again. Her battered heart was about to give up the fight. Suddenly from above a long arm reached down, grasped her wrist, and pulled her to safety.

TWELVE

MAN-DAR enjoyed the wind in his face as he and Kirack flew on the huge flat bolder, but he worried about when and where their flight would end. He had remembered the chants and tones, which set the rock moving, but no matter how hard he tried, he could not think of the sounds necessary to reverse the process. They would have to ride the stone until it stopped.

The sound of groans reached MAN-DAR's ears and he turned in time to find Kirack sitting up shaking his head. He was about to rise when MAN-DAR seized him and held him to the stone.

"Do not move about, Kirack. The gods have smiled upon us this day and awarded us transportation, but we no longer stand on solid ground."

MAN-DAR saw astonishment and fear fill Kirack's eyes as he realized he sat on a wide flat stone with the landscape speeding by below. At once he lay flat in an attempt to meld with the stone. His voice quaked as he called above the noise of the wind to MAN-DAR, "How is this possible. I know that the Atlanteans have airships but they have machinery, which cause their movement. This is solid rock. It must fly by magic."

MAN-DAR answered calmly, "Not magic, Kirack, simple magnetism propels what we call a ley stone. The procedure to levitate an object is known to any schoolboy in Atlantis, if he pays attention. This ancient system must have been installed in an early attempt to colonize Angleland. POL-TAR and Zarharrab obviously discovered the ley system and POL-TAR recalled the sound resonance necessary to activate it."

Kirack still looked puzzled and although MAN-DAR did not like the Euro, he could not pass up the chance to show off Atlantean technology.

"Although a barbarian would not understand, the process is simple. Natural magnetic lines exist in the earth. These lines emit a magnetic force. Stones such as the one on which we fly, contain a magnetism of their own. Magnets have a north and a south pole. Do you understand?"

Kirack still looked puzzled and shook his head no.

MAN-DAR wondered why he bothered with the barbarian, but continued. "I will try again. Some stones contain much Iron, like the metal of a sword. If the iron is magnetized, one end will have a positive side, the other a negative. Either side will attract, say a metal object, but when two positive or negative ends are placed together, they repel, or in other words, push each other away." MAN-DAR suspected Kirack's mind turned elsewhere but he continued in order to pass the time. "This repelling situation caused this stone to float. The magnetic lines of the earth give off a positive magnetic force, as does the underside of this stone, so the two positives push against one another to cause us to lift off the ground. If a particular sound is voiced, it can change one from negative to positive and if it is done in a chanting rhythm, there is a constant push pull effect, which moves the stone.

Kirack still looked puzzled, but surprised MAN-DAR

with an intelligent question "I believe I understand this push pull magnetism, but what draws it along a particular track?"

"When I discovered the huge upright stones covered with ancient Atlantean runes, I should have realized the runes indicated the beginning or end of one the earth's natural magnetic lines. Is that clear enough? We will stay on a straight line or ley line until we come to the end of the groundside magnetic force. My guess is that we will stop when we reach one of the standing stones."

Kirack still looked quizzical but MAN-DAR explained no further. A huge megalith ahead absorbed his attention. They had found the end of the ley line and he hoped none of Zarharrab's patrols waited.

MAN-DAR breathed a sigh of relief as the stone slowed on its own. He could see they would stop in a hilly desolate area, which contained few weed-vines. He thought an instant about the fact that he felt the vines might act as spies for Zarharrab, but quickly dismissed the idea as absurd and concentrated instead on the search for unearthling patrols. His eyes wandered over the low hills and to a large mountain still covered in green. He felt surprise when he realized the sun still shone on the mountain and wondered why Zarharrab's magic had spared it.

Slowly the flat stone came to a complete rest and settled to the ground next to a huge upright boulder. Immediately MAN-DAR and Kirack leaped to the ground and started to head for the green mountain. Both came to an instant halt when a spear flew past their heads. Then another. Both men realized they had flown into a trap and dropped to the ground. By the time MAN-DAR and Kirack raised their heads, they found themselves surrounded by fierce looking men with blood in their eyes and spears in their hands. They had no chance to defend themselves and MAN-DAR surrendered with hope of future escape. As he rose from the ground a solid kick caught him in the ribs and sent him sprawling.

"Stay put, stranger, or you may never rise again," snarled a rough-looking man with a long red scar down one cheek. "If you two vile creatures have a god, you better start to pray. For you will soon meet them in the spirit world." The man raised his spear to kill MAN-DAR when a cry came from the rear of the surrounding band of warriors.

"Wait! This man does not help the evil ones. I saw him in the camp of Reamann."

Without taking his eyes off his captives the scar-faced one replied, "What difference makes that? Reamann's heart holds an equal amount of treachery. They most likely spy for him. And if you were not the husband of Jerd's daughter, you too would have died, as these two soon shall."

"Jerd knows I lived in Reamann's camp to care for my dying mother. He shows mercy. He has not the soul of an animal like you, Oknee. Besides, if these two be spies, Jerd will want to know what they have learned. Then perhaps you can satisfy your blood lust."

"He speaks the truth, Oknee," one of the others added. "Perhaps it best to let Jerd decide what to do with the strangers."

Reluctantly Oknee concurred, "Bind their hands and cover their eyes. We cannot let them see the location of our encampment."

Two men hauled Kirack to his feet. He struggled to break

free from the rugged men, but an elbow to the stomach subdued him. MAN-DAR stood on his own and did not protest even when they tore Secura from its sheath. With both men tied and blindfolded, they were shoved in an unknown direction over rocky terrain. MAN-DAR heard no words spoken as they headed for the encampment and whatever misfortune lay ahead.

After they traveled a good distance over hilly terrain, MAN-DAR recognized the sound of camp life. By the din that surrounded him he knew they had entered a compound of some size. Soon, he and Kirack found their heads shoved down and their bodies pushed to the ground with orders to stay put. A few moments later, their blindfolds torn off, they found themselves in a tiny hovel with no windows.

Before MAN-DAR's eyes could adjust to the dim light, a group of men entered the hut. A large bearded man with a rough manner and an ugly vacant hole where his left eye should peer, spoke in a deep voice directly to MAN-DAR.

"I am called Jerd." The big man announced roughly. "I am leader of the survivors called the Hill People. I demand to know who you spy for."

"I am MAN-DAR of Atlantis and I spy for no one. I am here on assignment for the Empire. This man is Kirack," MAN-DAR nodded in the Euro's direction. "I was sent to bring him and his wife, Sulina, to Atlantis. Sulina has disappeared and we believe her to be in the hands of the wicked priest, Zarharrab."

"Tell me why I should believe this story. You arrived here

on one of Zarharrab's flying stones. No one but he knows the magic to make it fly."

"My people, the Atlanteans, installed the technology in Angleland generations ago. I learned from ancient myths how to make the stones fly. Most likely POL-TAR, or you may know her as Zerrina, Zarharrab's mother, also knew how to use the ley stones."

"A witness saw you in the camp of those who live in the swamp. Our enemies. We know you saved their leader, Reamann. That fact alone will ensure your death. Why did you save him?"

MAN-DAR surveyed the band of hate-filled men around him. He saw little chance of escape and tried to explain. "A wicked old soothsayer tricked me into the swamp. If I had not saved Reamann I would surely have languished until death in that awful place. I had to save Reamann to save myself."

"Some would say anything to save their skin. I do not believe you mean us no harm." Calmly he turned to Oknee, "Take them out and have done with them. Even if the Atlantean's claim be true, they prove worthless to us."

"Wait," MAN-DAR broke in. "Why do you hate the people of the swamp? You have a common enemy in Zarharrab and you should work together against him."

"Do not listen to him Jerd," Oknee interjected. "I would rather die at the hands of Zarharrab's creatures than to unite with the Swamp People. Besides, if this Atlantean is who he claims, it will be easy to settle. Let him prove it by trial. Let him fight the unearthling we caught in our trap. If he defeats the creature, maybe the Atlantean will prove useful."

A chorus of agreement rose among the men behind Oknee.

Jerd scrutinized MAN-DAR with his good eye and studied the faces of his followers. "So be it. If the Atlantean can defeat the unearthling he will save himself and his companion. If not, he shall die anyway and the one called Kirack shall soon follow. Either way, we rid ourselves of enemies."

MAN-DAR and Kirack found themselves quickly untied and dragged from the hovel to a pit not fifty paces from the campsite. At the edge, MAN-DAR peered down to view his adversary. What he saw made his blood run cold.

In a hole as deep as the height of three men and twenty paces across stood a snarling creature two heads taller than he. It had the body of a man but on its shoulders sat the head of a lizard with sharp glistening teeth; behind him a long tail lashed savagely in the air. Beside him lay a huge ax. When he saw the crowd at the edge of the pit he grabbed it and shook it menacingly at his tormentors. A horrible hissing roar flew from his huge jagged toothed mouth. The crowd fell back in fear and Kirack tried to run but was caught again and roughly dragged back to the pit.

Jerd turned to MAN-DAR, a gleam of amusement in his single eye, "What do you think of our pet, Atlantean?" Then he laughed, his rumbling voice overpowering that of his less ferocious followers.

MAN-DAR stood tall and looked the leader in his eye. "Do you intend to send me against the creature unarmed?"

"Oh no, Atlantean," Jerd answered sarcastically. "There exists no sport in that. We have little enough to amuse us in this terrible land. You may take your puny sword." And the big man laughed again as he handed Secura to MAN-DAR and pushed him into the pit.

MAN-DAR hit the pit's floor hard. The fall knocked the wind out of him and Secura flew from his hand. It landed with a dull clang on the opposite side of the hill people's death trap. Fortunately for MAN-DAR the creature's wits and reactions proved sluggish. The clamor from above had confused the creature, and by the time he realized one of his tormentors lay nearby, MAN-DAR had a chance to scramble to his feet. When the unearthling noticed he had someone to vent his anger on, he lifted his ax. With a hissing roar the creature charged straight at MAN-DAR who sidestepped. The unearthling crashed head on into the side of the pit.

Indeed, MAN-DAR thought, the creature does prove to be powerful, but slow. He now had a glimmer of hope he could survive this battle. The creature still separated him from Secura and his eyes searched for a weapon. Quickly he noticed that when the unearthling was first captured, he had fallen through the tree limbs covering the pit. In doing so he had carried a number of branches with him. MAN-DAR found the stoutest limb of the lot and stood to face his adversary once more.

The lizard creature looked ferocious. It had yellow slanted eyes with black slits for pupils, which nearly froze MAN-DAR in his tracks. But before the unearthling could charge again, MAN-DAR's crude weapon smashed the unearthling between his eyes. The creature's only reaction was to shake his head and issue and angry hissing growl. MAN-DAR knew for sure only one would survive this battle.

The lizard-man charged again, MAN-DAR stepped aside once more, but this time he hit the unearthling in the shins. A hissing scream of pain hissed from the creature's huge mouth, but as he did so, his great tail swung up and knocked MAN-DAR to the ground. MAN-DAR rose quickly and found himself closer to Secura.

By now the crowd had pushed themselves to the very edge of the pit. The closest two being Kirack and Jerd. Most above cheered, they hoped for blood soon, no matter whose.

The lizard creature now raged completely out of control. He saw only one enemy in his world, a puny earthman that he would easily kill. MAN-DAR felt the creature's rage and braced himself for another onslaught.

It came again as a lumbering charge. MAN-DAR stood his ground and when in range, he shoved the heavy branch into the pit of the unearthling's stomach. A puff of putrid air hit MAN-DAR's nostrils, sickening him as the wind flew from the creature's lungs. MAN-DAR's only thought was to reach Secura, but the unearthling recovered quicker than he expected and wheeled around, clipping MAN-DAR's head with its heavy jaw. MAN-DAR dropped to his knees and the unearthling landed a terrible blow to MAN-DAR's back with his tail. The Atlantean's face crashed to the ground and blackness began to fill his consciousness.

The unearthling roared in defiant victory, and moved to finish his enemy. Abruptly the earth under Jerd who was pressed to the pit's edge by his followers gave way and he tumbled headlong into the pit. Jerd lay still but his fall caught the attention of the dull-witted lizard-man who prepared himself for the second adversary. MAN-DAR regained consciousness in time to see the creature approach Jerd with his huge ax.

MAN-DAR saw fear in the single eye of the Hill People's leader as he looked up at the huge unearthling. The lizard-man had his ax poised for the kill. Jerd prepared himself to die, but astonishment replaced fear as the ax flew from the creature's hand. MAN-DAR had slammed the back of the creature's head with his heavy branch. The unearthling's attention turned back to MAN-DAR who had rushed to retrieve his Akarri. Meanwhile, Jerd dragged himself to relative safety behind the debris in the pit as the battle between MAN-DAR and the lizard-man ensued once more.

With Secura in hand, MAN-DAR felt the odds more even. The unearthling no longer employed the ax, but came straight at MAN-DAR; he believed his shear bulk could overcome the human. He was wrong, and missed his adversary. The creature utilized his tail once more; he swung hard at MAN-DAR who easily jumped it. As he did so, MAN-DAR drove the blade of Secura into the creature's side. A horrible scream gurgled from the bloody lips of the dying unearthling. He took a few faltering steps in MAN-DAR's direction and collapsed.

The crowd around the pit fell silent. MAN-DAR heard only his own heavy breathing until finally Jerd broke the silence.

"You saved my life Atlantean," the huge one-eyed leader of the Hill People said haltingly. "I would have let you die if our positions were switched. Why did you act so?"

MAN-DAR caught his breath and went to the injured leader. He held out his hand to help Jerd to his feet and answered. "The humans in Angleland are not my enemies. The enemy is Zarharrab, POL-TAR, and their horrible minions." MAN-DAR allowed his voice to rise so all who surrounded the pit could hear, and continued. "The people of Angleland must unite. You must take back this place you once called home. You must throw out the evil priest and his sorceress mother. You must cleanse your land of the unearthling creatures that have destroyed your crops, your livestock, your villages, and your women. It is time to fight. Time to take back your lives."

MAN-DAR looked straight at Jerd for confirmation and acceptance.

"I swear to you, MAN-DAR of Atlantis, I will lay down my life for you. I shall do what you ask, I will help unite the remaining tribes of Angleland for a battle against the evil which occupies this land." Jerd then lifted his head toward the rugged men around the pit and spoke. "Listen to me people of the hills. The time has come for us to be men once more. It is time we made peace with the other tribes of this devastated land. We will join together as one, and with the help of the Atlantean we shall build weapons and train for war. We will stand up and fight. We will be the men of Angleland once more."

The big one eyed leader of the Hill People threw his arms around MAN-DAR and the crowd circling the pit easily drowned out the half-hearted nays of both Oknee and Kirack.

THIRTEEN

"No, no, no, Reamann, how many times must I tell you? Keep your eye on the target and squeeze the trigger gently," MAN-DAR instructed the scraggly leather clothed leader of the swamp tribe. "A quick pull will jerk the crossbow up and you will hit nothing." Because of Zarharrab's spell on anything mechanical, MAN-DAR was forced to rely on cruder weapons. Reamann rearmed the rough crossbow MAN-DAR had taught the newly united clans of Angleland to construct and tried once more. This time his arrow struck the straw filled target mid-center and a large cheer rose from the band at the practice grounds.

MAN-DAR trained the men of Angleland hard, as hard as his father had trained him. He felt he had little time to mold the ragged peasants into a fighting force able to mount a successful attack on the Temple of Inanna. Most of the men handled their crude spears fairly well and a few, such as Jerd, had natural ability with any weapon scrounged from the desolate villages.

Jerd had proved to be a natural tactician and leader of all the men who joined together to rid their land of Zarharrab and his mother. MAN-DAR heard his name called and looked up to see the large one-eyed man haling him from the edge of the crowd. "Reamann, take charge of the training while I speak with Jerd. And do not let up until each man can fire an arrow into the straw." Reamann nodded in affirmation as MAN-DAR turned to Jerd.

As usual, a broad smile crossed Jerd's face when he saw MAN-DAR coming his way. "How goes the training, Atlantean? I see that you push the men hard, but the weapon you chose is unfamiliar in this land. I hope they can learn its use quickly."

The usually reticent MAN-DAR could not help but smile back at the big leader. He had found Jerd as open and easy going as he proved deadly when he felt he or his men threatened. "I must be firm, but if I am only half as hard as you it would be too much." The both laughed. "But seriously, Jerd, they must be pushed. They have much to learn in a short time. The creatures of Zarharrab are fierce as you well know, but their weapons are built for the brute force of hand-to-hand combat. The new crossbows will even the odds. Our ragged little army will have the ability to fight from a distance."

"You speak the truth, Atlantean. We have strength in numbers, but the power of Zarharrab's unearthlings with their great clubs and axes could easily defeat our numbers. I hope that along with your new weapon, in your mind is a plan of attack. With crossbows alone, we cannot breach the sturdy walls of the temple fortress."

"Correct my friend. The time has come to formulate a plan for war."

"Good. My men grow eager to do battle with those who have done so much harm to this land. Let us find a place to discuss this matter between ourselves." The big man threw his arm around MAN-DAR and led him to the quiet sanctity of a nearby glade.

The two men sat on the ground, a smooth patch of dirt between them. MAN-DAR spoke first. "Tell me all you know of the Temple of Inanna and its fortifications."

The big one-eyed man thought for a moment, picked up a stick and began to draw on the smooth ground. "This square is the walls which surround the temple. Here is the main gate, but to reach it you must cross a bridge over the moat. Right here." Jerd drew parallel lines indicating the bridge. "Also there are four guard towers, two at either end of the bridge. Other than that bridge, I know of no other entrance to the temple."

MAN-DAR adjusted his position on the hard ground. "That does not show much promise."

"That is not all, many slotted spires guard the wall around the entire temple and worse still, and the moat is protected by horrible creatures known as gall worms."

"Gall worms? That sounds like a myth."

"Myth or not, my men believe they exist."

"Do you say the only possible means of attack lies across the bridge?"

"Yes, across the bridge and through a heavy gate. On either side of the gate stand two of the towers I mentioned, here and here. But before we can gain access to the bridge, we must pass the other two small guard towers, here and here." Jerd drew the towers on his improvised layout of the temple on the opposite side of the moat from the main gate.

"I find it hard to believe only one entrance to the temple exists. None of your people have ever seen Zarharrab or his minions exit by any other means."

Jerd thought hard and MAN-DAR saw a look of recognition

cross his face. "Well, Atlantean, I have heard that a stone like the one you flew upon to reach this place, exits and enters through a large portal in the main temple building."

"That might have possibilities," MAN-DAR mumbled as he pondered Jerd's rough map. Leave me while I consider the best plan of attack." Jerd nodded his consent, and stood to leave when they were hailed by one of Jerd's men running toward the glade. MAN-DAR recognized him as the man who saved him and Kirack when they first met the Hill People.

"Jerd, master Atlantean, you must come quick! Reamann and Oknee have come to blows over who is next in line to command. You must come quickly. I fear blood will flow."

Before the man reached the two leaders, Jerd and MAN-DAR stood. As MAN-DAR prepared to leave for the camp-site, Jerd grasped his arm. "I will handle this matter," and he marched off swiftly in the direction of the camp with his follower gesturing wildly until they passed over the crest of a barren hill and out of MAN-DAR's sight.

MAN-DAR sat once more to study the rough map of the temple fortress but soon became disturbed by a prickly sensation on the back of his neck. He was sure someone or something watched him. Slowly MAN-DAR rose to his feet and wandered around the glade, pretending to be deep in thought. Soon he strolled into the long-dead woods and whistled an old tune as if he had no problem in the world, yet every sense in his body stood on alert.

As he walked he heard footfalls other than his own and knew for sure someone was there. When he passed a large bolder, he abruptly ducked behind it and drew Secura. Silently MAN-DAR waited for his assailant. His wait proved short, as the footsteps grew closer. Slowly MAN-DAR raised Secura in preparation for defense or attack. Stealthily a stranger walked past MAN-DAR's lair without a hint the Atlantean waited to strike. With surprise on his side, MAN-DAR sheathed Secura and leapt on the unsuspecting intruder and wrestled him to the ground. He lifted his fist to thrash his adversary into submission. Suddenly the heavy hood of the assailant fell away and MAN-DAR sat up abruptly as he realized he battled a woman.

"Great Baal, what have we here? I had no idea Zarharrab employed female assassins. Who shall he send after me next, children?"

The woman refused to give up easily and thrashed about under the weight of MAN-DAR. "Leave me alone you great brute, or MAN-DAR will beat you to the quick."

MAN-DAR could not help but smile at the ragged young woman and could not help but play along with the game. "What makes you believe I fear this one you call MAN-DAR? It sounds by his name that he is of Atlantis, and anyone can tell you that all Atlanteans are crawling dogs. I will have his ears in my soup for dinner."

"He is no dog, or coward. My mistress says he is the bravest of men, and he will slay you before you can say his name."

Still holding the young woman to the earth MAN-DAR continued, "So, you have a mistress, and she has heard of me. Who might I ask is this mistress you speak of? And may she be dressed in such finery as yourself?"

"She is a princess and if she were in my place, a spear would already pierce your ugly gut."

"A princess you say, my my, and existing in such a wretched land. Does this princess of yours have a name?"

"Yes, they call her Sulina, daughter of Molack, the greatest chief of all the plains people. Her totem is Muckdah, the strongest among the strongest gods."

The roguish grin left MAN-DAR's face, and without a word he helped Marrina to her feet. When he finally had control of his emotions, he asked, "Where is the princess now, and how did you come to meet her?"

Marrina tugged her earlobe and spoke. "My mistress bid me to speak of her only with MAN-DAR. Now let me pass as Sulina's life stands in danger and I must find the Atlantean."

MAN-DAR's attention became more acute. "Tell me by what name they call you, woman?"

"Marrina."

MAN-DAR looked deeply into the young woman's eyes. "I am the Atlantean called MAN-DAR, and I want to help your mistress with all my heart. Now tell me, Marrina. Is your mistress all right? Is she in the hands of Zarharrab?"

Marrina told her story to MAN-DAR. She included the facts about how Sulina had befriended her and saved her from the hunchback. How Sulina had given her the courage to make an escape. How they got caught in the sticky twine in the underground passage, and how Sulina had insisted she find MAN-DAR. Marrina cried when she told of her near death by the gall worm, but brightened when she spoke of the tall strange man who saved her and directed her to this camp. Finally she told MAN-DAR of the horrible experiments she and Sulina stumbled upon. She ended her narrative by stating she feared for Sulina's life.

As she sobbed she tugged on her earlobe again and pleaded with MAN-DAR. "You must help her. I know Zarharrab and Zerrina have terrible plans for Sulina, and I fear they will come to pass soon."

"Can you tell me more of this tall stranger who helped you?"

"He saved me from the gall worm, showed me where to find you and disappeared. He never told me his name."

After he listened to Marrina's account of the occurrences in the Temple of Inanna, MAN-DAR accelerated the training of the surviving tribes of Angleland. The evening after Marrina's arrival he gathered his troops around the fire to explain his plan for the attack on the temple. As he spoke, he could not help but notice how close together Marrina and Jerd sat.

"I know you have had little time to train, but from what the maiden, Marrina, has told me, we must act now. Zarharrab and Zerrina plan to launch a hideous scheme soon. I know not the details of their plan, but it will at least involve the final destruction of Angleland and possibly the world."

Scar-faced Oknee stood to complain, "As you said yourself, Atlantean, we have not had much time to train. Let us put off this misadventure. And what of this girl, this scullery maid? How do we know she is not in league with the High Priest and his mother? After all, she lived in the temple for many harvests. Why did she not escape earlier?"

MAN-DAR stared into the fire. He knew the same questions troubled many of the others. "I understand your anxiety

Oknee, but I believe we must act immediately. Remember, we gain the advantage of surprise by attacking now. Zarharrab must know we gather and train, his spies have told him at least that much. But he knows not when we shall attack. Besides, his ego would never allow him to believe defeat could come at the hands of mere peasants."

Reamann stood, "The Atlantean speaks true. We will have the advantage of surprise. Plus we have the new crossbow weapon, which should prove another fine surprise."

Jerd offered still another reason for an early attack, "Our food supplies grow low. If we wait longer, weakness will surely blunt our assault. But, if we take the temple soon, we shall have plenty to see us through the winter. So I agree with the Atlantean. Attack now." A cheer rose from the men who surrounded the fire, and all eyes turned to MAN-DAR.

"My plan is simple. When we reach the temple, we will wait for early light to attack. The day guards will not have arrived and the night guards shall have tired. Jerd, Kirack, and the main body of men will attack the front entrance to the Temple as a diversion. The first wave of attackers will sweep across the bridge and kill as many of Zarharrab's minions as possible. At the same time, a small force will use the ley stone to fly through the portal in the temple wall, kill any opposition, and open the gate. If they cannot reach the gate, they will take up a defensive position and wait for help."

Oknee, his long scar redder than usual, spoke up immediately with accusation filling his question, "And where shall the Atlantean stand while all takes place?"

MAN-DAR ignored the scorn in Oknee's insinuation. "While the main force distracts Zarharrab, Reamann and I will take three volunteers and paddle across the moat. We shall retrace Marrina's escape through sub-passageways. Then work our way up into the temple and join the force opening the gate, if they have not already done so."

MAN-DAR heard a question called from the rear of the small army, "Who shall lead this band that flies through the portal?"

To MAN-DAR's surprise, Oknee called out, "I feel I can handle the flying stone. I volunteer to lead the attack through the portal. Is there not three others man enough to join me?" Quickly three hands shot up, all willing to share the glory of being Angleland's first flying force.

"Now listen, men," MAN-DAR shouted over the excited din of his tiny army. "When light first strikes the top of the temple's highest spire, all three forces will attack."

Led by MAN-DAR, Jerd, and Reamann, the tiny Angleland army reached the Temple of Inanna after three days of forced march. MAN-DAR had ordered Marrina to stay behind but she insisted on joining the fight beside Jerd. Since she had entered the camp she had barely been able to lift her eyes from the gruff leader, and his single eye had constantly strayed to her.

As early light struggled to brighten the desolate Angleland landscape, MAN-DAR and his men climbed a small hill where a standing stone overlooked the temple. For the first time, MAN-DAR saw the Temple of Inanna. He stood awe struck by its size. Its huge walls held scores of tall spires, which reached, into the yellow mass of the murky

Angleland sky. A strange feeling of déjà vu swept over him and he almost retched.

Although not quite light, the temple looked formidable. Besides its massive iron gate with two huge towers guarding each side, he saw at least ten guards on duty. But, from his position on the hill, the sentries, all human, did not appear alert.

Most shrubbery had long since disappeared, but dead bramble lay strewn in large clumps before the two small guard houses on the closest end of the bridge. Jerd and his men would have no problem sneaking to within bow range. The bridge itself was built of huge logs and ended on an outcrop of stone only meters from the great gate and its two protective towers.

MAN-DAR had left Oknee in the camp for a few extra days of practice with the ley stone and just as planned, a high-pitched whine alerted MAN-DAR of Oknee's approach. The huge scar on the short-tempered Oknee seemed even more pronounced with his hair windswept from the flight. As Oknee leapt from the stone, MAN-DAR gathered the small army around him to give them final instructions and bid them good luck.

With the main force in position MAN-DAR went to join Reamann and three men by the edge of the moat at the opposite side of the temple. He found them waiting in the thick mist, which swirled off the slimy water.

The signal to start the assault would come from a crimson ribboned arrow, fired by Kirack. From his position near the megalith he would see the early light strike the highest spire, fire the arrow, and then join the attack with Jerd and his men against the main entrance. MAN-DAR and his contingent had just slid the small raft into the water and had clambered aboard when Reamann pointed skyward. A crimson arrow fluttered through the air and simultaneously an ear shattering war cry came from the opposite side of the Temple. MAN-DAR ordered his men to cast off.

Before they had paddled twenty paces from shore, a ripple appeared in the water. MAN-DAR knew from Marrina that such a creature as the gall worms did exist, but he doubted it would attack their vessel as it moved. Besides, he had assured his men, they were all well armed. After another twenty strokes a second set of ripples appeared. More than one gall worm exists, MAN-DAR thought.

Reamann spotted the actual worm as its head appeared out of the water to the front of the craft. "MAN-DAR, look!" The leader of the swamp people exclaimed anxiously while pointing at the head.

MAN-DAR searched in the direction Reamann pointed and was astonished at the size of the creature swimming to-wards their craft. "Do not fear Reamann, the creature will not dare attack a craft with five armed men." MAN-DAR'S beliefs about the creature weakened when another long men-acing head appeared above the water's surface to his right.

For such a large creature, the worm moved more swiftly than MAN-DAR could believe, and before he had time to re-act its tail flew out of the water in an attempt to sweep the raft clean of its occupants. Instantly the men dropped to the deck. "Stay low," MAN-DAR urged as the worm made anoth-er sweep, just grazing Reamann. One crewman panicked and called for a return to the shore. Reamann ordered the oars-men to continue on. He refused and another crewman joined the mutiny, "We must abandon this expedition. Chances prove slight that any passage exists. Marrina might well be a spy for Zarharrab." MAN-DAR drew Secura. He intended to force the men to paddle. Suddenly another huge snake-like tail splashed from water and wrapped itself around the pro-tester closest to him. At once the creature jerked the man overboard. He barely had time to scream when the head of the giant worm appeared above his writhing body and plunged, snout first, deep into his belly. MAN-DAR watched in help-less horror as the man turned white and the water red.

Before MAN-DAR recovered from the first attack, an-other crewman at the front of the vessel screamed as a tail wrapped itself around his leg. Quickly Reamann grasped the man's arm but to no avail. He was yanked from the craft and pulled quickly beneath the slimy waters. For some moments all fell silent. Finally MAN-DAR regained his composure, "Reamann, take the paddle. Pull hard for the temple. Possibly we can make it before they return." MAN-DAR ordered the third recruit to grasp the tiller and aim for a dark shadow in the looming temple wall.

"Paddle for all you are worth, Reamann. If they return, I will use the bow on them."

"Aye, Atlantean," Reamann answered," but at what vital spot will you aim?"

MAN-DAR had no time to answer as another of the worms surfaced beside him. Without taking careful aim he released an arrow, which caught the worm in the side of its long head. It did not flinch, but instead raised its tail in an attempt to reach him. In one swift motion Reamann unsheathed Secura from MAN-DAR's scabbard and cut deeply into the creature's tail. It submerged and MAN-DAR gave Reamann a look of thanks.

They had almost reached the far shore, when the raft shuddered and rose into the air. The other worm had swum under the craft with the intention of overturning it. Reamann and the other man wailed, sure they would meet the fates of their comrades. But the worm pushed in the wrong direction and flung the raft towards shore. All three occupants tumbled onto the rocky ground and scrambled quickly to their feet. The secret entrance to the temple stood only steps away.

Instantly MAN-DAR heard a splash and turned to see two worm's tails reach from the slimy moat in a final attempt to seize their quarry. "Quick, slip between the bars." But his words proved unnecessary, for before he turned back to the entrance the other two were already squeezing through the gate. MAN-DAR quickly followed.

Once inside the black tunnel the three survivors stopped to catch their breath and get their bearings. MAN-DAR spoke first. "Thank you Reamann, I owe you my life this day."

"Think nothing of it, Atlantean. For without you, my people would never have had the chance to escape the grasp of Zarharrab and his wicked mother, Zerrina."

"Do not count your bones too early, Reamann. There is much to accomplish before the people of Angleland may call themselves free." The other man said nothing but stared fearfully into the dark tunnel-like passageway.

"Let us move quickly now," MAN-DAR announced. "We must find a passage which leads to the main temple.

MAN-DAR saw the silent man's throat take a gulp in the dim light filtering through the heavy bars then he spoke, "Allow me to take the lead, Atlantean. I heard the directions given by the woman, Marrina, and believe I can find the way. If I die in the attempt, Reamann and yourself might still live to help open the main gate."

MAN-DAR felt moved by the commitment of the people he had called barbarians, and reluctantly agreed. With the simple farmer in the lead, the three set off into the dark passageway.

"Forward men!" Kirack shouted, as he fired the crimson ribboned arrow, but he held back. From his vantage point on the hill he watched Jerd and fellow archers kill the first set of guards at the near end of the bridge. His next responsibility was to use the sword Jerd had found for him and lead the main body of the army in a direct attack across the bridge. However, Kirack believed the attack a folly. As determined as the Angleland people were in their fight for freedom, he felt they had no chance. Zarharrab would prove too powerful.

Now is my chance, he thought, I shall leave MAN-DAR to his suicide mission and find the land route to Atlantis. I will tell the leaders of the Empire how bravely we all fought, but unfortunately I proved the only one capable of escape. I might even receive a commission in Poseidon Command.

Kirack smiled to himself as he dashed through the dead undergrowth and away from the battle. He could still hear the war cries of the charging force, but over that, he heard the roar of the ferocious unearthlings Zarharrab held in his power. None of the attackers would live through this day, of that he felt sure. None would live to tell the true tale.

MAN-DAR could not see the spider, but sensed it close by. He had realized they had stumbled into a giant spider's web when the lead man cursed and more curses issued from Reamann who found himself entangled in sticky twine. "Come no closer, Atlantean, this stringy mess must belong to a giant spider."

"Try not to struggle, Reamann. You may find yourself more entangled. I will use Secura to set you free." In the total darkness of the passageway, MAN-DAR slid his way along the wall until he felt the first strand of sticky web. As he sliced through it, a hairy object grazed his hand. Quickly he stepped back, but his retreat proved too slow. He felt four hairy appendages grasp him and suddenly he saw a pair of red eyes. Eyes bright enough to shed light on a set of pincer-like jaws. Jaws, which were about to crush his throat. Instantly MAN-DAR jammed Secura between the huge pincers and struggled to free himself.

Shocked by his inability to lock his jaws, the spider dropped its prey. At once MAN-DAR searched the darkened floor with his hands for a weapon. Soon rewarded, he clasped the long human thighbone. Nervously MAN-DAR stood ready for a second attack.

Suddenly he heard the metal clang of Secura hitting the stone floor. Reamann's voice followed immediately, "Something touched me!"

"I am here, Reamann. Stay calm." MAN-DAR hoped to

intercept the huge spider before it crushed the life from his friend. He reached Reamann and found him alive but still tangled in the web. Suddenly from the darkness nearby came a scream quickly cut off by the sound of crunching bone. MAN-DAR knew the other man lay injured.

The red glow of the spider's eyes moved directly at Reamann, and their brightness illuminated the horror stricken face of the swamp man. MAN-DAR swung the thighbone with all his strength. The large bone struck the spider with a sickening thud. Immediately the spider's attention turned to its antagonist. It rushed MAN-DAR and bowled over the Atlantean. His crude weapon flew from his hand.

MAN-DAR rolled to his right as the spider's jaws went for his leg. The spider missed. MAN-DAR found a sharp bone just as the ferocious creature hissed and charged again. The huge spider's limbs once more caught MAN-DAR, but before the deadly jaws could crush out his life, MAN-DAR drove the pointed end of his weapon into the spider's head. The bone pierced the insect's exoskeleton and slid into the soft tissue of its brain. The giant spider died at MAN-DAR's feet.

Quickly MAN-DAR felt his way around the tunnel floor until he found Secura. With its razor sharp blade he freed Reamann, and together they found their compatriot, dead. Cautiously they moved on, MAN-DAR in the lead, his Akarri ready.

The pair followed the passageway further into the bowels of the temple until they found an open door and saw a dim light in the distance. MAN-DAR guessed they were near the area where Sulina and Marrina had discovered the deformed bodies of Zarharrab's experiments.

When they turned into a torch lit passage, they encountered rooms filled with human females, both dead and alive. A few of the distorted creatures noticed them and screamed. But most sat or lay unseeing, as if in another world. MAN-DAR's spirits plummeted with the thought of what might have happened to his beloved Sulina. Reamann saw his despair.

"Fear not for the barbarian princess, Atlantean. I feel Muckdah shines on us this day and she will be safe."

"I pray you stand correct, Reamann. For I feel without this woman, I could no longer live."

As they continued to follow Marrina's directions, the passage grew darker and MAN-DAR sent Reamann to snatch a torch from the lighted hallway. With the help of the light they located the door to the room containing the garbage chute, which led to the main temple. As they pushed open the squeaky door rats scurried between their legs. Finally they located the chute and ascended the steep incline toward light. The climb proved difficult, but with a boost from each other, MAN-DAR and Reamann made it to the hole leading to the pantry.

Reamann slipped through the opening and MAN-DAR began to follow, but as he reached up to grasp the rim of the hole he slid back down the greasy incline. Unable to climb the chute alone, he called Reamann for help. No response came. Fear for his friend plied him with an extra burst of strength and he finally managed to scramble through the opening into the small room Marrina had described. He found no sign of Reamann. MAN-DAR figured that his companion must have scouted ahead and was about to exit the pantry when he heard a commotion. Hurrying toward the noise, he rounded a corner into a large kitchen and came to an abrupt halt. Reamann stood before him with a look of astonished pain on his face. Behind Reamann stood Oknee, his scarred face filled with a defiant grin. Oknee gave Reamann a slight shove and the leader of the Swamp People slowly fell forward into MAN-DAR's arms. As he did, MAN-DAR felt wetness and saw a knife in Reamann's back.

MAN-DAR's shock turned to fury as he realized Oknee's betrayal. "How could you do this?" MAN-DAR hissed through gritted teeth as he unsheathed Secura.

"Reamann was weak. He should have killed you in the swamp when he had the chance. Instead he let you live." The tone of Oknee's voice grew defiant and filled MAN-DAR with rage. Without another breath, he raised Secura and flung it into the gut of the sneering Oknee. But before the traitor had slumped to the ground, a round of cheering arose behind MAN-DAR. Turning sharply, he faced the hateful eyes of Zarharrab, Pogul and a half dozen armed unearthlings. Behind them stood a woman dressed in flowing black silk, who stared at him with cold eyes of differing color.

FOURTEEN

MAN-DAR felt excruciating pain and heard the muffled sound of battle in the distance. Restraints held him firmly in the metal chair, which tore his wrists and ankles with every movement. An iron spiked headpiece dug bloody gouges in his skull, but the torture of his body meant nothing beside the pain in his heart as he watched Pogul strap Sulina onto the ceremonial alter.

He had not seen Zarharrab since the priest's minions had roughly dragged him from the kitchen. The guards had beaten him severely, but once they had him shackled to the chair they had disappeared. MAN-DAR had since fallen in and out of consciousness and had no idea how much time had passed before Pogul entered the chamber with Sulina.

As he watched Pogul carry out his task, MAN-DAR struggled in a vain attempt to help the woman he had grown to love. Pogul saw his struggle and strolled casually to MAN-DAR. The giant rewarded MAN-DAR's efforts with a crushing blow to his abdomen. MAN-DAR lost consciousness again, and when his eyes finally opened, the room was empty save for Sulina.

"Sulina, my love, it is I, MAN-DAR, speak to me."

Even from the twenty-pace distance he sat from her he could see her eyes open, but vacant. Her eyes stared solely at the high vaulted ceiling above. The only sign of life MAN-DAR could discern was the slow rise and fall of her bosom as she breathed. He tried once again to gain her attention, "Sulina, speak to me or I shall die of anguish."

"You will most certainly die, Atlantean, but not of anguish."

MAN-DAR's head, held firmly in place, could not see his antagonist, but he could not mistake the evil voice. "Let her go, Zarharrab. It is I you want."

"Ah, but you are wrong, Atlantean. 'Tis true I seek the revenge I promised long ago, but I seek a much larger prize. Moreover that prize requires the use of the virginal barbarian princess."

"Let her go, or by the gods, I swear I will tear out those wicked eyes and feed them to the crows."

"Now now, Atlantean, I think you must admit you sit not in a position to make threats. Let alone carry them out."

"The men of Angleland fight at the gates of your Hades born temple. You will soon feel their wrath."

"Ha! You mean that ragged bunch of farmers. By nightfall they shall all be fodder for my unearthlings."

Anger slowly drained from MAN-DAR's face to be replaced by hopeless resignation. He feared Zarharrab spoke the truth. "What have you done to Sulina? Why does she not speak?"

"We have done nothing to her yet, save put her under a mild spell in order to relax her for the coming ceremony."

Angry again MAN-DAR demanded to know of what ceremony Zarharrab spoke.

"I am astonished, Atlantean, that someone as learned as yourself would not know I speak of the Trinity of Waves.

You must know it exists to help us usher in the new world order."

"I know nothing of any trinity or new world order. And less as to why it should concern this woman. You have had all the women of Angleland to choose from."

"All of Angleland to choose from," Zarharrab spit in disgust. "You mean choose from those superstitious peasants whose life force barely allows them to live in this dung-heap?"

MAN-DAR's struggled painfully as his anger rose to new heights. Zarharrab laughed sadistically at his torment.

"Certainly your swift fall into love with this tart must have given you some hint. Or do Atlanteans always fall in love at the drop of a tunic?"

"Do not speak basely of one who lives pure of heart, halfbreed. Our love exists on a higher level."

Tauntingly, "So you say Atlantean, but in other lifetimes your love was not always so pure."

"What do you mean, other lifetimes?" MAN-DAR demanded.

"Come now brave warrior, do you not recall a great sage who once told you of a puff of smoke?"

"What great sage? What smoke?" Anger crackled in MAN-DAR's voice, "Why do you speak in children's rhymes?"

Zarharrab smiled wickedly as he unfastened the straps holding MAN-DAR's head still. He then sauntered to the miniature harp and replied, "Let us see if this riddle stands fit for children." As he sung a strange chant the priest plucked the harp.

From his tortured vantage point MAN-DAR strained to see what Zarharrab contemplated. He immediately noticed a small trail of blue smoke rise from the harp. It formed a hazy circle, and in the circle he saw two people. One, a woman who lay on a bed, which rolled like the sea. The other, a man with hair on his lip who handed the woman a cup. She popped a few tablets in her mouth and took a sip from the drinking vessel. Slowly the images faded, and the blue smoke disappeared into the harp.

"You have no recollection of this, Atlantean?"

MAN-DAR answered through swollen parched lips, "It means nothing to me. The scene occurs in a strange land with strangely dressed people, how could I know of it?"

"Oh such a pity," Zarharrab droned sarcastically. "You do not even recognize yourself and your lady love in another life, a life in the future. You two have lived many lifetimes together as lovers, or should I say, as *soul mates*."

"Soul mates? What do you mean by soul mates?" I know of no such term."

"Ah, if only you understood the Sons of the Law of ONE. They know all about soul mates. But suffice to say, most entities, people, live many lifetimes. Most live out their lives without ever finding their soul mate. You and Sulina, on the other hand, are lucky, or should I say, were lucky. You see, your mate will soon lose her soul. And you, my fearless warrior will search for it in vain in a self made Hades. I can think of no better revenge, then to have the knowledge that you shall suffer loss after loss for all eternity."

MAN-DAR stared vacantly, not knowing whether to believe the evil priest. Yet, something about the couple in the blue haze had struck a chord in his heart, and he worried Zarharrab spoke the truth. MAN-DAR found no words of condemnation strong enough to hurl at his captor, but as the implication of what he had learned shook through his body, Zarharrab laughed while he reattached the head straps.

"Sorry I can no longer stay to enjoy the agony of your enlightenment. But I must see to the final destruction of your pitiful army, and prepare for the upcoming ceremony." Without another word, MAN-DAR watched as Zarharrab turned on his heel and strode purposely toward the chamber door. Suddenly the priest turned, a wicked gleam in his eye, and spoke once more. "But, I do feel sure I shall enjoy more of your helpless agony when you watch your mate's soul slip into eternal death."

Beside himself, MAN-DAR screamed through his agony, "By Kroll, I will kill you!"

"Will you now?" Zarharrab chided, and he disappeared from the chamber, laughing.

Sulina, barely conscious, found herself in the blackness of Angleland night. She barely heard a commotion somewhere in the distance, but felt cold stone against her back. Abruptly she realized leather thongs bound her wrists and ankles. She lay spread-eagle on the stone and unable to move.

She felt her long red hair cascade over the edge of the large stone slab. Somehow it reminded her of altars used for sacrifices to entreat the gods for a good hunt or to ward off demons. The awareness sent fear surging through her but behind the fear she also felt a surge of strange sexual pleasure. As more consciousness filtered into her mind she sensed she lay in an immense chamber. Finally, full consciousness reached her. She raised her head and saw flickering light growing from beyond the chamber door. Accompanying the light she heard the sound of a low solemn chant.

She strained to hold up her head, and watched four scantily dressed maidens enter the room. Each carried a huge mounted candle the height of a man. They moved in single file and marched in a slow rhythmic half step which matched their hushed chant. The light from the candles cast an eerie pall of flickering shadows across the chamber. For the first time Sulina saw the truly immense size of the chamber surrounding her. A few more tentacles of fear crept into her stoic body.

From her limited vantage point, Sulina craned her neck in a search for any avenue of escape. What she saw caused more fear to grip her body. A skull-encrusted throne stood to her right, and she instinctively knew anyone sitting on such a hideous chair must contain evil incarnate. She strained to see to the left, and her eyes fell on a huge table laden with large skin-bound books. Centered between the volumes stood a tiny harp.

As the maidens slowly drew closer she felt the discomfort of her constrained position on the cold stone ease. The rhythm of the chant not only eased her pain, but also her anxiety. She slowly became aware of a tingling throb deep inside, which matched the rhythm of the chant. The women's slow march continued until two maidens stood on either side of Sulina. They set the candles on the floor beside them, and held their position without movement, save for the solemn chant on their lips.

While the chant continued a sensual pleasure spread throughout Sulina's body, and another group entered the great

chamber. They consisted of three men dressed in black hooded robes. The first man carried a huge golden ladle and led
two men who carried a large cauldron between them. They
moved to the same slow chant as the maidens had and eventually deposited the vat behind Sulina's head. The man with the
ladle stood behind the vat, while each of the other two took
up a station between each pair of maidens.

Next through the portal came Zarharrab, his tall hooded
figure unmistakable to Sulina. He carried with him a large
pedestal and marched at the same pace as the others while he
chanted the same solemn words. Gradually he moved to the
end of the stone alter, and set the pedestal to his left. From her
position, Sulina could look between her spread legs and just
see the top of the pedestal.

Finally, a short striking looking woman entered. She
marched the same half-step march and chanted in the same
rhythmic chant. The woman wore long flowing black clothes,
and although they had never met, Sulina felt sure she watched
the wicked Zerrina or sometimes POL-TAR, that Marrina
had spoken of. Zerrina did not take up a position with the rest
of the procession, but instead marched to the tiny harp setting
among the books on the long table. Ceremoniously she lifted the tiny instrument and slowly carried it back to the alter
and positioned it on the pedestal next to Zarharrab. She then
placed herself to the opposite side of the alter from her son.

The low chant had continued, and with the placement
of the tiny harp shivers of sexual pleasure pulsated through
Sulina's body. She could see the instrument between her legs
and for the first time realized she was dressed in a costume
different from the one she had worn in her cell.

This garment, as black as the darkest night, was also constructed of a single piece of material. But the upper portion had been cut away revealing her breasts and the portion passing between her legs had a slit revealing her private parts. Suddenly she remembered a bath of scented oils given by several maidens shortly before she slept. The cleansing ceremony had sexually aroused her. Embarrassed, Sulina squirmed in a vain attempt to avoid exposure, but the leather straps held her fast.

In unison all nine members of the ceremonial procession slightly increased the rhythm of the chant. Sulina felt moisture between her thighs as she began an unsuccessful battle against the rising tide of sensuality flooding her body. When her hips moved involuntarily, she squeezed the muscles, which controlled her pelvis. She tightened her stomach to prevent the pleasure that inflamed her lower abdomen as it forced its way through her torso toward her throat. Her attempt at constriction proved useless as a sensuous moan issued from her lips. She found herself writhing against her bonds while each movement only increased her sexual desire. She could stand the excruciating sexual torture no longer and prayed to Muckdah for the relief of orgasmic explosion.

Suddenly the chant ceased; the chamber fell silent save for the rasp of Sulina's quick breaths. The sexual tide in her body subsided, her breathing slowed and finally her writhing pelvis relaxed into a languid squirm. No words were spoken but slowly the six novices stepped forward and as lightly as feathers, their fingers caressed her. Each caress soon turned to a stroke and a new level of sensual pleasure rose in Sulina. The new pleasure did not push her to orgasm as she had prayed, but lifted her beyond the old pleasure as if the process of arousal had started anew, on a higher and more sexually charged plain. Sulina sensed movement of the high priest and his mother. From her view they had moved to the end of the alter. Near her spread legs. Both stood still, save for their lips which issued a new chant. It held a quicker rhythm and different pitch.

Sulina remembered details of a ceremony Marrina had spoken of, and from deep inside Sulina found the strength to fight back. Through the maze of spell-induced sexuality she focused on Zarharrab and Zerrina. "You cannot do this. You want to turn me into one of those horrible unearthlings. Also I know you must have my consent, and I will never give it."

Zerrina lifted her hand and the novices returned to their places, she then replied, "So my pretty, you believe we wish to make an unearthling of you. Ha! What we want from you stands much greater than another single minion. We want much more and you shall help us by your own will."

"Never will I consent. No matter what tortures you devise for me."

"You do not think so my pretty princess?" Sulina saw Zerrina's eyes glance past her and a command issue from her lips, "Pogul, remove the gag from the Atlantean."

Vividly sharp pains of anxiety swept through Sulina as MAN-DAR called out her name, but before he could say more, Zarharrab gestured to Pogul and MAN-DAR's words were abruptly cut to a muffle, then to complete silence.

"What have you done to MAN-DAR?" Sulina demanded of the evil pair who stood before her.

"Nothing serious. Yet," Zerrina teased. "However, that may change soon, very soon, if you do not cooperate."

Sulina heard a muffled cry of pain from behind and realized MAN-DAR's life depended on her. The thought of any harm coming to the Atlantean threw her mind into frenzy. Her torture or MAN-DAR's life. Whatever the torture, she felt she must save MAN-DAR's life. Sulina had no choice. She blurted between quivering lips, You leave me no option. I will consent to your plans. But, you must swear by whatever vile god you pray. That no harm shall come to the Atlantean."

With a sly smirk, Zerrina answered, "You have our word. We swear by the supreme spirit, Agron, that we will not harm your devotee." To the others she smiled and said, "Let the ceremony continue."

Zerrina began another chant. At the same time Sulina saw her pluck the strings of the tiny harp. Zarharrab took up the chant, as did the surrounding novices. Soon the rhythm of the chant increased, as did the overwhelming sexual desire which pulsed through Sulina's body.

More chanting and string plucking brought a wisp of blue smoke streaming from the tiny harp. The smoke formed a large cloud-filled ring. Inside the smoky blue circle forms took shape. The shapes became a man and woman lying naked on a strange sleeping pallet. Furnishings she could not begin to recognize surrounded them. But for some reason the couple seemed incredibly familiar. The man had thick dark hair on his head and over his upper lip. The lips kissed the pretty woman with brown hair who responded in kind.

Suddenly Sulina felt the man's lips on her own. They felt familiar and filled her with even greater passion. Slowly his lips moved to her throat and he sucked lightly on her neck. She responded with a low moan. The man's lips continued down her body until they reached her breast. Sulina felt incredible pleasure and fought her bonds in order to feed him her breast. Slowly the dark haired man in the blue mist slid down the woman, kissing her lightly. He lingered at her navel before he continued his downward movement towards the lips between her legs. Slowly he licked and kissed those lips. The feeling sent Sulina into a rapture and her buttocks lifted rhythmically and forcefully as they slammed against the hardness of the stone alter. She heard herself moan. Soon a name formed in her throat then it passionately slipped from her lips, "Manny, oh Manny, take me." He answered, "Yes Iris." Only a moment separated her from the orgasmic release she desperately need-ed. Suddenly a deluge of ice-cold liquid splashed her body.

The images in the circle quickly receded into the blue fog. The urgent need to release subsided. Her hips ceased move-ment, although her body pulsed with undulating sensuality. She realized her tormentors had splashed her with water from the heavy vat behind her head. Again she heard the chanters. She felt the same pulsating need for sex match their chant.

Zerrina broke the rhythm, "Not yet my pretty princess. There still lies another level you must reach, and another friend you must meet."

With those words Sulina felt hands massage her wet body, heard the chorus quicken its rhythmic chant, and watched as Zerrina plucked the strings of the tiny harp once again.

Like magic Sulina's body matched the new rhythm. Almost instantly she reached another level of sexual tension. She surpassed that level, felt her wetness overflow and swam in the warmth of unbridled sensuality. Then she saw it.

Deep in the murky blue smog of the smoke ring another

image formed. Without a hint of what it might be, fear filled her being. A fear, which surpassed the unbelievable sexual level her body rode upon. Slowly, as the image formed, her fear mingled with her exotic pleasure. and rose to a point where her strength barely kept her spirit within her skin. Finally the image solidified and a scream of hysteria mixed with sensuous pleasure erupted from her throat. She knew it came for her, the *Demon of Agron.*

Suddenly the demon's serpentine face faded into the misty smoke. It was replaced by a vision of Uljeck. Still aware of the pulsating din around her, Sulina remembered her earliest sexual feeling. Feelings she had experienced when a touch could moisten her. When the rubbing together of her and Uljeck's clothed bodies brought a deep shake within. A shake that brought a small release, almost a tiny bit of death. She felt the rhythm they built together inside their soft leather skins. She felt the rhythm increase. She saw Uljeck and she removed their skins. Suddenly Sulina screamed above the pulsating rhythm, "We did not do that!" But the vision contradicted her, as Uljeck unclothed her. Sulina saw his man thing. It looked inhumanly huge, but when she looked up at his face she saw MAN-DAR.

Sulina forgot everything save for the fact that her man lay with her. She cried, "MAN-DAR, MAN-DAR, I want you so much. Release me, release me from this terrible pleasure." Instantly she stared into the cruel face of Kirack and screamed, "Get away. I hate you!" and her body fell limp.

Sulina did not lie still for long. When her emotional exhaustion waned, she felt the vibration of the chant increase. Her body responded in kind and at a higher level of sexual intensity. Her hips rose and fell with the exquisite pleasure and she felt herself build once more to uncontrollable sexual pleasure.

The novices joined once again, but not with hands. They lightly struck her with towels. They struck her throat, her stomach, her breasts and the tuft of red hair between her legs. It distracted her. At first it stole some of the pleasure. But soon the soft taps pushed her to higher heights and again she felt her buttocks strike the hard slab beneath her. She could stand it no longer. Her moans, her passion screams filled the gigantic chamber. The novices removed her bindings and tore the clothes from her body. She screamed, "Do it! Do it! I can live with this no longer!"

Sulina saw Zerrina pluck the harp as she took Zarharrab's hand. They both slipped into a trance. The novices moved back, dripping sweat from their own inflammation and joined in an increased level of chant. Finally the image of MAN-DAR appeared in the blue mist. He advanced toward her, his huge man thing stood erect and pulsated with the chant. He looked eager to release her from her horrible pleasure.

"MAN-DAR. Help me. I cannot do this, but I cannot stop. Please. Help me. Do it to me. If I stop they will kill you. Come to me. Finish it. Do it!"

MAN-DAR seemed to float to her out of a curly blue mist. His tongue licked her eyes, her cheeks, her lips. Sulina screamed with the beautiful agony pent up inside. "Do it. Do it, MAN-DAR. I can live this no longer!"

Sulina felt his tongue enter her mouth, his man thing pressed urgently between her legs. It would happen she could die. She shut her eyes as MAN-DAR entered. He plunged deep, deeper than she knew possible. Her eyes flew open. She saw the snake-like features of the blue demon. She expected an incredible implosion but she only screamed, "MAN---DARRRRRR!"

FIFTEEN

"Nooooooo!" Was the muffled cry from MAN-DAR as he sat helplessly gagged and strapped to the iron chair behind Sulina. He had watched the Trinity of Waves ceremony with rising horror. His head, held in place by the iron spike-filled headpiece, allowed no movement. His eyelids were fastened to his eyebrows by clamps and excruciating pain shot through his body at the slightest movement.

At first he screamed in an attempt to disrupt the ceremony, but Pogul quickly gagged him. He tried to block the ordeal by recalling the few pleasant moments he had had with Sulina, but the love he carried for her failed to overcome the present horrible reality. The pain in his heart grew with every level of passion Sulina transcended.

The pain had turned to rage as the chant climaxed and the vilest acts were perpetrated on Sulina. He had seen her body begin to vibrate wildly and rise into the air. On her face she held a look of terror and ecstasy as Zarharrab and POL-TAR had each grasped one of her feet and vibrated at the same rate. MAN-DAR understood they had completed the trinity. The circle of blue smoke engulfed all three as the vibration rate increased. The blue circle around them formed a large mirror and the three no longer looked of this world as they faded into the looking glass. MAN-DAR had watched in horror as their images faded into mere specs of blue. The circle had also shrunk and had receded into the strings of the tiny harp. Finally, the last images of Sulina, Zarharrab, and POL-TAR along with the Harp of Agron disappeared in a puff of blue smoke.

MAN-DAR had screamed. He had screamed out of pain and anguish the likes of which he had never felt. It had begun in his bowels, moved up to his stomach, then his throat and the horrible muffled wail he had emitted echoed throughout the Temple of Inanna.

He cursed Zarharrab, POL-TAR and all gods including Kroll. He had lost that which he had learned to believe was the most important thing in life, love. And worse still, he had lost it for all lives past and future. He no longer wanted to live.

So deeply immersed in pain, MAN-DAR failed to hear the rising tide of battle outside or Pogul who hovered over him. In one arm Pogul hefted a number of implements of torture, and the other he used to vigorously swipe at his nose. Pogul's presence continued unnoticed until his boom of deep laughter reached MAN-DAR's ears.

"You think you feel pain, Atlantean? You have not even begun to feel pain. The Lord high priest has left you to me. I may do as I wish with your puny body. And I feel like having fun before I put you out of your misery."

MAN-DAR did not protest. He did not complain. He felt the pain of torture might help mask the deep pain in his heart. Death might at least give him rest.

"You have nothing to say to a lowly servant, Atlantean? At least you can tell me how much you enjoyed the ceremony." Deep laughter rumbled again.

Still MAN-DAR said nothing. He gave no sign of

recognition to the pig-faced giant. Not even when Pogul tightened the clamps holding his head did he cry out.

"You bring no fun, Atlantean. Let us see if we can get a reaction with the tug of your fingernails."

Pogul took a pair of clamps and attached them to MAN-DAR's index finger then slowly pulled off the nail. Still, MAN-DAR did not flinch. Only a blank stare and a tear filled one of his clamped open eyes.

"Nothing yet, huh? This game tires me, officer of the Empire. I think it time to tinker with your manhood. We shall see what kind of meal can be made when we crack the eggs between your legs." Again the giant roared at his own cruel joke.

MAN-DAR showed no reaction as Pogul prepared yet another ominous looking instrument. Constructed of iron, it looked like a pair of ice tongs, except that two flat pieces of iron replaced points used to grasp ice. Pogul held the instrument up to MAN-DAR's eyes.

"See my little friend. You will soon not need worry about filling the land with your runty offspring." More peals of laughter.

Slowly Pogul lowered the huge tongs below the seat of the chair. The torture chair had an open bottom, which allowed MAN-DAR's genitals to hang exposed.

"Do not worry, my soon to be egg-less friend, I shall not slam this devise quickly and squash you with a painful whap. No. I intend to crack the delicate eggs slowly, crushing them bit-by-bit. We do not want nerves to deaden. You will have the honor of experiencing the entire event. Get ready, my Atlantean friend, I am sure this will get a response out of you."

Pogul laughed his terrible laugh and bent to his knees to better reach his victim's vital parts. Suddenly another sound blended with his laughter. At first almost imperceptible, below the noise of the giant's laughter, but its pitch grew higher, almost a whine, and as it grew Pogul's laughter subsided. Wary, he became distracted from his work and searched the chamber for its source. As he did so, the instrument in his hand started to vibrate. It vibrated with such intensity, Pogul needed all his great strength to keep the terrible instrument in his grasp. Soon he could endure the vibration no longer and a scream of pain escaped his gaping mouth. Abruptly the tongs exploded, shards of iron flew and Pogul crashed to the floor.

A slight spark of life appeared in MAN-DAR's eye as Pogul struggled to his feet, a grimace of astonishment pulling his ugly face askew.

"What do you look at, Atlantean?" Pogul roared as he savagely kicked MAN-DAR. "I have plenty more in store for you." But as the words reached MAN-DAR, another strange sound filled the room, the chamber door opened and MAN-DAR's sword, Secura, slowly floated in with no visible means of support. Pogul stood dumbfounded, his eyes locked on the akarri. The blade was coming directly at him. Too amazed to move, Pogul could not raise a hand in defense. The sword suddenly swung into the air then plunged downward. It split open his head down to his nose. Pogul thudded to the floor; a pool of his blood and brains forming around his dead pig-like head.

Slowly, out of thin air, a haze appeared around the hilt of Secura. The haze thickened and formed an arm. Attached to the arm a shoulder then torso with head, hands, legs, and finally feet appeared. The last image MAN-DAR saw before he slipped into the relief of unconsciousness was Lugaar.

MAN-DAR became aware of a hand which stroked his forehead. Painfully he opened his eyes and found Marrina's eyes staring sadly into his. He looked beyond her and saw the ceremonial altar, and remembered. He was suddenly aware of what had transpired. He then felt the tears of loss roll down his face. "Why must I live?" He sobbed openly and closed his eyes. A great cry of anguish filled the huge vaulted room. Mingled with the wetness on his cheeks, he felt further moisture. He opened his eyes again watched tears fall from Marrina.

She spoke. "Sulina is gone, MAN-DAR, but you must live."

"Why," he whispered, his voice horse. His eyes closed again and his head whirled as if full of intoxicating drink. Finally his world passed into blackness again.

When MAN-DAR awoke he saw both Marrina and Lugaar. Behind them stood a large window and the gray Angleland sky.

"Where am I? And where did you come from Lessor. I thought you dead.

"You still dwell in the Temple, Master. Safe, since the defeat of the temple garrison. After we released you from that horrid chair, we found your clothes, dressed you and carried you to this antechamber. I felt it unwise to move you any great distance until you appeared more fit.

As for me. I cloaked myself in invisibility with the crystal after the unearthlings attacked me and TAM-STX near our Vector."

Too emotionally drained to scold Lugaar, MAN-DAR grunted and asked, "Where is TAM-STX now? Is he alright?"

"I brought him back to his own Atlantean squad for recovery. The squad is also unable to contact Poseidon Command. They must wait the full time between harvests before a mother ship returns for them."

"What about the army of Angeland?"

"They are still recovering from the battle, but feared staying in the evil Temple of Inanna."

Without enthusiasm, MAN-DAR asked Lugaar how the temple came to fall.

"It proved almost impossible at first, Master. But once Zarharrab's minions learned he had disappeared, they ran amuck. Some attacked the human troops Zarharrab employed to defend the temple, while others pillaged the temple itself. Still others fought to the death among themselves. Even poorly armed, Jerd's men fought fiercely and easily beat their divided foe. They had believed in your plan and it worked. All went well except for Kirack. No one has seen him since the battle ensued. Most believe him killed by the unearthlings and eaten."

Marrina spoke up. "Do not let the Lessor's modesty fool you, MAN-DAR. The tide actually turned when he used the sacred crystal to make himself invisible once again. He then scaled the temple wall and opened the gate."

"It really was nothing, Master. You should have seen how fiercely Marrina fought at the side of Jerd. Together the pair took many unearthling heads."

MAN-DAR barely heard the description of the battle. His only comment at the finish of the narrative was to ask mournfully, "Why do I still live?"

Lugaar thought MAN-DAR meant his physical life. "You live because the crystal healed your wounds."

"Why did you do that?" MAN-DAR shouted at Lugaar. "I no longer wish to live. Not in this lifetime or in any other. At least death might erase for a time the terrible grief I carry for Sulina."

"I am truly sorry, Master, but I could not let you die. We must complete our mission. We must get back to Atlantis with the barbarians."

"Mission? You speak of Mission? Zarharrab will soon arrive here with an entire army of unearthlings. Their only mission is to destroy Atlantis!"

"That leaves you with even more reason to live, Master. You must warn the Empire."

"Do not tell me what I must do, slave. I have lost the one who should travel with me through all lifetimes. Her body lays dead, and with it her soul. She exists only in the place of the damned, where she will stay forever, neither dead, nor alive. Why would I think of a mission knowing love stands lost for all eternity!" Although filled with pain, MAN-DAR raised himself to his knees, got to his feet and moved menacingly toward Lugaar.

Marrina intervened. "Stop! MAN-DAR, the Lessor speaks the truth. You must not think of your own pain now. Your mission stands more important than ever."

"How can you speak so, Marrina? You told me you loved her also."

"It is true. I did love her. But my loss, and even the loss of Sulina's soul, pales against the loss of all the world's souls."

"What do you mean all souls?"

"If Zarharrab were to return from the underworld with the unearthling army as you claim. They could turn the entire world into a place such as Angleland. Is that not more important than my soul, or yours or even Sulina's?"

MAN-DAR sank slowly to a low stone bench, his flash of anger drained to despondency. He contemplated Marrina's words, but the thought of the loss of the world still did not raise any urge for action. Only the loss of Sulina filled his heart. Without her he could not see how he could gather the strength to help anyone. His expression took on a countenance of resignation until Marrina spoke once more.

"MAN-DAR, you must listen to the Lessor, Lugaar. He believes an avenue to save Sulina may exist."

"What can he do?" MAN-DAR asked contemptuously. "Even if the crystal he wears has the power of invisibility and healing, it cannot bring back life when it has departed."

"You stand correct, Master," Lugaar stated simply. "The crystal cannot bring life back from death. But, the Waters of Life can."

"Waters of life?!" MAN-DAR's ire rose again, "Is this more Lessor superstition? I have heard of no Waters of Life."

"I believe it true, Master. The water comes from a spring on the Mystical Mountain. While you lay unconscious I found reference of it among POL-TAR's books of magic. I searched through the books, hoping to discover a remedy to counter the hideous spell, which has held your will captive. While doing so, I learned in this land a place exists, a mountain actually, which still receives sun and on which life abounds. The mountain has resisted all spells cast by Zarharrab and POL-TAR."

Unenthusiastic MAN-DAR replied, "Yes, I have seen such a mountain. It stands as the only spot in this accursed land where great Sol still shines. But what has the water to do with lost souls?" MAN-DAR fell into despair again, covered his face with his hands and mumbled, "Speak to me no more of this farce. I have no longer the will to fight."

Marrina intervened once more. "You must listen to Lugaar. He has found a way."

His hands still covering his face, MAN-DAR slowly shook his head.

"But Master, listen. On this mountain, a magic spring endures. The sacred runes of POL-TAR's ledgers claim that three drops of the sacred water spilt on the soul-dead shall restore its life force."

A glimmer of hope flickered in MAN-DAR's eyes but quickly faded. "Even if such water exists, Lessor. How may I carry it to Sulina? Her soul has already passed across the timeless river of death."

Marrina put her hand on his shoulder, entreating further. "Listen to the Lugaar. He has a plan, a good one."

Despair still filled MAN-DAR's countenance as he mechanically inquired about Lugaar's plan.

"It stands simple, Master. All you need do is retrieve a vial of the magic water, travel to the underworld, revive Sulina with the water, and steal the magic harp."

"Is that all, stupid one? It sounds fine to me, very simple. If this magic water exists and if I can somehow retrieve it. Besides, I believe you forgot to mention two other small matters. Like how I enter the underworld, and how I get past the army of Zarharrab which gathers about him as we speak?"

"I have told you, Master. I studied the runes of the evil POL-TAR. I believe I found a way into the underworld. The crystal can act as the conduit as did the harp. We only need to duplicate the ceremony of the Trinity of Waves with a willing female."

"Is that all? A willing female. One who will risk life, her very soul for eternity? I imagine volunteers by the score stand ready at the temple gate. Forget the foolish idea, Lessor. All proves lost."

"All is not lost, MAN-DAR," Marrina broke in. "I am the female who shall help you enter the underworld."

"No. I cannot allow it. Even if we reach the underworld, your soul stands at risk for all eternity."

"I need not risk my soul. If you obtain the Water of life for Sulina, you can obtain it for me. Remember, MAN-DAR, I also love Sulina. I owe her my life. Lugaar's plan stands as the only way to save us all."

"She speaks true, Master. It is the only way."

MAN-DAR again covered his face and sat in quiet contemplation. Finally he answered, "So what if I reach the underworld? How do I foil Zarharrab and his wicked mother's plans? Only Baal knows how many creatures they might have at their command."

"Use the crystal, Master. I shall teach you its magic. It will allow you to become invisible to all you encounter. I am sure with all the commotion of a gathering army, you could easily slip to Sulina's side to administer the water. At the same time you could steal the Harp of Agron. Thus the evil ones would be deprived of much of their power."

The spark of hope glowed brighter in MAN-DAR's eyes. Seeing a chance to save Sulina, new strength cursed through his veins. Unhurriedly he lifted himself from the bench. He stood straight, his head held high. Without a word he paced the small room as new exuberance for life replenished his spirit. Lugaar's plan came to life in his mind and for the first time he dared believe he might see Sulina again. Suddenly he stopped, turned to Lugaar and exclaimed, "Great Baal, Lessor, I mean Lugaar. Possibly you have come up with a sound plan after all!"

Lugaar's face turned crimson with the recognition, and he almost wept with pride.

"Let us find this magic mountain. Let us acquire this Water of Life. Let us enter the underworld before Zarharrab and POL-TAR make good their hideous plan."

Hesitantly Lugaar commented. "Well, Master, to reach the mountain shall prove easy. You need only to fly the straight track to its base on a ley stone."

"Good, let us be on our way."

"It will not be quite that easy, Master. The runes claim two demons guard the sacred water. Two demons which you must defeat before you win the prize, the water from the magic spring."

"Only two demons. Have I not defeated the Rook of Styx? Sent him to his gods? And what about the time I took on Zargog or Miur? Was he not deemed unconquerable?"

"Yes, Master, but according to the runes, no water has yet to leave the Mystical Mountain. The demons stand undefeated. It is written; Yarbu the Sacred was unable to dip even a toe in the waters. And he is the only trespasser who escaped intact. Unfortunately his mind proved not so lucky."

"Tell me of these undefeatable demons," MAN-DAR demanded.

"One is called Stylus. The runes claim he stands no taller than a small reed."

"A small reed. I shall take Secura and chop him to splinters."

"Perhaps so, Master. Yet according to the runes, whole armies have fought the Stylus, none with success."

"I shall abide none of your defeatist yammer now that my mind is set. What of the other demon?"

"He is the trickster, Lop Nor."

"Trickster? What do you mean, trickster? Does he use treachery in combat?"

"The runes are not clear. Only the name appears, and the fact that he too has never met defeat."

"There is always a first time. Secura has conquered many a demon. If the Water of Life exists, I shall retrieve it and save my barbarian princess."

"I am sure you will, Master. Only allow me to teach you some ancient Lessor mind techniques. They may help you in your battle."

"Mind techniques? I have no use for mind techniques. All I need is strength and my akarri, Secura."

Once again Marrina intervened. "You must listen to Lugaar, MAN-DAR. This battle is for the soul of Sulina. And maybe even for the very existence of all mankind. If the mind techniques will help, you must learn them."

In the face of Marrina's powerful argument, MAN-DAR relented, but added, "I still believe it a waste of precious time."

Timidly, Lugaar interjected one final request. "You must also retrieve the sacred Rose of Nirvana."

SIXTEEN

MAN-DAR's hair fluttered in the breeze as the ley stone flew him towards the Mystical Mountain. Lugaar had located a diagram of the ley system POL-TAR had revived and learned MAN-DAR needed to stop at three megalithic stones to reach the mountain. When he approached the last megalith, he saw the mountain rise up in front of him. He immediately recognized it as the one he took note of when near Jerd's camp.

Mystical Mountain loomed like a torch in a darkened cave. Since he had entered Angleland, it proved only the second time MAN-DAR had seen the sun, which beamed brightly through an opening in the mucous cloud cover. The mountain itself glowed green and looked the picture of life. Slowly the huge flying slab of stone whined to a halt and MAN-DAR dismounted only a short march from the base of the mountain. This shall be easy, MAN-DAR thought.

Easy it proved not. After only his first few steps, MAN-DAR stumbled into the accursed weed-vines. He had dealt with the vines throughout his stay in Angleland, but none of the carnivorous vegetation had seemed as fierce and aggressive as the clumps of weeds he presently slashed through. The tooth-filled blossoms, twice the size of others he had encountered, actually snapped at his legs.

MAN-DAR found his movement slowed to a crawl by the vines and many times Secura was pressed into action to clear his way. It appeared the vines had piled themselves high around the mountain in order to build a wall to prevent MAN-DAR or any others from the green mountain.

With a great hack from Secura, MAN-DAR finally breached the fortress surrounding the mountain. He could easily see the demarcation line where the weed-vines ended and the realm of the mountain began. The sun kept the flora in glorious growth, as opposed to the brown-gray area occupied by the weed-vines. MAN-DAR stepped into the glow of the golden sun and lifted his face to feel its life-giving warmth. Relief filled him as he realized the first segment of his quest to save Sulina stood complete. The rest, retrieving the sacred water and the rose of Nirvana, would be easy.

He started up a small animal track which appeared to stretch to the summit of the mountain. At its end, Lugaar had told him he would find the magical Spring of Life.

With all the green surrounding him, MAN-DAR failed to notice the small reeds lying in his path and simply crushed them as he moved upward. By the time he climbed the lower portion of the mountain he found himself brushing off several of the half-arm length reeds clinging to his legs but paid them little attention. Not until he had traveled quite a way did he notice the clumps of the reeds holding stubbornly to his boots. In turn, the reeds collected others of their ilk as he traveled along. Slightly irritated, MAN-DAR halted and rubbed his boot on a fallen log to free himself of the encumbering sticks. It surprised him that he was forced to work quite hard to rid himself of the nuisance.

Eventually he managed to free himself of most of the sticks, except for a few on his left foot. He had only walked a short way when he noticed more reeds had gathered to the few he had failed to dislodge. As the mountain grew steeper, he found climbing with the clinging reeds laboring. In order to purge himself of the new encumbrances, he stepped on one pile with his right foot while he pulled his left foot free.

"Great Baal!" MAN-DAR cursed when he realized clumps of reeds now clung to each foot. Resigned to hauling this small burden up the mountain, MAN-DAR started off once again.

Soon the reeds attached to his boots gathered more of their kind. He now dragged along huge clusters of sticks reaching half way to his knees. MAN-DAR lost his patience.

He arrived in a small clearing where the path had leveled. He cursed the reeds and decided to put a serious effort into ridding himself of the grasping burden. "I shall be rid of you, pesky fellows. Secura has made short work of the weed-vines and I am sure she will have no trouble with a few twigs." Out flew Secura once again and MAN-DAR hacked at the reeds around his legs. As he chopped the slender reeds, they broke, cracked and splintered. Pieces of stick flew in all directions including onto MAN-DAR. They hung to his upper legs and even to his chest and arms. Abruptly, he realized each splinter grew instantly to the full size of its predecessor and soon found himself covered by a pile of reeds up to his neck.

MAN-DAR's good sense deserted him as he grasped Secura in both hands and whacked at the pile of reeds, which surrounded him. "Take that, and that and that and that, frail sticks," MAN-DAR roared as he hacked into the pile. Again splinters flew, but again, each instantly grew to full size. MAN-DAR began to suspect the reeds were alive, and finally recognized his only chance of escape was to push his way through the ever growing stack of twigs engulfing him.

By now reeds stuck to all portions of his body. He pulled them from his hair as he walked, only to find his hands stuck to his head. MAN-DAR now ran up the mountainside, reeds and all, but found the more he ran the more reeds gathered to the reeds already clumped around him. Before he knew it so many sticks clung to him he could barely see. His breath ran short and his pace slowed to a walk, and then to a crawl. Still more reeds gathered to him, and he could not see at all.

With the remainder of his strength, MAN-DAR screamed in frustration, tugged, squirmed and finally fell to the ground without freeing himself. He struggled, but the more he battled the larger his burden grew. Soon the tiny reeds had trapped him beyond escape. Worse still, the weight of the sticks crushed and smothered him. MAN-DAR saw the end close by and thought of the shame it would bring his father to know he had succumbed to a simple reed. With his breath almost gone he screamed, "Great Ball! If I fail to retrieve the sacred water, Sulina's soul will die. Of what consequence is my father's shame? Merciful gods, give me strength." Every fiber in his strong body fought to free itself, but to no avail. All seemed lost when suddenly awareness struck and he cried out again. "The reeds are the demon Stylus!" With his life draining, hope filled him as he remember Lugaar's lessons.

The Lessor had spoken of inner peace. How MAN-DAR must calm himself. He remembered Lugaar's words about resistance. "The more you struggle with Stylus, the stronger he becomes. MAN-DAR followed the technique Lugaar had taught him. He calmed himself and cleared his mind. Although little air reached his lungs, he relaxed. He built a picture in his mind of a staircase with ten steps and stepped down counting backward from ten. At any second he could lose consciousness, but he forced himself to relax and concentrate. He pictured an inner space where nothing existed but himself. In that space he felt Oneness with the universe. His breath was almost gone but an inner peace filled him. Abruptly the sticks began to release their deadly grip. Almost simultaneously a breeze stirred the air and the reeds withered like burnt grass and blew away.

MAN-DAR could not tell how long he stayed in the state of Oneness, but when his eyes opened, the reed god Stylus had gone. He kept his breath shallow and his mind at peace as he slowly rose to climb the second half of the mountain. While he climbed he recognized once again that he owed his life to a lowly, Lessor.

With his mind completely at rest MAN-DAR hiked at a slow steady pace, and finally reached the mountain's summit. As Lugaar had predicted he found a large bolder. From a crack in the bolder spewed a spring of clear water. The water sloshed down the side of the rock and ran for twenty paces before dropping into a small crevasse in the mountainside.

MAN-DAR had not encountered a second demon and hoped he would not. With one more look around for assurance, he walked swiftly to the spring, took two clay vials from the belt, and knelt to fill them. As he dipped the first vial into the liquid the water vanished. Astonished, MAN-DAR found himself scooping only thin air. Instantly the spring reappeared. Again MAN-DAR dipped the vial into the stream, and again the spring vanished, only to return when he lifted the vial. MAN-DAR attempted once more to fill the vial, only to have the spring vanish again. Frustrated, he cursed out loud and heard a light singsong voice like that of a child.

"Do you have a problem, friend?"

MAN-DAR wheeled to see a chubby dwarf, half his size, who sat on a stone not eight paces away. The dwarf had a jolly round face sporting a tiny goatee. His mouth carried a malicious grin. His clothes were colored forest green and on his feet he wore boots which curled at the toes. But the most astonishing fact about him was that as he sat, he juggled three creatures, a chicken, a rat, and an opossum.

"Yes," MAN-DAR answered the dwarf, trying to return the smile and ignore the animals. If the dwarf proved to be the other demon, Lop Nor, then caution was his best tact. However, MAN-DAR thought if this chubby little man is the demon, he is not a very imposing one. "It appears that this spring has a mind of its own. It refuses to give up its water."

At the word, spring, the dwarf sprang into the air. MAN-DAR thought for sure he would drop the creatures he juggled, but all turned to swallows and flew off towards the sun. No sooner had Lop Nor landed then in his hands appeared three fish. He juggled them as he spoke to MAN-DAR again in his child like voice.

"Well. Why might I ask, should the stream give up its water? If the spring walked to you and scooped out your blood, would you allow it?"

Lop Nor made the statement with such an impish grin that MAN-DAR could not help but laugh. MAN-DAR's levity died abruptly when two enormous liquid hands rose from the spring and grasped him. One hand-held MAN-DAR to the ground while the other turned into a pointed, razor sharp scoop. The scoop slashed down towards MAN-DAR's heart when Lop Nor suddenly let his three fish flip into the air and dive straight into the scoop about to puncture the squirming Atlantean. The fish seemed to appease the vengeful water. The hands released MAN-DAR and receded back into the stream. At the same instant three lizards appeared in the juggling hands of Lop Nor who giggled as MAN-DAR shook himself dry.

MAN-DAR did not smile in return, but instead queried the dwarf angrily. "That spring retired when you fed it your fish. Did you have anything to do with what just occurred?"

"Maybe I did, and maybe I did not. But at any rate, you can now see that things are not always what they appear. Why do you come to the Mystical Mountain, strange dark man? Uninvited." He continued to smile and juggle as he spoke.

"I came for the Waters of Life in order to save the soul of the one I love. Maybe to save the soul of the entire world."

Now that sounds like a task worthy of a hero. So might I ask how you are called, stranger?"

"I am called MAN-DAR. I represent the Empire of Atlantis. I have come to this land to lead a delegation to the city of Poseidon in order that they may take part in a conference on the plague of Gigantica Beasts."

"Plague of Beasts." Lop Nor laughed. "But we have no plague of Beasts here. You must go before you anger the gods of the spring further. Three little fish may not appease them the next time."

"I will not leave without the water. I shall take it by force if necessary."

"By force you say." The dwarf laughed while the three lizards left his hands. They landed in front of MAN-DAR and when their tiny feet touched down, all three exploded to the size of the creature MAN-DAR had killed in the pit at Jerd's camp. With a swipe of his tail, the first swept MAN-DAR off his feet. The second one sat on him, and the third prepared to bite off his head. Quickly Lop Nor snapped his fingers and the giant lizards turned into three slimy worms and slithered down a hole next to MAN-DAR's ear. By the time MAN-DAR caught sight of the dwarf again he stood close to the spring juggling three apples.

Lop Nor did not take his eyes off the apples as he spoke. "Well now, MAN-DAR of Atlantis, what force did you intend to use. For you see, no one may take the Water of Life. That is unless he is able to solve three riddles."

"Solve three riddles? How hard could that be? Riddle on, little one. I have always held riddles as my favorite game."

"There is only one catch, man from Atlantis. With each riddle you fail to answer correctly, you lose a part of your body. If you fail all three, you lose your life." The grin on the dwarf's face disappeared, and three weasels appeared in his juggling hands.

"Riddle on, trickster, I have no fear of what you might ask. The gods shall guide me. They would not let the world fall to the evil ones, Zarharrab and POL-TAR."

"It is your choice, Atlantean," Lop Nor answered as the weasels turned to three snakes. "So answer this riddle. You think you are so deft. Subtract fifteen from eighteen and tell me what is left?"

"I believed demons to possess great cunning, tiny one.

That riddle is too simple even for a child. The answer is obviously three." As the word three left his lips MAN-DAR fell to the ground. Upon attempting to regain his feet he realized both sets of arms and legs had vanished. He was left with only torso and head. He heard the giggle of Lop Nor again and strained his neck to see the trickster now juggling his arms and legs. Beside himself with anger he screamed at the dwarf, "You liar. I have not lost the riddle. By whatever magic you possess, you must return my parts this instant!"

"You guessed wrong my friend, the answer is four. You forgot the number zero, which adds one more."

"That is treachery," MAN-DAR screamed hysterically. "Zero is no number!"

"Zero may not represent a number amount, but it is a number, one number. And three plus one does make four."

"But that is a trick."

"So it is, but are riddles not tricks? So my son, are you ready for another? You might get lucky and return to your mother."

"This condition leaves me little choice. Riddle me again, dwarf."

The trickster, Lop Nor, continued to smile and juggle MAN-DAR's appendages. "Then this is the riddle, the second you'll hear for after the third, you shall have no ear. Listen quite closely so no mistake will be made. If there is no sun, who could lie in the shade?"

MAN-DAR pondered the riddle from every angle. If there was no sun, no one could lie in its shade. It could be the only answer. "No one."

"Ha, my friend who soon will be dead. Look at yourself,

you are only a head. Anyone knows, especially me, that I can lie anywhere, even under a tree." Lop Nor giggled and giggled as he juggled MAN-DAR's arms, legs, and torso.

Again MAN-DAR had been tricked. He could not believe he still lived with only a head. Not even a heart to circulate his blood. He did not get angry this time, just wary and frightened. His simple trip to procure water began to look like the beginning of the end. But again he thought, how could I exist without a body? Then he thought of Lugaar. What he had told him of physical reality only existing in the mind. It must be true. I am only a head and yet I live. And if the world is made of probabilities we create in our mind. I can ward off what this evil trickster might do by using the laws of probabilities against him. "Let us continue the game, Lop Nor. Get on with your last riddle and let us be done with this game once and for all."

"Game it is and rife with fun, for with this riddle, your life will be done. Now, if a tiger on the run, leaps on your head, what then can be done?"

MAN-DAR had no need to think for from the nearby brush leaped a huge tiger. His first thought was of the huge animal tearing his head to shreds, but he immediately pictured a big X across the image of his mauled head. Instantly the tiger disappeared. Along with the tiger went the juggling trickster and MAN-DAR found himself whole and alone by the quiet stream.

Wasting no time, MAN-DAR filled the two vials with water and corked them. As he stood to leave he spied a rose bush across the stream. On the bush grew the most beautiful red rose he could have ever imagined. He believed it could only be the rose of Nirvana Lugaar spoke of. Without hesitation he leaped the Spring of Life and attempted to pluck the rose. Unfortunately, the plant would not give up its flower easily and MAN-DAR found himself pricked by thorns several times before he had success. He wrapped the beautiful rose in a soft cloth provided by Lugaar, and placed it in his belt next to the two vials of liquid. He was about to hurry down the mountain when he remembered Stylus. Quietly he sat on a nearby rock, saw a staircase in his mind and counted down from ten to zero.

SEVENTEEN

When MAN-DAR returned to the Temple of Inanna, Lugaar had already made the preliminary preparations for his and Marrina's passage to the underworld. Lugaar had used the crystal to heal Marrina's bruised body and had bathed her in scented oils. He had exchanged Marrina's rags for a white ceremonial gown he had found among POL-TAR's wardrobe, and when MAN-DAR cast his eye on Marrina he could scarcely believe this beautiful woman was the same filthy scullery maid he had first encountered near Jerd's camp. A momentary flush of guilt and apprehension swept through him when he remembered what the coming ceremony entailed. Since he had met Sulina he thought it impossible to even think of making love to another woman. Now he found himself in a position where failing to make love to another could cause the loss of Sulina for eternity. He had to follow through with the ceremony, but the blossoming of Marrina had made the task easier.

Lugaar also appeared different. The constant stoop of his shoulders had vanished, and his face radiated serenity along with a new air of self-confidence. Lugaar, also dressed in a magnificent white robe, looked straight into MAN-DAR's eyes. MAN-DAR saw for the first time that this creature was not just a slave, not just a man, but more, he was a true friend.

"Lugaar. No words I could utter will make right what I

have done to you and your people. But whatever comes of this day, I humble myself before thee and ask your forgiveness." MAN-DAR held out his hand to Lugaar.

His eyes glistening, the big Lessor clasped MAN-DAR's hand but said nothing.

When they separated, MAN-DAR cleared his throat and spoke. "Let us proceed quickly with the ceremony Lugaar; we have no idea when Zarharrab will return with his hideous army.

"All stands ready, Master, except for your cleansing ritual and the reading of the spells necessary to help you and Marrina reach a proper state of mind."

"You need not call me, master, Lugaar. Not because you bear some kind of homage to me, but because I am your friend."

A tear streaked Lugaar's big face and he choked as he spoke. "It will be hard to change old ways, Mas...., I mean MAN-DAR."

"You have saved my life many times now. It is I who must change his ways. Again, let us make haste with the ceremony. I fear time grows short, and you claim I need a bath which I understand. But, why must I submit to a spell of any kind?"

"The spells assure the total concentration you shall need to help Marrina reach a level of sexual implosion without release. A spell to increase her sensuality has already been placed on Marrina."

"If what you say is true, why did Zarharrab and POL-TAR not use a spell on Sulina to reach the underworld?"

"They did place her under a spell, but only a slight one due to her high sexual aura. Even that spell would not have been necessary except the evil ones sought to transport three be-ings across the river of death. We send only two. Using both your sexual auras, the Crystal of Arrhamis can create the vibrational rate necessary for the Trinity of Waves."

Marrina spoke for the first time since MAN-DAR had returned from the Mystical Mountain, a slight shiver in her voice told MAN-DAR she still held fears. "If we reach the underworld, how will we return?"

"Simple." Lugaar stated. "According to POL-TAR's runes, you will have already torn open the dimensional barrier with your projection to the underworld. Once the gate has opened you must only visualize *this* chamber while humming the chant I shall teach you. When you have completed the underworld challenge, the crystal and chant will return you. The return trip will prove much easier for you than Zarharrab. He and POL-TAR must bring back an entire army. The reason they searched for one with the high sensual aura of Sulina was to open a larger tear."

"Zarharrab will have no chance to return with his army, Lugaar. I intend for him and his unholy mother to rot forever in Hades."

"Be that as it may. It is imperative you escape with the magical harp. The instrument must be secreted away from the likes of Zarharrab and POL-TAR."

"If I retrieve the harp, does it mean they could never leave the underworld?"

"No. POL-TAR's runes show the Trinity of Waves ceremony has already created a passageway through which they can return. I also learned they performed further ceremonies to help their safe return with an army. Only their deaths will prevent their return."

"That task I relish. Now, let us move along with this cleansing ceremony. Time shall not wait for us."

Quickly Lugaar stepped to a curtain in the wall on the far side of the chamber. He drew it back he exposed a steaming pool. As MAN-DAR stepped into the water sweet scents entered his nostrils. Several different aromas wafted in the hot heavy air, all of which put him in a state of arousal. He turned to Lugaar. "These scents cause a stir in me. You claimed a spell was necessary for the ceremony."

"That stands true, Master. But this venture contains a process. A great task stands before you. You must prove equal to it. If you fail to reach a level of arousal you may fail to judge the height of Marrina's. Do not forget, you must elevate her to the levels of passion few reach without spilling over the top."

"But what if I lose control? What if the juice of life escapes before we travel far enough along in the ceremony?"

"That will not happen, Master. One of the spells put on you shall prevent you from going too far. Neither you nor Marrina must come to the final release. Especially Marrina."

"How will I know when she has reached the proper level of excitement?"

"Did you find the sacred rose which grows by the Water of Life?"

MAN-DAR reached for his clothes and removed a piece of cloth. He unrolled it to expose the huge red rose he had picked from its prickly bush.

"This is good, MAN-DAR. With this flower you will help Marrina reach heights of arousal even POL-TAR never believed possible. Listen once more to your humble servant while I explain." As MAN-DAR rose from his bath, Lugaar whispered to him the small chant he would use with the Crystal of Arrhamis to make himself invisible in the underworld.

Marrina shifted her hips involuntarily as the first wave of excitement shivered through her body. She had joined the act of the Trinity out of her own free will in order to save her friend, Sulina. Sulina had shown her kindness where others had shown only scorn and pain. By performing the marriage act with MAN-DAR she could save Sulina's life, the life of her true friend.

As Marrina lay on the stone ceremonial altar, she found it hard and uncomfortable. Lugaar saw her discomfort and immediately placed a soft lambskin coverlet beneath her. The warm fuzzy sensation of the soft wool increased the sense of arousal. She had begun to feel its warmth when Lugaar had held the crystal before her and murmured several words in a language she could not fathom. Yet even before the crystal, she had felt a special tingling from the scented bath Lugaar had gently given her.

The Lessor had explained the ritual during MAN-DAR's absence. He told her he would use the magic crystal to put her in a light trance. The trance would relax her and allow her to open completely too sexual stimulation. He had cautioned her constantly throughout the bath that she must avoid sexual release at all cost. It would destroy the opportunity for the transition to the underworld and could even leave her in a state of insanity, much like the poor woman she had seen in the bowels of the temple.

Marrina understood fully what she had committed herself

to. She loved the wild barbarian princess who had saved her from the hunchback. She knew she could die in the attempt to save Sulina, but she had every confidence the two vials of sacred water held by MAN-DAR would revive both her and Sulina.

As for the handsome Atlantean, he held another story. MAN-DAR proved strong and brave, as did Jerd who also caught her eye. When in both men's presence she sometimes felt wetness between her legs. But she knew MAN-DAR truly loved Sulina. She had kept those feelings secret. With that thought clearly set in her mind she felt herself free to explore the experience of the ceremony with the Atlantean. Almost simultaneously she felt guilt. Did she betray her friend by expressing the passion Lugaar claimed necessary for the Trinity of Waves to succeed?

Suddenly all doubts vanished as MAN-DAR gently removed her garments. She did not know if the spell cast by the Lessor caused the increased urge to mate, or the heat she felt from the Atlantean. However, each time his fingers brushed her skin as he peeled away layers of fabric, she felt the flame of desire rise. Marrina's sexual passion had increased tenfold with MAN-DAR's advances. Already she felt it would prove difficult to prevent herself from releasing the hot pressure building in her loins.

Marrina attempted to relieve the immediate stimulation and thought of her friend Sulina. Lugaar had told her about the ceremony performed by Zarharrab and POL-TAR. He had said some black magic was used. They had degraded Sulina and coerced her into the high level of excitement necessary to attain the Trinity of Waves. They had forced Sulina to view unnatural acts produced by Agron in the blue smoke of the harp. They had stimulated her woman's part with visions of lovemaking from other lifetimes, especially with one called Manny. They made her believe through spells that she was indeed making love with MAN-DAR and not to the demon. At that point she had gone over to the other side. Lugaar had assured her that the ceremony he planned had no such extremes. She would reach a spiritual implosion only. He said he would use an opposite method, the method of the rose of Nirvana.

The very thought of becoming more sexually aroused than her present state caused moans to escape from Marrina's lips. Along with the soft moans came a more violent writhing of her hips. Never had she wanted to feel the push of a man inside her. In all the times she was forced to submit to sex in the temple, very rarely had she felt anything but pain. This felt different and she worried she could hold her explosion no longer. Already she wanted release.

Suddenly she felt the sharp slap of Lugaar's hand on the soles of her feet. Anger filled her and she cursed the Lessor. "Why do you not let me go? I can no longer stand this exquisite pain."

Lugaar answered softly, as if belying the fact that he had just done violence to her. "Lay still and breath fully, my child. You have not as yet reached the point where your body becomes pure spirit. You must become excited, but do not let it carry you away. Not before the time is right."

Marrina nodded in acquiescence, the beautiful pangs of desire, which had filled her, had subsided with the sharp interruption of Lugaar. Then she felt the rose.

It brushed her cheek and its wonderfully sensuous scent filled her nostrils. The touch had been so light she would never have felt it save for the oil scents and light spell cast by Lugaar. Gently the rose brushed her lips and the smell filled her once more. Sexual excitement again set her hips to move and she attempted to grasp the flower. It flitted away.

Once again the rose brushed her cheek, and the soft petals grazed her ear. Another small convulsion rippled through her. A slight cry slipped through her lips. The strokes of the rose felt light yet heavy with passion. She wanted to feel it harder, but the blossom gently flowed over her jaw as it followed a path to her neck.

Upon feeling the first few flicks of the bloom at her throat, Marrina moaned again and tried to crush the rose between her shoulder and jaw. The blossom slipped free. She relaxed herself and felt its flick once more. With each touch desire intensified and spread like fire before the wind.

As the beautiful hunger grew, she sensed wetness stain the soft wool beneath her. Her hips strained and the rose continued its stimulatingly gentle path. The blossom merely brushed her skin, but Marrina felt the aura of her sexual being pushed outward to create further pressure.

Marrina kept her eyes shut yet she heard Lugaar chant in the background. She heard a slight whine and lost all awareness except an increased level of sexual arousal and the soft petals of the rose as it moved further down her body to her breasts.

When the petals first touched the hard red center of her nipple she thought she would explode. Heavier pressure from the petals increased her passion. Abruptly MAN-DAR snatched the flower away. "Please, do not stop now." But it was too late; it had vanished, as had her extreme stimulation.

A short time passed, like days for Marrina before she felt the rose brush her other breast. She felt her passion explode to a new level which reached the edge of control. Along with her moans she cried, "I must be dying, I could not survive this exquisite pain and live." Her body pulsed. An incendiary sensation convulsed her hips until they pounded on the lamb's wool. Again the soft strokes of the rose passed over and around each breast. She wanted to scream but held back. Her inaction raised the level of her heat one more level.

Marrina gasped as the rose slid down her abdomen. She tried to reach between her legs to release herself from the delicious agony. Again she remembered Lugaar's warning that she must hold her explosion. She took several deep breaths, relaxed into a numbing sensuousness and allowed herself once more to be possessed by the rose and the strong sensitive Atlantean who performed the act.

Marrina felt her arousal reach still another level. She both wanted and needed release. She wanted to explode. She pictured a gush of her womanly juice flooding the chamber, but her only outlet was the thrash of her hips. Once again she heard the whining sound. Instantly she calmed.

Marrina lay on the altar as still as the rose which lay on the curly hair guarding her woman's entrance. She hoped the respite would be brief and she opened her eyes to find Lugaar placing the sacred crystal around MAN-DAR's neck. Lugaar chanted a few more syllables in the strange tongue.

Gently MAN-DAR held her hand and Lugaar took up a stance at the foot of the altar stone. He chanted in still another unknown tongue and Marrina saw a golden glow about the Lessor's hands. MAN-DAR's free hand still held the rose of Nirvana.

Marrina closed her eyes when struck by the new wave of sensuality, which flooded through her body. Again she felt a scream in her throat but suppressed it. The contained sexual energy boosted the exquisite pain deep in her belly then filled her completely. The rose brushed her thighs, her stomach and again between her legs. She wanted to scream.

Then it happened. The rose caressed the tiny swollen head between her legs. Petals brushed gently, lightly, like tiny breaths of air. But the slight pressure proved enough to send her into an ecstasy of excitement so intense MAN-DAR's hand almost lost the rose. Marrina felt the rose perched full on her own petals. MAN-DAR applied more pressure and teased the magic spot. The pleasure took her breath away. Even the trance proved useless as she screamed with pleasure. The scream matched the whine of the crystal and for the first time the aura of her ecstasy tried to burst through the top of her head.

The whine changed pitch and the pleasure retreated back between her legs. Yet again she felt the pressure of the rose as it slowly rotated, easing her entrance open. She felt MAN-DAR's hand on her wrist and the excitement of the stimulation rushed there. From MAN-DAR's wrist it rushed back to the rose and the need for exploding pleasure surged through her being once again. Marrina felt her sexual aura take control of her body. It had a life of its own. It wanted to grasp the rose and shove it inside. Fulfill her, make her release.

The whine changed pitch again and the rose exerted more

pressure. She could stand it no longer. She had to explode. The feeling burst from her groin to her breasts, to her throat to her head. She felt the swirl of a swoon. She was dying. She was flying. She was exploding from her body.

EIGHTEEN

MAN-DAR's head swirled as the energy from Marrina burst from her body and traveled through his. With his hand in her's the two lifted from the earth in a cyclone spiral. They flew with the cyclone, and floated downward in a misty cloud-like tunnel.

As they passed down the tunnel, they had paused five times. Although MAN-DAR could discern no light source, he could see clearly. At each pause he found them perched on the edge of a great precipice with no sky and only a bottomless drop below. Along with each interval he heard an increasingly loud unidentifiable sound, and Marrina grew weaker.

Their last pause was on a wide ledge. They stood before a cave guarded by a roaring two-headed lion. The creature stood as tall as MAN-DAR and was tethered by a thick chain to a ring embedded next to the cave.

Marrina spoke for the first time since their ordeal began, her voice barely a whisper. "Look, MAN-DAR, in the cave, another spiraling cloud. It must be the final passage to the underworld. But how do we pass this hideous creature? Either head could snap us in two."

MAN-DAR had little time to decide as the chain restraining the lion snapped, leading to an immediate attack. MAN-DAR set Marrina down just as the dripping fangs of one of the heads latched onto his shoulder. The strength of the lion proved enormous as it picked the flailing Atlantean into the air and flung him like a child's toy. MAN-DAR landed on his back with a thud, just shy of the edge of the great precipice. His head blurred, and his only sense was of the sound audible over the roaring lion; a sound which came from deep in the dark cave.

The huge two headed cat instantly forgot about MAN-DAR. His two heads turned to Marrina and his feet pounded directly at her. A hysterical scream brought MAN-DAR back to awareness. He found a stone under his back and pelted the lion's rear. The creature turned abruptly on MAN-DAR who already had Secura drawn. Teeth exposed, the lion attacked without pause. He lunged at the arm holding the Akarri. MAN-DAR swung Secura with all his strength in an attempt to behead the creature but before the blow reached its target, the twin head grasped MAN-DAR's arm. Secura clanged to the ground as a roar of agony escaped MAN-DAR's lips.

Again the first head went into action. Its great paw attempted to secure MAN-DAR by the throat, but a swift blow to its snout forced it away with a howl of pain. MAN-DAR tore himself from the other head and used the thick chain from the lion's collar to pull himself onto the cats' back. With the heavy chain, MAN-DAR beat both heads. In a rage, the lion strained to reach the antagonist, its vicious jaws snapping and snarling. With each blow the canine heads yelped in a painful frenzy as it leaped into the air to free himself of his antagonist. MAN-DAR hung on.

Finally, one of the heads drooped, blood poured from its ear and a tooth fell from its jaws. The other head snapped more furiously at its tormentor in a useless attempt to reach

MAN-DAR. With the Atlantean still clinging to its back, it too finely succumbed to the vicious blows. With a screeching roar, the two headed lion crashed to the ground, unconscious. Now the only sound he heard came from the ever-growing noise from the cave. MAN-DAR pondered its meaning as he dragged the two headed comatose lion back to the huge ring which had held it at bay and reattached the chain.

MAN-DAR then staggered back to the dying scullery maid. He lifted her into his arms, and carried her through the still thick mist toward the dangerous sounding noise coming from the dark cave.

Still carrying Marina, MAN-DAR followed the growing racket deep into the cave. As he carried Marrina through a darkened tunnel, the rising din swelled to an almost ear shattering roar. The rising deluge of sound pounded MAN-DAR and further weakened Marrina. MAN-DAR continued down into the dark mist filled tunnel.

With Marrina still in his arms, MAN-DAR finally felt more solid ground beneath his feet. He knew they had reached the underworld. The swirling mists surrounding the couple had also dissipated. He soon found himself and Marrina behind an outcrop of stone on a small knoll. The terrible din which assaulted his ears now grew to a hideous cacophony. Laying Marrina on smooth ground, he thrust his head over the stone and saw the reason. A growing army of unearthlings gathered before him in a gigantic cavern. A cavern so large, even the score upon score of torches held by the unearthling army left MAN-DAR with no sight of its end.

Enormous spike-like formations of stone hung from the ceiling and rose from the floor of the mammoth cave. MAN-DAR knew them to be stalagmites and stalactites. Scattered near and far were molten pools of lava, spewing a stench, which almost made him retch. From his vantage point MAN-DAR saw numerous tunnels. From each tunnel streamed even more endless lines of unearthlings. MAN-DAR knew they assembled at the command of Zarharrab and he immediately took Lugaar's crystal in his hand and chanted himself invisible.

MAN-DAR stooped to check Marrina and prepare her for the Water of Life. As he took the first vial from his belt he heard a series of grunts behind him. Wheeling around, MAN-DAR instantly lurched to the side as two burly unearthlings bent over Marrina. They had failed to see him or Secura as MAN-DAR drew the sword from its sheath. Just as MAN-DAR readied to dispatch the two creatures, an entire horde of unearthlings rose above the edge of the knoll and gathered around the dying scullery maid. A huge fish-headed creature, gestured for the others to bring the women and follow him. Vastly outnumbered, MAN-DAR had no choice but to fall in silently behind the unearthling troops and wait for a chance to rescue Marrina.

MAN-DAR followed the unearthlings through endless outcrops of rocks, pointed stones, and molten pools. Occasionally the unearthlings made detours around groups of creatures who gathered in any open space. Many sharpened weapons and spoke of war and how they would finally gain their soul's freedom. Still others practiced mock battles and spoke of the carnage they would bring on Atlantis. Some fought each other to the death for no reason MAN-DAR could discern. The smell of the unearthlings assaulted MAN-DAR's nose almost as badly as the sulfurous pools. Finally the unearthlings he tailed pushed through one last throng the size of a small army, and MAN-DAR stifled a cry as his shocked senses absorbed another blow.

Inside the circle of creatures stood two rough stone thrones, one occupied by Zarharrab, the other by POL-TAR/ Zerrina. Between them on a small boulder sat the magic harp and on an iron spike placed before the thrones hung the tattered body of Sulina. Dead.

MAN-DAR swallowed a cry, and the overwhelming urge to attack the wicked priest and his mother. With all his heart he wanted to annihilate them for what they had done to his love. Instead, he wept silent tears and prayed the Water of Life would restore her to the beautiful princess he had known.

The unearthlings MAN-DAR followed flung Marrina to the ground at the feet of the amazed new King and Queen of the underworld. MAN-DAR saw a look of cognizance on POL-TAR's face as she glanced about. She no doubt realized he must have somehow accompanied the scullery maid to the underworld. POL-TAR whispered in her son's ear and Zarharrab summoned several of his chiefs to organize search parties. He heard the word Atlantean mentioned.

MAN-DAR knew he must move swiftly while the underworld stood in a state of confusion. He went to Marrina and again prepared to administer the sacred water. He intended to revive her first, then Sulina, and to use the continued confusion to mask their escape. MAN-DAR knelt over Marrina, ready to sprinkle the liquid when he suddenly felt a hand on his shoulder. Startled, he turned to find POL-TAR, a wicked smile on her face, standing over him.

"You are a fool Atlantean. If you actually believe Lessor magic surpasses mine."

MAN-DAR quickly glanced at Zarharrab whose attention still focused on issuing more orders for his capture. The priest had not yet realized his mother had moved from the throne. MAN-DAR said nothing.

"I see you as well as I see anything in this world."

Still MAN-DAR refused to answer.

"Although it proved clever for you to use the scullery maid to enter the underworld. You shall find your scheme has only caused her and your death. Soul death." With the word death a glow grew in POL-TAR's eyes, a glow which instantly weakened MAN-DAR. As his strength waned he dropped the clay vile of water. Anguish spread through him as he heard it shatter and POL-TAR laugh her heinous laugh.

POL-TAR's spell could not restrain the anger and willpower of MAN-DAR. He stood, unsheathed Secura and stared straight into the eyes of the Atlantean priestess. As he moved closer, he spoke through clenched teeth. "No, POL-TAR, it is you who will die. You who have caused so much pain to so many."

Abruptly POL-TAR's eyes shifted from MAN-DAR to Secura. Instantly the sword grew hot and MAN-DAR dropped it from his burning hand. He heard it hit the rocky ground.

"Who shall feel pain, Atlantean?" And with those words, the glow from POL-TAR's eyes intensified.

MAN-DAR's attempts to avoid mesmerizing the look

failed and he once again felt the strength in his body begin to ebb. His legs weakened and he fell to his knees.

"I must say though, handsome Atlantean, it is appropriate that you should bare witness to the gathering of this great army. To witness what final end your soul mate has met, and to see your pain now that you realize you have caused the identical fate for the stupid scullery maid. It pleases me to let you live until she dies. It is fitting that this occasion be the last sight your eyes behold. Look!"

MAN-DAR could still hear Zarharrab shouting orders and the dimwitted unearthlings mulling in confusion, but his head was forced by POL-TAR's secret powers to follow her pointing finger to Marrina who lay struggling for air at the foot of the throne. He had failed his mission, failed his love, and failed one who willingly sacrificed herself for a friend. He felt utterly defeated.

Barely able to speak, MAN-DAR whispered, "Finish me POL-TAR. What could be the use of prolonging this pain? You have won."

"Don't worry, Atlantean, you will die soon enough. But you have the choice of making it quick and easy or slow and hard."

"You have already taken away everything which means anything to me. I have nothing left to give."

"Oh, Atlantean, but you surely do. You have the Crystal of Arrhamis, and I want you to hand it to me. Kind of a parting gift." POL-TAR cackled again.

The laugh brought anger along with a moments clarity to MAN-DAR. His thoughts raced. If the power of the crystal is so much weaker than POL-TAR's, why must she need it? Why can she not just remove it when I die? Perhaps her strength over the crystal was another of her lies.

With the last of his faltering strength, MAN-DAR forced a tone to rise in his throat, flick over his tongue and slide from his lips. It was the tone Lugaar had taught him to activate the crystal. As he hummed the chant he pictured his strength growing as POL-TAR's weakened. He was able to lift off his knees. As he did so the glow of power began to dim in POL-TAR's menacing eyes. When he felt they were at equal strength, MAN-DAR pictured Secura returning to him. Before the thought was even completed, Secura flew to his hand.

Astonished, POL-TAR backed away from MAN-DAR. He menacingly followed and raised his akarri for the kill. Suddenly Zarharrab appeared, drawing MAN-DAR's attention from the evil Atlantean priestess.

Zarharrab lacked the needed forces to see invisible MAN-DAR. He only screamed at his mother, "I have stood under your power since the death of my father. I have hated you through every instant. At this moment, it is my turn to control the power. We shall see who wields the blue force now, sorceress mother." With a fiendish grin he held the Harp of Agron to his mother's face.

A satanic smile slid across Zerrina's mouth. "So, you think it that easy to steal the power of the harp from your mother? With a chant or two I could have the Demon of Agron eating your head. What do you think of that, my vile son?"

"I think nothing of it, my depraved mother." With those words Zarharrab's fingers slightly stroked the strings of the tiny harp. A sound escaped from the harp and all the unearthlings in its reach snapped to a rugged attention. Quickly Zarharrab laid eyes on a tiger headed unearthling. Seeing her son's movement, Zerrina's lips began a defensive chant. Before she could finish a nod from Zarharrab triggered the tiger head to slam his hand on Zerrina's mouth.

Tiger head saw another grisly looking nod from Zarharrab. Immediately he knew its meaning. He dragged Zerrina to the edge of a shallow crevasse and threw her in. She landed on her back with a stalactite sticking through her stomach. He realized she wasn't dead when her lips began forming another defensive chant. He screeched wildly. At once a gang of unearthlings appeared at Zerrina's side. Without so much of a blink from tiger head, the unearthly crew tore the vile princess to pieces. Other than her head, what was left of POL-TAR, the gang wolfed down in a gory orgy.

Suddenly a bolt of lightning flashed around the massive cavern. It stopped at the heart of Zarharrab. The evil priest stood tall as the power of life and death burst through his body. His arms raised, he screamed in triumph at the surrounding unearthlings. "There is no stopping us my ungodly children. The entire world will now be ours to devour!"

MAN-DAR was about to return to the task of reviving Marrina, when he stepped to the crevasse and noticed POL-TAR's bodiless head. He peered closer as a shiver of fear ran through his being. The corners of POL-TAR's lips curled into a vicious smile. Suddenly life returned to her dead eyes. Along with her renewed life came her atrocious laugh. MAN-DAR cringed, but hoped the hideous sound would attract the attention of the unearthlings.

It did. A number of the unearthling creatures, curious about the cackle, wandered from the confusion still surrounding Zarharrab. The sight of scarlet liquid seeping from the Zerrina's neck instantly drove their blood lust into frenzy again. With a hideous cry, the horrible creatures tore at what was left of their unholy ruler. The screams of protest from her lips fell on heedless ears. Finally the shrieks were squelched when the jaws of tiger head crushed out the last of Zerrina's power.

Without looking back, MAN-DAR returned to Marrina. He knelt over her and saw her life had almost slipped away completely. He was about to pull the small water flask from his belt when he remembered. A cry of anguish swept him. He screamed out loud, "I hold only enough liquid to save one woman!"

To his shock, Marrina's eyes flew open. She spoke, her voice barely audible. "MAN-DAR you must use the water to revive Sulina."

MAN-DAR's heart and brain fought like lions and tigers. "I can make no such decision." he said to Marrina.

"You must." She answered. "You love her. I love her. You both must live together for eternity."

"I cannot let you die either, Marrina. You at least still live. As much as I love Sulina and have loved her in other lifetimes, she has already passed. I shall save you. You have sacrificed everything."

MAN-DAR removed the vial from his belt and began the chant needed to save Marrina. He was about to remove the stopper from the vile when a tremendous blow struck the back of his head. The vial of sacred water flew from his hand but he managed to retain consciousness. His eyes blurry, MAN-DAR looked up to see Zarharrab standing over him with a club.

"So, you think me still blind, Atlantean. It is I, Zarharrab who now holds the power of Agron. But unfortunately you will not be around to see me conquer the world." Zarharrab then raised his club to let loose a final deathblow to MAN-DAR. Just as he was about to swing a fight broke out between two nearby unearthlings. One unearthling swung his big club at the other but missed. The other unearthling swung his even larger club at him but also missed. He did hit something. Zarharrab's hand.

Zarharrab's club fell from his grip. His scream of pain grew into a howl of anger. Giving MAN-DAR time to recover.

Before Zarharrab found his club, MAN-DAR rolled to the side, grabbed Secura and jumped to his feet. "You will soon join your malevolent mother, Zarharrab."

No answer issued from the priest. He only picked up his weapon and with a great cry charged his tormentor. MAN-DAR sidestepped and the club swished through thin air. Meanwhile the dull unearthlings wailed in confusion as all they could see was Zarharrab swinging the club at nothing.

His attention on Zarharrab, MAN-DAR failed to see Marrina as she dragged herself to Sulina. In her hand she held the vial of sacred water. By the time MAN-DAR realized her intent it proved too late. She had already finished the chant and leaned against the great stake while pouring liquid over Sulina.

"Marrina, no!" MAN-DAR screamed. Before he could do more than shout, another blow whooshed by his head. As he ducked the bash, he fell into a pack of unearthlings and lost sight of both women. The battle between Zarharrab and the invisible Atlantean raged on. MAN-DAR saw from the corner of his eye that Marrina lay dying in Sulina's arms. Although his heart wept for Marrina, it leapt for joy at the sight of a living Sulina.

He redoubled his efforts to terminate Zarharrab. "Your end falls near, evil priest, along with your plan to destroy Atlantis."

"It is not finished yet," Zarharrab exclaimed as the blaze from his piercing eyes gripped MAN-DAR.

Since his mother's death, Zarharrab's power seemed to have doubled. The chants MAN-DAR hummed did nothing to enhance the crystal and his strength began to dissipate. His arms grew weak and he could hardly hold up the Akarri to fend off the blows Zarharrab rained on him. A smile drew Zarharrab's lips upward into a wicked grin as MAN-DAR retreated.

"So, who stands winner now Atlantean? I shall blame you for the death of my mother, after I have conquered Atlantis. Prepare yourself for death." Zarharrab raised the huge club to strike again.

MAN-DAR, too weak to resist, failed to even raise an arm in defense, but the blow he expected never fell. To his astonishment he saw a huge unearthling wrap his arms around Zarharrab. Other creatures soon joined the fray. The only explanation MAN-DAR could think of for the unearthling's behavior. Could be that by Zarharrab madly swinging his club at thin air, they believed he had gone mad with grief over Zerrina. If that were the case, he may have a chance to escape the soulless underworld.

As Zarharrab screamed, cursed, and struggled in the arms of the unearthlings, MAN-DAR climbed to his feet, weaved his still invisible self through the throng of confused unearth-lings and found Sulina and Marrina.

MAN-DAR pulled Sulina close to him and whispered to the startled woman, "It is I, MAN-DAR. The Lessor's crystal has made me invisible. We must act quickly. Marrina lies dying, but we might still save her." Sulina nodded weakly as MAN-DAR pushed back through the unearthlings to Zarharrab who was still held by the creatures. MAN-DAR found the small instrument the few steps from where Zarharrab had dropped it and he retrieved the Harp of Agron.

After forcing his way back to Marrina and Sulina, he told them to join hands. Once they did he took up the small harp, plucked its strings, and chanted. When finished he held the harp in one hand as the other grasped the hands of both Sulina and Marrina. Soon a swirl of blue vapor engulfed them all as MAN-DAR envisioned a picture of him, Marrina, and Sulina back in the ceremonial chamber.

When Sulina, Marrina, and MAN-DAR along with the Harp of Agron, materialized in the ceremonial chamber, Lugaar, who stood studying POL-TAR's runes, gaped in as-tonishment. "How have you completed your task so swiftly, Mas...MAN-DAR? You left only moments ago."

"Moments to you Lugaar, but it proved almost an eternity for us. Please help quickly, Marrina dies as we speak, and I know no magic to save her."

Lugaar rushed to the trio, his old lumbering self com-pletely gone. As he moved, his trained healer's eye quickly surveyed the people before him. MAN-DAR appeared fine save for an air of exhaustion. The barbarian princess also exhausted leaned against the Atlantean for support but showed no outward signs of imminent collapse. Marrina definitely proved to be most in need of help. He quickly retrieved the crystal from MAN-DAR and held it to the scullery maid's forehead. "She has almost passed over. I am not sure I can help her."

"Try Lugaar. You must use all the knowledge you and POL-TAR's magic can provide. If not for Marrina, we would not stand before you now."

"Help me carry her to the sacrificial altar. Between the power of the crystal and what I have learned of the Harp of Agron, we might save her."

As MAN-DAR helped lift Marrina gently to the altar, Lugaar felt the urgency in the Atlantean's voice. "We must hurry Lugaar, POL-TAR lays dead, but her son survives and may appear any moment with his hideous army of unearthlings."

At once Lugaar left MAN-DAR cradling Marrina's head while he helped Sulina to a more comfortable seat on POL-TAR's throne. He then retrieved the tiny harp from the chamber floor and placed it on the pedestal at the foot of the altar. "Take the sacred crystal, MAN-DAR, and hold it to Marrina's forehead. I shall use the harp to summon the demon, Agron."

Alarmed, MAN-DAR challenged Lugaar. "You cannot, the demon proves evil."

"I have learned from POL-TAR's runes that whoever summons the demon to this world has control of his power. It is the only way."

Lugaar watched MAN-DAR shake his head in disbelief as he followed the instruction silently. Lugaar began a low

chant, increased its pitch and plucked the harp's strings until
he found a cord, which matched the tone. Almost immediately a wisp of blue smoke curled from the harp and formed
a large circle. Blue mist materialized in the circle and from it
came the Demon of Agron.

"Who hasst ssummoned Agron?"

"It is I, Lugaar, protector of the Sacred Crystal of
Arrhamis."

"Why doth thou bother me, lowesst of the lowesst casste?"

Lugaar stood straight and answered, "I wish you to join
powers with the crystal and heal the young woman before
you."

"Why sshould the Demon of Agron save the life of a ssim-
ple sscullery maid?"

"Because I summoned you to this world and you must
obey."

The demon did not reply, he merely projected far enough
from the mist to flick the feet of Marrina with his tongue.
When he did so a flash like lightning passed over Marrina to
the sacred crystal and back. Instantly the blue smoke returned
to the harp, disappeared, and Marrina's eyes opened.

Jerd and the survivors of his army stood in silence at the far
end of the great wooden bridge, which led from the Temple of
Inanna. MAN-DAR took heart at the sight of the big one eyed
man and urged Sulina, Marrina, and Lugaar, who carried the
tiny harp, to hurry across the moat. Once on the other side he
ordered the bridge torched in an attempt to slow Zarharrab and
his unearthlings who had already begun to appear just as they

had fled the ceremonial chamber. MAN-DAR hoped the confusion of the undisciplined army and the burned bridge would give them time to reach the great Pass of Zorin. He had learned from TAM-STX that the pass led through the mountains on the route from the temple to the Forbidden Causeway. Jerd had sworn to guard the pass with his life and that of his followers. Marrina, happy to be at Jerd's side, had sworn also.

MAN-DAR took the lead in the direction of the Forbidden Causeway; to his surprise he encountered only withered weed-vines. He questioned Lugaar about them.

"Soon after you and Marrina disappeared with the Wave of Trinity ceremony, the vines died."

"What could have caused such a thing, Lugaar?"

"You have told me that POL-TAR died in the Underworld. I believe it was she who created and controlled the hideous vines. With her death came theirs."

MAN-DAR could think of no better explanation and grunted in affirmation.

When the remains of their tiny army straggled into the Pass of Zorin, MAN-DAR immediately set Jerd's men into the best defensive positions. He then climbed a rugged slope where Jerd and Marrina waited to bid farewell. Solemnly the two men and Marrina met.

"You need not do this, Jerd. You and your people have done more than enough already."

"We attacked the temple for ourselves, my bronze skinned friend. We defend this pass for the world. If you fail to reach Atlantis and warn the Empire, we are all doomed."

"I need not tell you that you are too few to hold this position for long."

"Yes, but if it buys enough time for a good lead, our sacrifice shall be worth it. Now you must go, my friend, or you will be in battle along with us."

"And you Marrina, are you sure you want to stay."

"Yes, MAN-DAR. My place is with my people and with my man, Jerd." Marrina's head turned again to MANDAR. "I have already spoken to Sulina and we have said our goodbyes. She understands the power of love over life, and though she cried tears of sorrow at our parting. She also cried tears of joy for the happiness I have finally found with Jerd."

MAN-DAR saw the joy in her face and addressed Jerd. "I must ask. Do you know if Kirack died in the battle?"

"I cannot say for certain. My men heard him call the charge, but that proved the last seen of him. Some believe he died when a Gall Worm attacked the bridge during the battle. A few even thought him eaten by Zarharrab's unearthlings who went wild. Personally, I believe he ran away. But it matters not, MAN-DAR. His heart is dark and if he did run, he became food for weed-vines or got caught in one of the deadly traps at the Forbidden Causeway. Does his widow grieve for him?"

"I think not, Jerd. Theirs was not a marriage consummated by the gods."

Jerd smiled knowingly at MAN-DAR who blushed under the big man's look, then stated. "It stands as no secret that he and I lacked companionship for one another. But I have a mission to complete and he is part of it. Poseidon Control will not care that the man had no honor. They only wish to see results. Returning home with only half the delegation shall not be considered a success."

"That may be so, Atlantean, but if Zarharrab and his forces reach Atlantis, me thinks they shall not be worried over one missing delegate, or twenty."

"I hope it comes not to that my friend. Just remember, whatever happens, songs shall forever honor what you and your people do here this day."

"Speak no more of it, Atlantean. I must lead my men in prayers to Muckdah and you must make haste."

"May the gods smile on you, Jerd and Marrina."

"And may they go with you, Atlantean.

The two men clasped both hands and wrists. Then MAN-DAR embraced Marrina. MAN-DAR saw a strength in the two he never would have thought possible in these backward people. No matter how this turned out, his perception of Angleland had changed forever. His throat tight, MAN-DAR quickly turned on his heel and he hurried down the steep path where Sulina and Lugaar waited.

NINETEEN

MAN-DAR, Sulina, and Lugaar marched rapidly in silence. Occasionally they halted as Lugaar knocked down a megalith to prevent a ley stone air attack. Otherwise much time passed before MAN-DAR finally ordered a rest.

Sulina broke the silence. "How much further to the Forbidden Causeway, MAN-DAR?"

"Jerd said many seasons had passed since anyone dared locate the Causeway, but he believed it a three-day march from the pass."

"Did he speak of my husband?"

MAN-DAR hesitated. "His men believed Kirack had died in battle or had run away. No one knows for sure."

"Running away sounds more like Kirack," she said sarcastically.

Not wanting to dally on the subject, MAN-DAR stood to indicate it was time to move on. What passed for daylight in Angleland diminished and he wanted to put as much distance between them and Zarharrab as possible. MAN-DAR felt Jerd could hold the pass for a day at best. It did not give them much of a lead, especially when they must seek ways around the traps lain by ancient Atlanteans.

When the blackness of night finally fell, the trio halted. Exhaustion left no energy to build a fire or even talk. Sulina snuggled against MAN-DAR's chest and Lugaar slept not far away. When day lightened the landscape enough to travel, they moved on. They had not traveled far when they heard a faint clamor of a battle behind them. The sound hurried the trio forward at double speed. All three prayed to their gods for Marrina, Jerd, and for the tiny army of Angleland.

"Look out, Jerd!" Marrina shouted as an ax flew at the one-eyed leader from his blind side. He dodged just in time and Marrina shot an ugly man with the hoofs of a goat between the eyes with one of her few remaining arrows.

Jerd took the time to smile at Marrina. "Thank you my love, I do not know how I have survived these many long years without you looking over me." As he finished his statement he was forced to duck as a spear flew over his head. When he rose again, Marrina was pointing anxiously down into the deep pass.

"Look Jerd, the monsters pull back once again. Maybe we have defeated them." Marrina said about the retreating army of Zarharrab. "They left piles of dead as they streamed back through the pass."

"I think not my Marrina. They only retreat to regroup and rearm. Zarharrab's army is almost limitless and they are sure to try once more."

"But we have killed so many. It is suicide for them to return."

"Yes, but our numbers dwindle also, as does our spears and arrows. By the next charge or the charge after, we will have but stones to reign down on the creatures."

"Then we will surly die, Jerd." Marrina's words were a statement, not a question.

"It appears the gods see it that way, my love. But we shall hold till the last drop of blood flows from our bodies." Then staring into her eyes he added. "It need not be so for you, Marrina. There is still time for you to escape. You are fleet of foot and could easily outrun the clumsy unearthlings."

"I could not leave you Jerd," Marrina said as she put her slender arms around the waist of the big man. "We may only have moments left to live, and I do not want to live any of them apart from you. In but a few days you have fulfilled my life. If we die it will be together."

Jerd took the tiny maiden and kissed her softly. "We will be together for eternity, Marrina."

"I know," Marrina answered as they turned to face the horde of monsters swarming into the pass.

By noon the trio had stopped again out of shear fatigue. They consumed a small portion of provisions Lugaar had packed. The Lessor had stored as much food as possible in the largest carrying sack his huge body could haul. Lugaar knew if they could safely reach the Forbidden Causeway, they still had weeks of windy traveling to reach the Azores Mountains on the most northern tip of Atlantis.

They listened in silence to the din of the fierce battle taking place behind them. "The battle rages still, MAN-DAR. Perhaps Jerd will stop Zarharrab completely."

"I regret to say, I think not, Lugaar. Even without his magic harp, Zarharrab stands as a formidable enemy. The Pass of Zorin is narrow and he will lose many of his unearthlings. But, he has many unearthlings. And at that they are also fearless fighters. His army fights with blood lust in their eyes. I even heard many vow to die rather than return to the underworld. They believe their time has come to reign on earth."

Lugaar continued. "But surely if they reach Atlantis, the technology of your race will easily annihilate them."

"Perhaps so, Lugaar, but they have large numbers. If we do not warn the Empire, they shall also have surprise on their side. Most of the Atlantean army has grown lax. As you well know, we have relied mostly on the Lessor conscripts in the wars against the Beasts."

"I know well Mas…. I mean MAN-DAR. Beasts killed my grandfather in the second war."

"That proves my case, Lugaar. The Beasts have no technology and in that war we barely defeated them. I fear for my homeland, and for yours."

"I fear for us all, MAN-DAR," Sulina broke in. Especially for you and I if Kirack has escaped death."

With the mention of Kirack, MAN-DAR rose abruptly and started down the track toward the Forbidden Causeway. As he passed Lugaar, the Lessor grasped his shoulder. "Listen."

MAN-DAR turned his ear to the direction they had come from. He heard nothing; the battle for the pass had ended and he knew it could not have ended well for Jerd and his people. Gloom covered his face and he walked ahead so the other two would not see his pain.

When they stopped for the night, they again ate a small portion of their provisions. Sulina urged MAN-DAR to build a fire against the chill, but MAN-DAR still would not allow it.

"Zarharrab may have fast moving scouts on the lookout.

It is best we give them as little help as possible. Move close Sulina, my love shall keep you warm."

"It is not the cold which makes me shiver, MAN-DAR. It is my fear that Kirack lives."

"If he lives, do not fear. I will protect you."

"You do not understand. If Kirack lives, I am still his wife."

"What of it? You do not love him. When we reach Poseidon, we shall petition the priests to dissolve your marriage."

"You must listen, MAN-DAR. I love Kirack not, and would dissolve the marriage in an instant if possible. But it is not."

"What do you mean, not possible? The priests only need utter a few words and it shall be ended. You do not understand the ways of Atlantis."

"And you do not understand the ways of Euros. I not only pledged myself to Kirack before Muckdah, I also pledged before my father, and more so, before the graves of my mother and sister. I cannot break this pledge."

MAN-DAR fell silent. He understood Sulina's strong will and sense of honor. For all the love he held for her, he knew he could not ask her to break her word. Sulina saw his turmoil and spoke again.

"I too am hurt beyond words, MAN-DAR, but I had to tell you. Kirack is a bad man. He is as ambitious as he is selfish. If he found any way to protect himself, no matter who it hurt, he would do so. If we cross the causeway and learn Kirack lives, I fear we shall never share this lifetime together."

MAN-DAR turned away in anguish.

Sulina gently placed her hand on MAN-DAR's cheek, and turned his face to hers, "Listen to me. We have found a great love in this lifetime. Few have felt what we feel for each other. Let us seek happier times. Let us seek times when we will be content together."

MAN-DAR's consternation showed on his face. "What do you mean?"

"We have the harp. Lugaar knows how to evoke its power to view other lives. Let us seek another time when we existed happily together. Let us feel our happiness in the past or the future. Then even if destiny forces us apart, we shall know in our hearts eternal joy."

"Sulina, I know the harp helped save Marrina, but I fear to evoke its powers."

"It can be done, and Lugaar has the crystal to protect us if necessary. He assured me it is but a simple chant. Let us try, MAN-DAR. Please, it may be our last chance to find happiness in this lifetime."

MAN-DAR finally relented, and beckoned for Lugaar. The Lessor must have sensed what his master wished for he carried the small harp with him. As he placed the tiny instrument on the ground before them, he spoke without a word from MAN-DAR, "You need only hold hands and think of yourselves together. I shall perform the necessary ceremony."

Before Lugaar had finished the instructions, his fingers struck a chord as the lovers joined hands under a dead tree on a small hill in Angleland. As Lugaar chanted, MAN-DAR saw the familiar curl of blue smoke rise, circle him and Sulina, and meet again with the harp to form a large smoke ring. MAN-DAR looked into Sulina's eyes and she in his. Their minds mingled with the smoke and flowed into the harp with it. The smoke clouded MAN-DAR's eyes and when they met with Sulina's again he said, "I love you, Iris."

"I love you too, Manny, you shit."

They both laughed as Iris drove her little blue VW bug around the sharp curves of the California coastline highway on their way to Salinas. The scent of eucalyptus trees enveloped the car and they passed a bottle of wine between them. Manny couldn't believe he could love anyone as much as he loved Iris that day.

The kisses and wine they shared smoothed the day into a kaleidoscope of cliffs, ocean and love. They stopped at a cozy little restaurant to eat and had the place to themselves. The waitress sensed their intimacy and gave them space. They ate slowly, swallowing the love in each other's eyes along with the delicious food. After dinner, they moved on to a tiny jazz bar, where the piano player tingled the keys just for them.

The feeling Manny had for Iris exploded. "I love you so much I can't keep my hands off you."

"Same here, and I don't give a shit if the whole world's looking."

They kissed over their drinks at a few more funky little bars. They kissed getting into the car for the ride home. They kissed on each landing leading to Iris' apartment. They kissed at the door. They kissed in the foyer. They kissed as they lowered themselves onto the waterbed and in unison Iris and Manny said, "I'll love you for eternity."

Manny's arms enveloped Iris, and water in the bed made them feel like they floated on a cloud. They kissed and hugged and Manny opened his eyes. He was in a cloud, a blue cloud. The cloud dissipated before his eyes as he wrapped his arms tighter around Iris, but this time he said, "I love you, Sulina," and the cloud drew quickly back into the tiny harp which along with the last traces of the wispy blue smoke, vanished.

Kirack studied the landscape before him. He had crested the top of a small hill which led down to a gentle meadow. The meadow meandered down to the sea. A spit of land reached out from the shore and traveled westward as far as he could see. A smile crossed his face. He had found the Forbidden Causeway. As he stood ready to take the last few steps to the meadow, he suddenly heard a low rumble behind him. Instantly Kirack recognized the sound as the movement of a huge army. He turned quickly to hurry on and barely stopped himself as he was about step off a steep cliff into a bottomless crevasse. He could not believe he had failed to see the cliff only moments ago.

Kirack peered over the edge of the precipice and dropped a stone. He shook with fear when no sound of rock hitting bottom reached his ear. He stepped back a few paces and noticed the lay of the land created an illusion that the crest of the hill met with the meandering meadow. Immediately he searched for an alternate route. He was scared and limping.

Since he had fled the battle at the temple he had fought one terror after another. He especially recalled the unearthling who had lunged at him from behind a bush. He had become so unnerved he had lost his sword in the chase across the terrible Angleland terrain. Luckily he stumbled across a pair of ragged youths playing by an algae filled pool. He had lured the children within reach with a promise of food and had managed to capture them. Kirack then traded their lives for his when the unearthling finally had him trapped.

In the days it had taken to reach the causeway, the weed-vines had plagued him terribly. One blossom had gouged his leg and in an attempt to avoid another he had miss-stepped, tripped over a log, and twisted his ankle. As he fell, the vines entangle him, but just as the blossom's fangs closed on his neck they inexplicably died and dropped from their withering vines.

Finally he had reached a spot where he could smell the sea. Strange Atlantean written signs hung on the hulks of rotting trees and the bony remains of many creatures lay about. He had no doubt he was getting close to the Forbidden Causeway.

The crevasse he had almost stumbled into had been only the second trap he had come upon. The first proved simple and easy to avoid. Mainly because the mechanism used to spring the row of sharpened spikes had rotted over the millennium. Until he had reached the crevasse he had begun to suspect the superstitions about the booby-trapped causeway were merely that, superstitions. Now he realized the dangers of the causeway were far more subtle. It was only a trick of perception that made the open spaces look like meadow instead of a bottomless chasm. Had he not stopped to listen to the rumbling army, he would have fallen off the edge, and as far as he knew, he might still be falling.

As Kirack searched for a route around the gorge he limped down the hill in the direction of the distant rumble. Suddenly the movement of three figures caught his attention. They moved in his direction and even with his swollen ankle, he ran for cover in a small draw. From his new vantage point he could watch without being seen. If the trio proved to be more un-earthlings he would stay out of sight since he now lacked children to feed them. If they proved to be natives who escaped Zarharrab, he did not want to be seen either. For they would surely realize he had deserted and would not take it kindly.

To his surprise, in the distance he recognized MAN-DAR Sulina and a Lessor. They climbed swiftly up the same hill he had just descended. They were heading for the crevasse. With relish, Kirack decided to let them walk to their deaths. At the same time he realized the rumble and dust further in the distance must be the unearthly army of Zarharrab. He began to formulate a plan on how to save himself, and at the same time gain power through leadership of the awesome army.

I shall make a deal with Zarharrab, he thought. After saving him and his minions from the plunge over the cliff, he will surely make me one of his lieutenants. After the conquest of Atlantis I shall find a way of ridding the world of the half-breed priest. Even if I were to allow Zarharrab and his army to fall to their deaths. I could still find my way to the leaders of Atlantis and explain to them the enormous service I have done for the Empire.

The rumble of the army close behind them was becoming a roar. The unearthlings Zarharrab commanded moved faster than MAN-DAR had anticipated, and at each rise he saw their forms more clearly. That included a huge black steed with a black cloaked rider leading the way, Zarharrab.

MAN-DAR cursed himself for stopping the night before.

That was when he and Sulina had regained consciousness from their other-life sojourn. Unfortunately, they both had fallen into a dreamless sleep.

Suddenly he felt Lugaar roughly awakened him. As he had stood to wipe the sleep from his eyes, an eerie light had led him to believe the Angleland dawn had arrived. Lugaar proved him wrong when he excitedly gestured in the direction of the pass. MAN-DAR turned to find the light came not dawn, but from an untold number of torches carried by the huge unearthling army. At once MAN-DAR realized Zarharrab had pressed his army to march through the night. They had made up for much of the half-day lead the trio had gained on them. The distance of the light told MAN-DAR they were still safe from the high priest. If they hurried they could reach the causeway ahead of the monstrous army.

At once he had awakened Sulina and they had fled as fast as possible into the black Angleland night towards the causeway. With a last look over his shoulder MAN-DAR had felt in awe over the sheer number of torches, which lit up the night sky behind them.

By mid morning, they had discovered signs written in ancient Atlantean, and Lessor. The signs had warned of danger and death upon trespass. So far they had found only one trap. It had been ancient and incapable of harm. MAN-DAR had prayed to the gods for any remaining traps to be as useless.

A sea breeze, wet with the smell of salt water wafted across MAN-DAR's face. He sensed the causeway stood no further than over the next hill. While MAN-DAR urged his companions on at greater speed, he turned to observe the progress of the army at their heels. Fear gripped his heart as he realized he could almost make out every gaunt feature of Zarharrab as he pushed his black steed to travel faster.

MAN-DAR felt certain Zarharrab had seen them by now and prodded Lugaar and Sulina to hurry. Suddenly a slight movement ahead caught his eye. At first he believed it only the paranoia of the chase, but he glimpsed movement once again and motioned for Lugaar and Sulina to slow their pace. Possibly some of the unearthlings had gotten ahead of them, or maybe the movement represented one of the expected traps. At any rate he could not chance racing into an ambush.

As Zarharrab's army bore down on them, MAN-DAR sent Sulina and Lugaar ahead while he crept off silently to out-flank whoever or whatever hid in the outcrop of rocks near a small draw. He slipped from rock to bush to rock again, while he kept an eye out for a surprise attack. Slowly he made his way to the far entrance of the draw.

From his new vantage point MAN-DAR almost gasped when he saw Kirack peering at Lugaar and Sulina. They had already traveled to the bottom of a small hill. From where he stood, he could also see Zarharrab and the army rushing to overtake them. When he looked back at Sulina and Lugaar, they had climbed half way to the hill's crest. He could see the hill led down to a large meadow which rolled gently down to the causeway parting the sea below.

A slight smile appeared on MAN-DAR's lips as he realized he could rid himself of Kirack, once and for all. He had no com-pulsion against killing the coward who had deserted them in battle. Besides he thought, with Kirack gone Sulina would be free of her vow. A mere chop with Secura would end MAN-DAR's dilemma and without a sound he moved towards Kirack.

He halted a few steps behind his prey and withdrew Secura from its sheath. MAN-DAR took two more steps toward Kirack. He raised his Akarri to finish his adversary but as he set his feet for the blow, his foot kicked a stone and alerted Kirack.

With startling speed, the Euro swung around with a walking crutch in hand. Without hesitation he viscously smashed MAN-DAR's knee. Caught off-guard, MAN-DAR lost his footing and fell. His head hit a stone and Secura clambered to the ground. Kirack pounced on him at once. Another blow caught MAN-DAR in the ribs knocking the wind from his lungs. Dazed, his vision blurred, he barely saw Kirack lunge for Secura a few paces away.

MAN-DAR felt defenseless as Kirack wielded Secura over his head. For an instant he believed he would never see Atlantis or Sulina again. Then without warning Sulina and the Lessor came into view over Kirack's shoulder. They had almost crested the hill and would soon enter the meadow leading to the causeway. With great effort MAN-DAR swung his leg out and kicked Kirack in the ankle. The blow had barely glanced Kirack but he inexplicably fell down in a heap. With the strength he had left, MAN-DAR threw himself on Kirack and wrenched Secura from his hands. As he was about to finally end Kirack's life, the Euro's eye caught MAN-DAR's and he spoke, not with fear, but with malice.

"If you kill me she will die!"

MAN-DAR did not wish to hear the pleas of the coward who stood between him and Sulina. He raised the Akarri to kill his rival.

"Wait Atlantean. I swear to you she will die. I am the only one who can save her."

MAN-DAR hesitated, but again decided Kirack must die. One swipe and Sulina's oath to her father would be broken.

"Listen to me. She walks into a trap. I can save her. You must spare me or she and the Lessor will surely die."

"If this be a trick, you shall die a thousand deaths, coward."

"I swear, it is no trick. They will die."

MAN-DAR paused; he could not chance Sulina's death, even if Kirack lied only to save himself. He lowered Secura. "Tell me of this trap and speak quickly. My blade longs for your neck."

Hoarsely, Kirack told MAN-DAR of the deadly crevasse. "Sulinaaaaa!!!!!!"

Zarharrab halted his army. He raised himself on his horse and looked over the crest of the small hill. Below he could see four figures rushing down a sloped meadow toward a spit of land which ran out across the sea. So, this is the great Forbidden Causeway he thought. The rumors around it turn out to be no myth. Even still, I shall run over the puny figures running before me. Then I will continue straight over the passageway to Atlantis. Soon I shall rule as Emperor, not only of Atlantis but of the world. Too bad my mother cannot share this moment. However, at least *my* dreams shall be fulfilled.

A sly grin crossed Zarharrab's face. He felt no remorse for his dead mother. Her death had worked in his favor. He knew she would have hated sharing the power, and he would constantly be forced to look over his shoulder to see what treachery she played.

The High Priest of Angleland gazed once more at the small

band that had almost reached the causeway and laughed to himself. The time has ended for you MAN-DAR. I shall crush your Atlantean body into the ground as your legs rush to carry you over the causeway. Without another thought, Zarharrab raised his arm and bellowed to his army of unearthlings, "Chaaarrrrgggge!!!"

Zarharrab's entire army rushed forward in a great hurry to conquer Atlantis. An instant later, Zarharrab recognized his shocking mistake. The earth no longer stood beneath the hooves of his snorting black steed. In an anguished moment of clarity he realized he and his entire army had plunged over a cliff and into an bottomless abyss.

Lugaar swung the heavy carrying sack from one shoulder to the other. The straps had begun to hurt after only the first half-day's journey across the windswept causeway. He tried to displace the thought of more pain. He knew they had many more days to travel before they reached Atlantis.

The pace of the trip had slowed considerably since they had watched Zarharrab and his minion's dive headlong into the endless crevasse. Kirack had saved them from the same fate and most likely his name would continue in legend and song. Kirack would call himself the savior of the Empire. He had destroyed the hideous army of unearthlings. Furthermore his voice had led to the death of their evil leader, Zarharrab, the High Priest of Inanna.

Lugaar sighed as he watched the back of Sulina who walked in front of him and behind her husband. He felt intense sorrow for MAN-DAR who walked solemnly at the head of their tiny column. MAN-DAR would never possess the woman he would love for all eternity. Not in this lifetime, not while Kirack lived. He prayed that MAN-DAR would forget the woman eventually but he knew in his heart it would never happen. However, he thought, I know he will never forget the promises he made; the promise that he would never again enter the games against a Lessor. That he would confront his father, SAN-DAR. That he would join SOL-RAM in the cause for equal justice for Lessors. And especially, MAN-DAR would honor his promise to help all Lessors reach their promised land.

Lightning Source UK Ltd.
Milton Keynes UK
UKHW011936100822
407146UK00008B/113/J